Praise for
Hristo Karastoyanov

"On the surface, this is a far away story in a far away time, but Karastoy-anov masterfully brings his reader in close, immersing each of us in the action, anarchy, and art of a fierce political resistance."

—DW Gibson

"A poet and an anarchist in the same year, 1925, both their last. The men's voices and narratives breathlessly intersect, take hold of one anoth-er, then mix into the blood and terror of Bulgaria's undeclared civil war, which would vanish them without a trace. A poignant novel, at once tense and fractured, brutal and lyrical. Powerful voices that haunt you long after the ending."

—Georgi Gospodinov

"Karastoyanov never lets us forget that this story, like every history, is a could-have-been narrative refracted through the prism of the present moment. . . . Izidora Angel's translation skillfully captures the author's (and the characters') sardonic commentary, while still conveying Kara-stoyanov's deep connection to and concern with events that even now continue to shape Bulgarians' conception of their own history."

—Angela Rodel

"A writer of true European spirit."

—*Berliner Zeitung*

Translated from
the Bulgarian by
Izidora Angel

HRISTO
KARASTOYANOV

THE
SAME NIGHT
AWAITS
US ALL

— Diary of a Novel —

OPEN LETTER
LITERARY TRANSLATIONS FROM THE UNIVERSITY OF ROCHESTER

Library of Congress Cataloging-in-Publication Data: Available.

*This project is supported in part by an award from the National Endowment for the Arts
and the New York State Council on the Arts with the support of
Governor Andrew M. Cuomo and the New York State Legislature*

*This book is published within the Elizabeth Kostova Foundation's program
for Support of Contemporary Bulgarian Writers and in collaboration
with the America for Bulgaria Foundation.*

Printed on acid-free paper in the United States of America.

Text set in Garamond, a group of old-style serif typefaces
named after the punch-cutter Claude Garamont.

Design by N. J. Furl

Open Letter is the University of Rochester's nonprofit, literary translation press:
Dewey Hall 1-219, Box 278968, Rochester, NY 14627

www.openletterbooks.org

Translator's Introduction

"Art can blossom only when it is planted in freedom.
If you censor the writer, you would be killing art itself."
—*Geo Milev*

Hemingway, in writing about Bulgaria for Toronto's *Daily Star* in 1922, said of the country, "There are no internal problems in Bulgaria, there are no troublesome minorities . . ." And of its leader, Alexander Stamboliyski, he said "[He] is chunky, red-brown-faced, has a black mustache that turns up like a sergeant major's, understands not a word of any language except Bulgarian, once made a speech of fifteen hours' duration in that guttural tongue, and is the strongest premier in Europe, bar none."

Caught between Germany and Russia's titanic post-First World War appetites, the tiny Eastern European country of Bulgaria suffered many internal struggles for power financed by external interests, and within a year of Hemingway's dispatch, fascist forces would descend onto Bulgaria and Stamboliyski, the leader of the Agrarian Union, would be dead—brutally tortured and then murdered by the Internal Macedonian Revolutionary Organization (IMRO) following the military coup of June, 1923, which brought down his democratically-elected government and inserted a fascist one in its place.

Hristo Karastoyanov's novel opens eighteen months later, in May of 1925, with the brutal murders, imagined here on the same night, of two key Bulgarian figures: the erudite, exquisite poet Geo Milev, and the notorious anarchist Georgi Sheytanov. Karastoyanov then rewinds and takes us back to the year and a half leading up to the men's deaths, bookending the narrative on one side with the aftermath of the September Uprising in 1923 (the hastily organized and brutally suppressed response to the June coup, which claimed as many as 30,000 lives and effectively led to the communist party being outlawed), and on the other end with the unprecedented terrorist attack in Bulgaria's capital, Sofia, on the St. Nedelya Church in April 1925, which took the lives of 150 and injured 500, and is still considered one of the bloodiest terrorist acts in Europe. The attack was planned and executed by the communists in an attempt to eradicate high-standing members of the police force. The attack resulted in violent repressions led by the Military Union with the fascist government's implicit consent. In the aftermath, nearly 450 people were executed without trial, including the poet Geo Milev.

In 1923, we see a Bulgaria on the verge of tyranny, amid an identity crisis, a nation still reeling from the five-century Ottoman yoke. And we see anarchists whom today we'd hardly hesitate to call terrorists. And yet, it is precisely an anarchist, Georgi Sheytanov, who sponsors Geo Milev's magazine.

It is perhaps very natural to frame the book around the question "Who killed Geo Milev?" It's a loaded question, raising many more with it in regard to Bulgarian and European early twentieth-century history, politics, and culture. But perhaps before attempting to answer who killed Geo Milev, we need to know who Geo Milev was and what he died for.

Despite losing part of his skull and with it his right eye while fighting for his country in the First World War, in early 1920s Bulgaria the international literary promise of this young visionary poet—German-educated, avant-garde writer, multilingual translator, and magazine publisher—was unbound. Contrarian, brilliant, and erudite, he worked fanatically and almost obsessively in a race against time to expand the horizons of the Bulgarian literary landscape. A fierce apologist of modernism and expressionism, he authored potent poetry and sweeping political commentary, and translated into Bulgarian no less than Lord Byron, Shakespeare, Goethe, Pushkin, John Keats, Browning, and de Musset, to name some. In turn, he was despised by the conformist literary circles, the pseudo-intellectuals, and, of course, the government.

Georgi Sheytanov was only a year younger than the poet and one of the most famous anarchists in Bulgaria in the 1920s—the single most wanted man by the police, in fact. Like Geo Milev, he too was a bright and extraordinarily erudite political commentator, and, repulsed by Lenin's communism, the world traveler, anarchist, and perpetual escape artist left Russia for Bulgaria, where he inspired and became a patron to Geo Milev's cause: to awaken the sleeping people at any cost.

The two created the magazine *Plamuk* (Flame), which was not only excellent, but also incredibly successful, and somewhat leftist. *Plamuk*, after only a year of existence, fell prey to the censorship of the authorities, who, after the September Uprising, and especially after the attack on St. Nedelya, persecuted both dissidents and anybody else who dared to think with equal fervor.

Karastoyanov brings Geo Milev and Georgi Sheytanov back to life in a lush, dark, and "true fictional" account that is, as the author himself notes, "maybe not all true, but certainly faithful to the truth."

It wasn't until 1954 that Geo Milev's remains were uncovered in a mass grave at the outskirts of Sofia, nearly thirty years after his secret execution. He was recognized only by the blue glass eye in the right socket of his skull.

It's difficult to overstate the parallels of the Bulgaria—even of the world—of today with the Bulgaria—and the world—of a century ago. Karastoyanov employs a diary construct with the precise goal of disintegrating the distance of the ostensibly faraway dates he chronicles, drawing unabashed parallels with the culture and politics of today: press monopolies concerned more with entertainment and selling papers rather than with ascertaining facts; weak, pusillanimous politicians; ruthless cops with ruthless ambitions; even the fundamental pandering of literary awards and the eternal struggle between real intellectuals and politics. He dares to ask: What has changed, if anything?

> *"The ivory tower, the refuge of poetry and hiding place of poets, lies crumbled in ruins. From the dust of dreams, from the ruin of fantasies the poet emerges—stunned, astounded, no longer blind—and confronts the bloodstained face of the people, his people . . ."*
>
> —From Geo Milev's manifesto in Plamuk, *which included the poem "September," about the September Uprising*

—Izidora Angel

Translator's Note

Breaking apart Karastoyanov's dense, vigorous paragraphs from the inferential mood of that "guttural tongue," as Hemingway calls the Bulgarian, and forming them back into English was nothing short of heartbreaking, gut-wrenching, and ecstatic.

Idiomatic English is stunning in its complex beauty, but the complexity and richness of the Bulgarian comes from an entirely different source—a deeply nuanced grammar comprised of over 40 tenses across different aspects and moods. Karastoyanov employs one such mood—the inferential—throughout the entire novel. It's a retelling of events bound by an admittance on the part of the narrator that he wasn't present when they occurred. Aside from a few instances of "allegedly" and "surely," I had to let that mood go.

There are also some incredibly potent single-syllable relays in Bulgarian that are near impossible to render—"*a*," a kind of sharp right turn that could mean "but," "moreover," "therefore," and "there you have it." Karastoyanov starts an inordinate number of his sentences with "I," meaning "and," but to have retained these in English would have diluted the potency of his storytelling; he also ends an inordinate number of sentences with exclamations; that too was difficult to let go of, but ultimately necessary.

Karastoyanov's language in the novel is beautifully archaic without being impeding—he doesn't give his characters 1920s slang, which I was grateful for, but there are still some great older words like "*dodeto*," essentially "to what extent" or "close to"; "*podir*," meaning "behind" or "in his wake"; or the more transitional "*ta*," meaning "and so," or even the novel's ubiquitous "*tai bilo*," meaning "that's how it was" or "that's how it happened," which the author uses to great effect when he wants to poke his head into the narrative and remind us this is a reimagining.

So, although this potency was inevitably sometimes lost in translation any time "*tai bilo*" had to be rendered into something so ostensibly trivial as "*and so it went*," my hope and vision for the novel is that it travels well, and that I've left enough Bulgarian words in to strike a chord and leave an impression.

Translator's Acknowledgements

There are far easier things than living with a writer, although the conversation is always interesting and the bourbon is good. Christo, your tireless support of and contribution to the artistic process, even during extraordinarily difficult times, has meant more to me than I can ever say. My pack of female anarchists—Sofia, Alexandria, and Mirielle—being your mother is an honor.

Thank you to Kaija Straumanis and Chad W. Post for giving me the luxury of three uninterrupted weeks of writing in Rochester, and for believing in—and editing, and publishing—this novel. I have immense gratitude for the Elizabeth Kostova Foundation's support of this translation, and specifically Milena Deleva—the work you do is incredible, and with this novel you've affected my life forever.

I'm also deeply grateful for receiving the support of an English PEN grant while still translating the book. And to DW Gibson—thank you for inviting me to Ledig House, in the company of true heavyweights, and for making it so that Hristo Karastoyanov could see New York, and the Empire State Building.

THE SAME NIGHT AWAITS US ALL

— Diary of a Novel —

"The same night awaits us all,
And the road to death is to be trodden once."
—*Horace*

[One]

ще мога да задоволя напълно интереса
Ти относно дружбата на нашит
[да лехъ ни]
мили покойници - Гео и Георги.

"... I'd be far from able
to fully satisfy your interest in the friendship of
our two dearly departed—Geo and Georgi."

—From a letter written by
Mila Geo Mileva to the
Plovdiv-based anarchist
Dr. Konstantin Kantarev,
October 30, 1944

[Saturday, December 29, 2012]

"This is it," Georgi Sheytanov must have thought as they unfastened the shackles chaining his ankles to those of some gruff, petrified villager from Nova Zagora, and shoved him toward the dark, unlit car parked at the train station. He must have been certain it would all end that night. He'd cut and run from everything and everywhere, including the Sofia Central Prison, where his escape was but a given fact and they'd kept a watchful eye on him, not, as it turned out, to actually prevent him from fleeing, but rather from the itch to see how the infamous anarchist would do it. But how closely had they watched him, really? True to form, he stayed just long enough to incite a riot and then vanished, and life once again lay before him, whatever that meant.

Yet in that moment, at the train station at the foot of the mountain, he must have felt a deathly fatigue.

In any case . . .

The chains they took off, the ropes they left on, and they forced him, bound, into the car, steering the automobile up the sharp mountain road. And he would never find out what had happened to the poet, Geo Milev.

[Sunday, December 30, 2012]

The headlights of the heavy vehicle cut through the darkness ahead, only illuminating the boulders on the side of a road eroded from that spring's incessant rains and riddled with black puddles that the car tore through, spraying the drops far and wide like precious gems. The driver took the turns up the steep road violently; Sheytanov, all knotted up in the back seat, had no way of grabbing the bronze handle on the inside of the door, and instead lurched side to side with the car.

They took him across the mountains to Gorna Dzhumaya, where his arrival was met by the same pathological slaughterers whose names had been on everyone's lips that year—the year an undeclared, loathsome war pitted neighbor against neighbor. And it is said that these thugs then began to *contemplate his verdict*. But he wasn't about to have any of it.

"Me," he said, "you don't sentence. Me, you either shoot or you let go."

But who can say if that's how it really happened? It may not be all true, but it's certainly faithful to the truth.

[Tuesday, January 1, 2013, New Year's Day]
Sheytanov must have known that exactly two weeks prior to his own capture, Geo Milev had already been to court and that his lawyer had conveniently not shown up on time, which had necessitated the poet to act as his own attorney—that much was reported in the newspapers. The case itself had been absurd: a poet on trial for writing a poem. The people in the dust-filled courtroom had not taken in a single word from the poet's defense—that everything he'd written was in the name of humanity, brotherhood, and love and peace on earth, that this was an idea anchoring his entire body of work, and that the real question at hand for the Bulgarian court was: would it convict a poet for his words? But when have a poet's words ever been taken seriously by a court? Geo Milev was convicted, and it was then, in the middle of May, as he lay low in the Balkan mountains amid the tentatively verdant forests above Kilifarevo that Sheytanov likely first read the resulting headline inside that rag known as *Utro*: "*Guilty: Author-Provocateur of 'September' Poem Convicted for Instigating Class Division and Hatred!*" And perhaps while reading that same paper he had also learned what the poet's sentence had been, and who knows, maybe he'd simply groaned that a year in jail along with a twenty thousand leva fine was the lesser of two evils. The twenty thousand wouldn't be a problem to get hold of, just as the five

thousand leva bail before it hadn't been; he had been the one to bring the money to Mila, the poet's wife, after they'd first arrested her husband back in January. Mila had been running around in despair then, making the rounds at all the publishers her husband worked with, the bookstores and newspaper stands whose owners still owed him money—managing to collect a hundred leva here, two hundred there—all the while growing faint and nauseated with the realization she'd never actually come up with the full amount. Sheytanov brought her the accursed five thousand leva in the afternoon: ten lousy bills the color of dirty violet . . . Her eyes, behind frames thin as a spider's web, had looked distraught, and he, seeing her so scared, had lied for the first time in his life; he said *everything would be all right.* But they both knew the ten worthless pieces of paper solved nothing, that the bail money would not bail out the poet, that January was not the end, but only the beginning . . .

The twenty thousand in question now didn't seem like a big deal, either, and the twelve months in jail . . . well, what's a year in jail? Nothing. He'd done it himself.

"He got off easy," he said to Mariola and tossed the paper aside. "What's a year compared to eight! I bet the prosecutor and the judge were fans . . ."

Indeed. The prosecutor, one Manyo Genkov, really had tried his best: instead of asking for the minimum three-year sentence he had pleaded for a year, and the judge had groaned with hasty relief and banged his gavel. And as Sheytanov sat there amid the Kilifarevo forests, he likely wished for nothing more than to have been inside that courtroom, slinging jokes at the poet to cheer him up, shouting: "Milev! I disagree with the ruling. This man is making a mockery of your work. Only a year for that poem?! For shame! These people aren't taking you seriously, Milev. You should've been hit with the maximum for writing that fine piece!" Or something in that vein.

But who could've possibly told him that while he read the now three-day-old newspaper, the poet had already been summoned for an "informal inquiry" in connection with his now seemingly settled case?

And how could he have known that the poet wasn't summoned to the courthouse as he should have been—but to the Police Directorate?

And that was that.

[Tuesday evening, January 1, 2013]

In late afternoon on the fifteenth of May, nineteen twenty-five, the poet's wife and her sister Maria made their way to the Police Directorate right next to Lavov Most, Lions' Bridge. The Directorate was a white-stone building with a pentagram above it, yet unhaunted by the ghosts, vengeful vampires, *karakonjuli*, and angels with blood-drenched wings that would one day reside there. The women brought the poet's coat, because they'd sent him off at dawn with nothing more than a handkerchief, and it was frigid out. It had been so cold, in fact, that both women's fingers had frozen inside their lace gloves—as if winter had returned that spring day.

It goes without saying that the women weren't at all allowed in, and while they stood outside and the murk over Sofia descended, they caught sight of the poet behind a window on the top floor.

But Sheytanov, up in the Kilifarevo hills, had no way of knowing any of this.

The poet too had no way of knowing that the last thing he would ever pen was his signature acknowledging receipt of a three hundred leva loan from the secretary of the Union of Handicapped Officers. Which he would never repay . . .

[Wednesday, January 2, 2013]

The poet had a strange attitude toward Death. He'd lived through her once, when she'd held him in her dark embrace for seven days and seven nights. She had to all appearances unhanded him, but in fact she followed him no matter where he went and what he did. It was for this reason Death had become tedious—she reminded him of herself all the time. It was enough to simply look in the mirror. Or to feel the guilt-ridden shiver in the eyes of those who saw him for the first time . . .

Only Mila had not so much as flinched when she met him at the corner of Legé Street and Dondukov Boulevard on that December day in nineteen seventeen. Only she had not been even the slightest bit repulsed by the hideous, weeping, dark abyss behind the black bandage he wore to cover what had once been his right eye, or by the disheartening scars all over his entire face.

The poet would be forever grateful for that.

[Thursday, January 3, 2013]
The reminder of Death's nod most infuriated him while he was in the midst of giving one of his lectures. As soon as he'd reach the pinnacle of the discourse, either due to the intensity of public speaking or because of the penetrating reek of the tar they used to seal the parquet floors in those claustrophobic community-center salons, or perhaps it was due to the muted lighting above the podium where he stood, it was without fail that rivulets of amber mucus would wind up trickling down his right cheekbone. Agitated, he'd briskly turn his back to the uneasy audience, take off his glasses with the darkened right lens, rapidly wipe his face, then shake the lock of hair back into place above his right eye and start up again exactly where he'd left off. But he'd grown petulant in the process, coming across as if he were now berating his audience, rather than giving a speech on expressionism and futurism.

At any rate, the Dutch doctor from Leiden, Johannes Esser, esteemed member of the University of Berlin and a widely respected plastic surgeon, had done an outstanding job, but the German-made glass eye had proven overwhelmingly uncomfortable and the poet had had to purchase another one from Schlesinger & Co., the specialty optical atelier on Alabinska Street.

It was as though Death somehow lived inside of him, in the pulsating throb above the blown-out right brow and in the piercing chest pain, where Esser had removed part of his rib, reconstructing some of what had been destroyed by British shrapnel. But aside from that, his brain was covered only by skin, and if it weren't for the lock of hair falling over his right eye, the blue veins pulsating beneath would be bared for all to see. He could only sit bent over his writing table for an hour before his head would pound with unbearable pain. In moments like these, he'd ask himself whether it wouldn't have been a good idea to have stayed for those last two surgeries in Germany as the good Doctor Esser had suggested that February day in nineteen seventeen. But he, still sunken into a sticky, tar-like sweat following yet another dose of anesthesia, had cut the doctor off: "I will not. This is it for me. Aren't fourteen operations enough? Let whatever happens, happen. I'm leaving!" The doctor had then pleaded with his wife. "My dear lady," he assured her. "It is only one more surgery! I promise you, he will have his looks back. Tell him, I beg of you." But the poet snapped that *his* wife would never disagree with *her own* husband, and on the first of March, Geo and Mila Milev set off to Budapest from Berlin. From there, on to Orşova, and from Orşova, to Lom, and after twenty days of trains and hotels and cruise liners, they arrived back in Sofia . . .

The pain got to him, but the poet walked around with the dark pride of a swan to spite it. He'd trip up on occasion when he misjudged the height of stairs, and he looked both ways apprehensively before venturing to cross the tram-filled boulevard. And so it went.

In that respect, Death really did live life alongside him. At home, nobody had raised the subject for ages. He'd forbidden them to. His only concerns were the magazines, the books, the printers, the zincographers, who never got the engraving plates for the vignettes right, and the illustrations and the inks and the paper. And the booksellers . . .

. . . And the money, of which there was never enough for any of these things.

[Friday, January 4, 2013]
. . . The idiots assessing Sheytanov's verdict in Gorna Dzhumaya—all those Vanchovs, Ionkovs, or Perovs—shut themselves in the other room to decide his fate; he'd been left alone with two of their goons. They had

dark faces, reeked unbearably, and glared at him with empty opium eyes. He knew their type—they killed without a second thought.

"Not that these scumbags have any *first* thoughts to speak of," he may have thought to himself, and vowed to remember the joke and share it with the poet in the coming days; the latter would probably put it in one of his poems or his trademark philippics.

Sheytanov couldn't have known that a second group of black-coated messengers of God had already cracked the poet's skull with a bludgeon thick as a man's arm. That's how it went down: the others just got strangled, but the poet, they shattered his skull first.

Geo Milev's skull had cracked from the left temple all the way to the nape of the neck at the first blow, but the goons kept going until they broke him entirely. Only then did they throw a black rag over his face and strangle him with the nearby rope left out for the very occasion.

[Saturday, January 5, 2013]
Sheytanov sat, hands tied, inside a room that reeked of rotting wood, sour wine, and opium. It was quiet and dark, save for the rusty voices scraping the silence in the next room over . . . The two smug goons sitting across from him assumed they had frightened him to death, but they'd only made the whole thing tiresome for him. "What do I have left to be afraid of?" he thought.

He suddenly laughed.

"Excuse me, friends, but have either of you ever heard of a bath?"

The goons froze.

"My apologies, gentlemen, looking at you—I just couldn't help but laugh," he continued. "You're quite pungent. Do you at least change your underwear? Why am I even asking . . . You probably don't even wear any, do you? You just pull your breeches up right over your bare ass—am I right? Come on, you're still young men. You'll make the ladies gag."

Then he sighed and added that clean underwear is half the battle to good health.

"Civilization," he went on. "How can you not love it?"

And the goons? One of them shot snot out his nose and wiped it on his leg; the other mumbled a vile expletive.

[Sunday, January 6, 2013]
A gray morning followed on the thirtieth of May, but the Vanchovs and the Ionkovs kept on bickering in the room next door. He put his head down on the cot and fell asleep, still tied up. He'd been so exhausted; he slept for ten hours and by the time he awoke, it had already darkened again. The goons across from him had changed, but it was as though they were the same—like they'd crawled out of the same mother.

"What's happening, *druzia*? Anything new?"

The goons groaned in lieu of a response and put a hand on the Mausers sticking out of their belt holsters.

"Never mind," he sighed. "I thought we could make some small talk to make the time go by faster, but I can see you're not much for words . . ."

He shrugged and shut his mouth, and they stood there in silence as the night passed, all while the voices of the Perovs and the Vanchovs muttered behind the locked door. They didn't come into the room that night, and they did not come in the following day . . . In fact, they didn't appear at the door again until late on the night of the thirty-first of May, and, tired and sour, informed him he'd been sentenced. Then they nodded at yet another pair of goons to take him out of the shack.

They took him out to a yard enclosed by a stone wall, where either Vancho or Ionko or another of the king's men going about their business in these volatile places cut off his head. The others wrapped the head in rags, stored it away in a leather saddlebag, and stuffed his body back in the car.

All this happened at the precise hour in which the wrecked body of the poet, jammed into a sack, was thrown from a black truck into a muddy hole by the Ilianski Base* on the outskirts of Sofia. The men inside the vehicle threw some scraps of garbage and five dog

[Monday, January 7, 2013]
carcasses on top, lest someone come digging around.

[Tuesday, January 8, 2013]
[Before I forget! On the afternoon of that same fifteenth of May, when the agent took her husband away to the station for an inquiry, Mila Geo Mileva sent a telegram to her brother-in-law, Boris. She'd already been to the Police Directorate to ask after her husband, but when she was told no person by that name was there, she'd become perturbed. She summoned Boris to Sofia immediately without revealing why . . .

Boris was, at that time, secretary to the Stara Zagora governor—Stavri Andreev someone-or-other. As soon as he received the dispatch from his sister-in-law, Boris's heart sank. That year such telegrams were never a good sign. He *knew* how people disappeared that spring, he knew about the so-called rogue agents*—those in charge of murdering political opponents—he knew about *all of it*. The very first thing he did when he got the telegram was to call that same Stavri Andreev and ask him to arrange a meeting with the director of Public Safety in Sofia, Vladimir Nachev. Andreev picked up the phone at once and the man on the other end, Nachev, confirmed that Geo Milev was indeed at the Police Directorate, not to worry, but Boris caught the overnight train to Sofia nevertheless.

He arrived before sunrise the following day, now the sixteenth of May, and took the first taxi, or maybe the first phaeton, and headed straight to see Nachev. Not at the Police Directorate, either, but right to the man's house—because he and Nachev went back to the army days and had served together in the same regiment . . . Nachev, astounded, told him that his brother had never been there, and who would tell him such a thing! Boris, even more astounded, reminded him of the previous night's conversation with Stavri Andreev, but Nachev swore that he hadn't spoken to Andreev in weeks! He went as far as to cross himself.

"Honest to God!" he said. "Boris, brother, don't talk like that. Have I ever lied to you?!"

That is what he said and gave his word that he would personally look into the whole thing, and call Boris back the very next day . . . Boris only let out a groan and went to Maria Luisa Boulevard to reassure Mila and Maria that everything would be all right.

But the next day was a Sunday and of course Nachev didn't call, so on Monday Boris marched right into Public Safety. There, Vladimir Nachev told him immediately that he had checked everywhere and now only the worst could be assumed: that his brother may really have been taken by rogue agents . . .

Boris erupted and demanded to know what Nachev was insinuating—that his brother was done for and there was no use in searching for him?

"Is that what you're saying?" he yelled. "Or are you telling me that you can protect the Sakarovs and the Bakalovs and Kabakchievs,˙ who have been propagating communism for years, and whom you now coddle and protect, because God forbid, what's Europe going to say! But my brother, who is scarred from head to toe from fighting for this country, you can leave him like a toy in the hands of some so-called rogue agents? I hope that isn't what you are saying!"

He continued, questioning what this pathetic little country had come to, and pounded Nachev's desk with his fist. He then snapped that he would quit, he wouldn't stay secretary to the governor for one more second.

"Don't be stupid," Nachev said.

"Watch me."

Boris slammed the door.

He went right to Captain Kocho Stoyanov, with whom he'd also served, and whom the Minister of War, Vulkov, and the Minister of Internal Affairs, Russev, had now appointed Police Marshal of Sofia.

This same Stoyanov jumped to his feet as soon as he saw Boris and bustled around him, asking after his father and what could possibly have brought him here, but Boris cut him off:

"I demand to know the whereabouts of my brother—the writer Geo Milev!"

Kocho Stoyanov stood confused: "Oh, Geo Milev? He's your brother? That Geo Milev—your brother?"

When Boris looked into the eyes of this former *friend from the regiment*, he knew instantly—not only did this person know exactly his brother's whereabouts and his fate, but he had personally ordered the execution. Boris felt his world collapse and his knees buckled with a helplessness he'd never before felt; he realized he would no longer be looking for his brother, but for his brother's body. And the most he could hope for now was to give his brother a proper funeral . . .

He suddenly remembered how, when they were children, he trailed after his older brother, his *batko*, like a little puppy, and his batko had seemed so much older and so much bigger—an entire year bigger! His batko was always drawing and drawing and drawing . . . And if he didn't like the drawing—he ripped up the paper and Boris scurried to pick up the scraps. Batko drew, then ripped the paper and threw it away, and Boris picked it back up, over and over again. And when Boris got all the little scraps—he'd glue them back together in his own little notebook . . . then hide the notebook in very secret places, and his batko just laughed and laughed . . .

Boris remembered too how he and his batko—barely five and six-years-old—were coming back from the vineyard one autumn with their father, Milyo Kassabov. Their father, their *tatko*, picked up an acorn from the lawn outside the train station and told them that this was where all the big trees they saw all around came from. Both of the boys rushed to gather up all the acorns they could find, planting them right next to the well, where the earth was moist, because that's what their tatko said to do.

And it really happened! The very next spring two little oaks sprung up from the ground. The boys immediately encircled them with nice big stones and watered them: just as their tatko had instructed them.

The following year, Boris's little oak dried up, but his batko's only got bigger and bigger. It grew quickly and unstoppably, surpassing the stone wall, then the shed, and then the house, until it reached the sky. And that's where it stayed—in the sky. Their little sister Maria loved to lay by the thick, trimmed box tree and look up at the clouds through the oak branches. "Did you see the fairy up in the cloud?" Geo would ask her. And she'd swear she had. "Batko's little poetess!" he'd exclaim.

. . . And Boris wept, then stood up and left.

Kocho Stoyanov yelled at his back, "I know nothing about this matter, I haven't even the slightest idea about any of it!" And he repeated this until Boris had exited the building, leaving the gaping door behind him . . .

. . . Well, who's to say if this was the way things did or didn't happen? . . .

The world is fucked up, and so is Bulgaria.]

1.

[Thursday, January 10, 2013]

Towering and swarthy like a raw-boned raven, the young man from Yambol marched next to Sheytanov in the humming Sofia dusk. It was the fall of nineteen twenty-three, the first day after the government had lifted the martial law; the young man was convinced he knew the poet Geo Milev very well, and was recounting the latter's visit to Yambol the year before last, where some idiot, some witless moron, had had the nerve to arrest him.

"Can you believe it, Sheytanov?" The young man gesticulated wildly and kept tripping over his own feet along the sidewalk. "He had, you know, long hair over his eye, and can you even guess who that idiot mistook him for?! . . ."

Sheytanov said nothing and only smiled, but the young man went on to say the dumb cop had mistaken the poet Geo Milev for none other than Georgi Sheytanov himself! The cop had arrested him, even dragged him down to the station . . . Yambolian bullshit. The young man had immediately run after them, demanding to know whether these people were out of their heads—did they even know whom they'd detained?

"And so I tell them," he went on, "that this is the apostle of contemporary Bulgarian art, and they respond well how the hell are we supposed to know that he's an apostle, Krustev! . . . To us, they tell me, he's just some strange-looking guy, and it's our duty to find out who he is and what he's doing! You dimwits, I tell them, you, I tell them, I know you don't read newspapers, but don't you at least read the placards? They're everywhere! Have you heard nothing about tonight's lecture? He's a Bulgarian writer who gives lectures—that's it, I tell them. We're embarrassing ourselves. I lay into them real good, I'm telling you."

Sheytanov wasn't acquainted with the young man—he knew his father, the bookshop owner Vassil Krustev. He'd often stop by his shop on Coburg Square in Yambol, right next to the tram stop with the two municipal horses tied up in front of it. But on this day in October, it so happened that when Sheytanov went to Professor Kazandjiev's lecture at the university, someone pointed out the young Krustev during the break, so he went up to him and introduced himself. The kid practically jumped out of his skin. The anarchist only smiled and suggested the kid work on not getting so startled in the future.

[Years later, when this same young man from Yambol was deep into his wise years, he'd tell anybody who'd listen that he hadn't been the least bit startled when he met the anarchist. He told everybody how he'd immediately spotted the gun underneath the frightening man's polished suit, but hadn't been the least bit scared. Not *in the least*! And then he'd remember something even scarier: the gun hadn't actually been underneath the overcoat, but inside that wide-brimmed hat Sheytanov was known for, and he held it folded in his hand like a bag, so that when the young man had peeked inside, he saw not only the gun, but a bomb, too. And Sheytanov had said: "Just in case!"

Sometimes those listening to the stories laughed under their breath disrespectfully. "Come on now, Bai Krustev, what gun, what bomb inside a hat are you going on about? What would he need a bomb for, he was on his way to meet a poet, not take out a general. You," they'd say, "you're starting to lose it a bit, eh?" He looked at them, young and disbelieving, mocking him . . . but he held his head high and shrugged it off: "Those were the times! Everybody in Yambol," he'd yell, "went around with guns and bombs . . . You wouldn't understand."

Then he'd wave his hand and go on.

"I too am still wondering," he explained assuredly, "where I got the courage that night to go for a stroll in such company. I suppose I had no fear then."

Anyway, when he—the *most wanted man in the entire kingdom,* whose name derived from *sheitan,* Turkish for "devil"—had come up to ask the then-young Krustev whether he'd introduce him to the poet, he had responded without so much as blinking an eye: "You bet I will! Let's go." Now the elder Krustev kept jabbering and believing everything he said.]

[Friday, January 11, 2013]
"He was really pissed, I'm telling you," the young Krustev wouldn't shut up afterward on the street, zigzagging between the throngs of people. "He says to them, 'I am a Bulgarian writer, and who the hell are you!' And before that, we've got him on a caïque. We're taking him to one of our people across the river in Cargon . . . Romantic, right? But then the boat starts swaying, and our guy's practically screaming . . . 'What the hell are you doing? Goddamn it, are you trying to drown me in your Tundzha? Is that what you want, you giftless scumbags! Ha ha, I'm only joking!' He said he was joking, but he seemed really pissed off to me! . . . So we bring him to my house straight from the station. My mother starts setting the table for him—taramasalata, yogurt, crepes, this and that, and he turns to me, 'Hey Kiril, a minute ago you tried drowning me in that damn river of yours and now you want to starve me to death. Look at me, do I look like someone who can get by on taramasalata and crepes? I need *manja*! I,' he says, 'love nothing more than to eat manja and converse.' Well, I got embarrassed. I got up right away and ran across the street to the Little Kazak, where I grab, no joke, an entire pan of stuffed peppers, and run back home . . ."

Krustev and Sheytanov drifted through the jovial Sofia crowds and the kid from Yambol kept on shouting excitedly, lest Sheytanov assumed all they'd done with the poet was eat and drink, which they surely had, of course—entire Dionysian suites followed the poet's lecture at the Yellow Salon. And he'd said it exactly like that—*Dionysian suites,* nonchalantly adding that what he meant were *bacchanal transpositions from ancient Dionysus,* of course. The poet had drunk them all under the table, for the man could drink. The young men—in all their Bohemian glory!—had barely finished a tin of wine (they all drank from petrol tins which they called *amphorae of modernism*), but the poet, he had drained one entirely by himself. The kid was impressed. The poet had been a great aesthete otherwise. And he had immediately agreed to contribute to their magazine in Yambol . . .

Sheytanov had heard of their magazine, yes, and smiled. They'd started it in Yambol—in all their Bohemian glory!—in the spring of twenty-two with all the ferocious earnestness and exalted impertinence in the world, and had not only convinced the poet to write for them, but had somehow contacted the famous Italian poet Marinetti himself. Their magazine halted publication after only the second issue, naturally. At the time, Sheytanov had been at the commune near Ruse, but frequently came back either to Sliven or to Yambol, and when he did, he was sure to stop by to see the young man's father, Vassil Krustev, at his bookstore, where he had learned of their magazine with the bombastic name: *Crescendo*. As a joke, he and Vassil Krustev wagered a bet to see just how long these literary Qizilbash would last before they abandoned the whole thing. The bookseller laughed bitterly and told him that he'd sold a whole four copies of the first issue, three from the second, and that if the philosophizing slackers had really pushed, they could have gotten to six issues out of pure pig-headedness—just long enough to spend the last of their literary patron Petkov's money. Sheytanov bet they'd make it to five issues. But in the end, both guessed wrong.

And so it went . . .

[Friday, January 11, 2013]

It was as though Sofia had come to life again following the bleakness of martial law on this Wednesday, the tenth of October, nineteen twenty-three: the confectionaries were once again sweet with the aroma of caramelized sugar, cakes and *boza*; the cafés rolled up their blinds with a bang and the waiters ran around drawing the colorful awnings and setting the tables on the sidewalks; the beer halls were already brimming with men and easy women, and flower girls and cigarette girls squeezed between the tables; charcoal pans smoked with the first chestnuts of autumn; the shops took down the shutters from their window displays and set out whole sacks and crates of uncovered goods; and the servant girls hurried along with their baskets, picking out dinner for their masters . . . And so it was! And besides, who enjoys sullen times? By the afternoon, everyone had already forgotten about the two horrible weeks that followed the September mutiny, when the streets were patrolled by a military watch day and night and the horses of the sour-faced mounted Sofia police clopped along the pavement, and the plateless black trucks rattled back and forth, loaded with things no one in the city wanted to imagine.

But now the city hummed with an air of jubilance and the pointy-roofed newspaper stands opened once again,

[Now I remember! Some newspapers managed to get their evening editions printed earlier that afternoon, filled with the panicked declarations that so and so, following the unparalleled September endeavor of such and such, had cut all ties with the so-called communist party and conjured the esteemed public not to mistake them ever again for those villains the communists.

This trend had appeared as early as June of twenty-three, when dozens of frightened people—downtrodden deadbeats with beggars' habits and vile dispositions—clamored to denounce the agrarian union.

And all these newspaper columns were positioned right alongside the news about how the now brutally murdered prime minister Aleksandar Stamboliyski's closet inside his villa in Slavovitsa was, apparently, overflowing with lace slips and women's silk culottes, not to mention how entire milk-cans of perfume had been found at his homestead in Zaharna Fabrika. It would appear the village tribune practically bathed in perfume!

But so what, nothing new under the sun . . .]

and the walls and the ad pillars, variously colored by the newspaper placards and vibrant posters, announced everything imaginable. The Drummers Cabaret, showcasing *Stamboliyski in the Heavens* from Borio Zevzeka; the public lectures of the famous Russian professor Aleksei Etastovich Yanisheski from the Sofia medical faculty and his lecture "Fear and Bravery"; the traveling healer Nesterov—a scientist, supposedly, but really a charlatan and incomparable whoremonger—with his noisy scholarly essays on psychological phenomena and their application in treating nerve-related illnesses; the Italian acrobat Montagnani, the king of the tight rope; there were new and already old placards for German films (*Nosferatu: A Symphony of Horrors* at the Modern Theater down Maria Louisa Boulevard; Paul Wegener's *The Golem* at Gloria Palace); Russian concerts, all things of that sort . . . and the two of them, the young man from Yambol and Sheytanov, marched all around that kaleidoscope of color, first down Shipka Boulevard, past Sofia University, then past the King's manège, by the Alexander Nevsky Cathedral, built long-ago yet still unconsecrated, down Moskovska Street, and from then on toward Dondukov Boulevard, where one could barely get past the crowds and where the vitrines of the famous butcher shops of Dokuzanov and Krusharov were festooned with smoked pigs' heads and legs, salamis gilded in foils, and countless sorts of *sudjuk*, where the trams turned with a scream down the even louder Targovska Street or pushed straight ahead to the Sveta Nedelya Cathedral.

From Dondukov Boulevard they turned by the Macedonia bookstore and descended down Targovska Street toward the Berlin Hotel, where the jovial babel of the first customers rose up from the garden. From there down to Banski Square—through the garden, where a street organ was breaking the hearts of bystanders and a parrot pulled fortunes out of a nearby box, and a hundred grinning shoe-shiners tapped on their boxes, and phaetons and expensive automobiles were lined up along the curb . . . The construction sounds of gas chainsaws screamed and grated down the tiny side streets in all directions, and extending above all of that was the ineradicable twittering of the billions of Sofia sparrows and the hollow cooing of the pigeons.

"Krustev, Krustev . . ." said Sheytanov to the young man. "How funny life is. Just look at these people. Loosen their leash just a touch— and off they go, celebrating . . ."

"No shit!" he said, repulsed. "Philistines."

[Saturday, January 12, 2013]
. . . The two men arrived at the poet's apartment building, which was across the street from the Banya Bashi Mosque and was practically glued to the side of the Market Hall. A pharmacy stood at one end; at the other end a sign enthusiastically advertised the boza beverage company Radomir; right next to the main building door, yet another sign publicized an import-export bank with branches in Varna and Burgas, and a "Post Office" sign hung above the door; and above all that, between the second and the third floors, the dark blue blinds of the Bulgarian offices of the company Longines stretched all the way from one end of the building to the other. The two men crossed the boulevard with its red trams rattling on their way to Lavov Most, and headed over to the dark mass of Sveta Nedelya and pushed open the heavy wooden front door. Sheytanov spotted the doorbell bearing the poet's name and saw "77 steps" written right next to it, which made him laugh.

"Are you laughing about the steps?!" the young man exclaimed. "It's absolutely, exactly seventy-seven, I counted!"

Then they both spotted someone had scribbled "Cyclops!" below the doorbell and the young man, angry at the sight of the reference to the one-eyed monster, shouted:

"Bastards! Come on, let's go, and try not to swear."

They climbed up the red carpet, fastened by brass rods to the wide staircase, and went straight to the fourth floor . . .

When the poet opened the door, Sheytanov held out his hand:

"Sheytanov."

"I know," the other responded, "Milev."

"I know."

[Sunday, January 13, 2013]

Sheytanov had spent nights in all manner of locations, been all over, including lux hotels—places of quiet, calm debauchery, sophisticated brothels, really, with an endless supply of hot water, silk sheets, and feather duvets; the hallways were covered in carpets a centimeter deep and the hotel whores were bathed, discreet, and polite. But he'd also laid his head down in hovels with dirt floors, blackened straw-mattresses, and snorting cattle. This place, however, truly impressed him. Originally designed as a regular apartment, the poet's abode was now a vast single room he'd cleverly partitioned with curtains, like an enfilade. There was a vestibule, a bedroom, a kitchen, and between them a hallway adorned with dozens of prints from famous paintings by Marc Chagall, Heinrich Zille, and Edvard Munch. There was also a little room behind a colorful cotton print for his oldest daughter (who was already a little miss of three, a hair before four, even, and she couldn't possibly be expected to sleep in the same room as some baby!), an office for him, and even a guest room by the window facing the boulevard, where the first electric streetlights came on as dusk fell.

And the ceilings . . . high as the sky.

"Well," the poet spread out his arms, "here we are, this is our life, maybe not the one we want, but for now, the one we have . . ."

"You have a great place here," Sheytanov reassured him. "Very nice. Cozy and comfortable . . ."

"Ha-ha!" the other laughed. "Well, I'm not complaining! I can rearrange it at any time, and the most important thing is that with walls like these, there's no need for us to yell from one room to another . . . But the kids love it too—they can potter about without having to worry about opening doors. Apart from that, the coziness is entirely Mila's doing, and the comfort—well, that's all me."

He continued laughing and added that if they were to ask Kiril, he'd tell them that in a bourgeoisie apartment, the orderliness of only two rooms mattered: the *bath-room* and the *toilet-room*! . . . The young man's face went scarlet as he began to explain himself, arguing that the poet had in fact quoted the Soviet writer Ehrenburg, but the other cut him off again.

"Ehrenburg, Shmehrenburg—you're both wrong! The most wonderful place in a bourgeoisie apartment is the *dining room*, Bai Krustev . . . The dining room!"

And he let out an even louder chortle . . .

The poet led them to the guest room and excitedly pointed to the window. This was the best part about living on the fourth floor, he explained—you could watch the world from up high, both the people and the city, and he wasn't quite sure which he liked more, watching the city or the human ant trail underneath. But he most loved watching the trams—the way they followed the straight line from the bridge all the way down the entire boulevard with certitude, then obediently made their turn up by the church. He noted how only the minaret across the street was higher than his building, but that didn't bother him since the mosque was so old and grand—a true masterpiece created long ago by Mimar Sinan himself.

"So, there you have it," he said, "nothing more to say about our place, really. Oh, yes, and I don't need curtains on the windows, either—it's not as if the muezzin's going to be peering in from his minaret. Let's sit, and please, make yourselves at home."

They sat around the round, lace milieu-covered table, while the poet's astonishingly beautiful wife quickly brought glasses and a bottle of wine as her youngest daughter pattered behind her, still a baby at barely two years, and the eldest marched with a grandiose waddle wanting very much to show everyone that she cared about nothing else but the doll in her arms, likely sewn by her mother. Aromas mingled all around—the tart scent of the washing, the bouquet of an autumn stew, and of milk, from behind the canvas to the kitchen.

And the smell of books . . .

[Sunday, January 13, 2013]

At some point the little girl couldn't stand it anymore and stepped out from behind her kingdom of disinterestedness, went up to Sheytanov, and tugged on his sleeve. When he looked at her, the little girl politely said:

"How do you do? My name is Leda-Evgenia Georgieva Kassabova! Nice to meet you!"

And he responded:

"Likewise young lady—Sheytanov, Georgi Vassilev! . . . You have a very pretty doll."

Then he scrunched up his face a little and repentantly asked:

"But shouldn't I have introduced myself first?"

"Oh, no," Leda explained. "That's only how grownups do it. Kids should always go first, so that the adults aren't always saying 'what's your name, little girl, what's your name, little girl? . . .'"

Sheytanov put a hand to his heart in relief, about to ask her something else, when she beat him to it and reproachfully queried:

"Where is your wife, Mister Sheytanov? Is she in Stara Zagora or Berlin?"

The poet's wife started to scold her, but the little girl sighed and went on:

"Is she expecting?"

Now everybody laughed and the poet's wife picked up the child to carry her to her room. Leda looked over her mother's shoulder and still managed to get out:

"Isn't that what women do? Expect children?"

Her mother lifted the printed curtain to her room, and Leda Georgieva Mileva waved her hand, courteously declaring:

"Good night, sleep tight, don't let the bedbugs bite!"

"The third will be a boy," the poet declared proudly. "We've made our decision . . . My mother and father started with two boys. I was first, followed by my brother, Boris, and then four beautiful girls, one after the other. We'll do it just the opposite—two girls and four strong boys!

[Monday, January 14, 2013]

They spoke at length next to that window, behind which the gray night had already fallen. The first tattered Sofia fog fumed between the streetlights, and beyond the fog, the cupola of the sign for the Splendid Hotel seeped through like a silver halo. They drank up the wine while they conversed, and Sheytanov gave the young man from Yambol money to run across the street to Turgovska to get some more before the public houses shut down for the night on account of the police curfew. They kept talking throughout that first night—the poet asked questions, Sheytanov answered, then vice versa . . . Sheytanov set forth to the poet his own take: there was no other god but ordinary man, and it was he who sat at the center of the universe, not the state.

"The state," he said, "is a badly written fable, an abominable pyramid scheme for cowards and marauders, and it is man who stands at the center of the universe . . ." The poet slammed his hand on the table and challenged him: were Tsankov, Russev, and Vulkov,* the current prime minister and his two generals, were *they* in fact the ordinary man?

Sheytanov told him to leave the Russevs and the Vulkovs alone . . .

"They," he said, "are a fluke, an anecdote. And a sinister one at that, but an anecdote nevertheless, as was the miserable Stamboliyski,* with his pitiful ministers and his delusions of grandeur, attempting to bring down Tsankov and getting slaughtered. Not to mention the others, the Dimitrovs and the Kolarovs,* who couldn't even incite a proper civil war, instead fleeing through the border and writing letters from Vienna. All of them," he said, "are miscreants."

The poet acquiesced. He knew from his own father that Ivan Vulkov's father was known as *Urdechkata*—the Goose—in Kazanluk.

"How low have we sunk to if we've got the sons of geese for generals? General Goose. What has Bulgaria come to!"

They went on until ten o'clock, when Mila had long put the little girls to bed behind all those draperies and curtains. She'd brought a glass for herself too and sat quietly next to them, looking at her guests with the wide eyes of an actress, while the last trams, vacant due to the unrelenting curfew, made their way to their depots.

After a minute or two of silence, Sheytanov calmly asked the poet:

"Milev . . . What do you say we start another magazine?"

The poet froze. "What magazine?" he snarled, but Sheytanov saw in the poet's good eye such a quick, fierce hope, that he hurried to smile.

"A magazine," he said. "A literary magazine."

[Monday, January 14, 2013]

The poet jumped from the chair, leaned sharply over the table, and hissed:

"Sheytanov! Are you mocking me, my dear man?"

Sheytanov looked at him, incredulous. "Me? Why would I do that?"

"You tell me!" the poet remained furious. "You obviously are. You have the gall to bring up a magazine in the house of the damned. Have some respect!"

Sheytanov only sighed and asked the poet to forgive him if he'd felt insulted, that he'd be on his way at once. The poet's wife stood and carefully wiped the tear rolling out from beneath the black lens of her husband's glasses.

"You'll wake the children," she calmly said. "Hear the man out, then decide if it's worth getting angry for."

The poet glared at her as though he were going to slap her across the face, then calmed down as quickly as he'd boiled over. He sat back down in his chair and mumbled that he hadn't been right to lose his temper, but that he'd been through a lot lately. He still found it hard, he said, not to get angry over losing the magazine he had so hoped would push this pitiful Bulgarian literary landscape forward. Instead, no one saw past his own nose and every ego was more inflated than the next . . . He gave an irate flick of his wrist and reached for his cigarettes.

He smoked violently, as if he were murdering someone, and lit up frequently. Often, as he pulled out a new Sultan cigarette from his officer's cigarette tin, the previous one would still be smoldering in the small Japanese ashtray next to him, only half smoked. His better half would only sigh, reach over, and quietly put it out, and then he'd already be on his third. When he gesticulated with his hands, the smoke curled up like a whirlwind around him and the ashes scattered everywhere.

Sheytanov politely heard him out, and when he was done talking, he just as courteously asked him if he could offer an observation.

"Go on," the other snapped.

Sheytanov shrugged. "At the risk of offending you a second time, Milev, I do have to admit that *Vezny* simply didn't resemble a real magazine . . ." And just as politely he added, "I apologize for having to put it that way."

"I see," the other snarled combatively. "And what exactly do you mean?"

"Well, what I mean is . . ." Sheytanov smiled. "You simply can't call a pamphlet folded in eight and printed on terrible paper—with no cover to speak of—a magazine. Especially if, inside that very same publication, you are writing about aesthetics."

The poet bristled again and tried explaining that it didn't matter what a magazine looked like—what mattered was what was written *in* the magazine!

Sheytanov stopped him.

"Really?" he asked thoughtfully. "Should we ask the young man how many issues of *Vezny* his dad sold in Yambol?"

"I know exactly how many he sold!" The poet lost it again. "I know perfectly well how many! One. That's how many. That beanpole over there was my only subscriber."

He vehemently pointed to Kiril as the latter began to fidget in his chair, grew red in the face, and started loudly protesting that he could explain. It was because his friends came over to read it with him, and each had felt relieved from the material obligation of purchasing it, you see, which was why they hadn't all subscribed, the dogs. And he would've gone on, but the poet cut him off.

"Kiril, shut up, my friend. Just listen to yourself, goddamn it, you'll get your tongue up in a knot. Material obligation, my ass. You're all nothing more than petty conmen, every last one of you. And don't give me that face. You still owe me that hundred leva for the translation, and aside from that, eighty-four leva for the subscription for the German magazine you never sent me! Now sit your ass back down and shut up."

"Why don't you," Mila spoke up then, "leave Kiril alone for a minute and hear the man out?"

She then turned to Sheytanov with a gentle expectancy. He simply shrugged and repeated that he wasn't here to pick fights, but that, in his humble opinion, a magazine ought to look good, too.

"In any case, how something is presented is quite important. A person is more likely to buy something beautiful, and, if it also happens that it ends up being of value to him . . ."

"You think I don't know that?" the poet burst out again. "You think I don't know what quality paper is, you think I don't want a thick cover and a spine, so that you can put the magazine in your bookcase, like a normal person? Huh? You think I don't know what an illustrated magazine is supposed to look like? So you can publish prints, so you can have paper at the very least on par with *Illustrated Week*, so you can put photographs on every page, illustrated supplements . . ." he sighed and waved his hand hopelessly.

"That's exactly what I had in mind," Sheytanov calmly responded. "Just like *Illustrated Week*, why not?"

"And did you think about the money? Where's the money going to come from?" the poet looked at him sideways. "Do you have any idea how much paper costs now? And I mean regular paper—I'm not even talking about chrome paper. Do you have any idea how greedy those miscreant printers have become? They tell you they're buried under urgent print jobs, thirty thousand labels and God knows what else, and that you, with your measly print of three thousand, would just be getting in their way. And they're looking for handouts. I give them a piece of my mind, and I go someplace else, but it's always the same story.

"A guy just like that has the guts to say to me, 'Well Mr. Milev, you know the printing press is a lot like the millstone at the flour mill. When it turns,' he says, 'the flour falls into the miller's bag, but the person who brings the grist to the mill gets a little toll too, right?' 'Okay I get it,' I say to him, 'nothing wrong with a little toll, but this bag you have, *djanum*, is bottomless!'

"Extortionist prices everywhere . . . My father can't take it anymore, either. I'm asking him for money to buy paper, he writes that he can't believe the numbers. I'm wracking my brain how to keep the business going, how to make it reputable, and he's writing back that we need to cut back. And he sends me a case of miniature bust portraits so that I can sell *them* to buy the printing paper. Who am I supposed to push this stuff to? My grandmother? I left seventy with Chipev—he sold one in three months. One! Ibsen's. Lenin's is not selling that well for some reason. So Chipev—who's avoiding me at this point—am I supposed to try to sell him more of these? They're asking an arm and a leg at the royal presses too. It's madness. 'Is this some kind of joke,' I ask them, and they answer, 'No joke, that's how much it costs today, and we can't guarantee how much it'll cost tomorrow.' And this, at the royal presses, where they're meant to have the most reasonable prices . . ."

And he didn't stop at that. He grabbed a piece of paper and a pencil, wiped yet another trickle off his cheekbone, and began to scratch towering columns of numbers.

"See here," he said, "this is how much they wanted last year just to publish Verlaine's collection of selected poetry. I went and bought paper from Lazar Kotev, because it's smaller, seventy centimeters to a hundred and eight, and it's lighter, around thirty-five grams to the sheet. So, for forty kilograms, I don't get a thousand sheets like if I were to buy them from Chipev, but instead fourteen, almost fifteen hundred. Win, win. Add the numbers: forty kilograms times sixteen leva, what is that? Six hundred forty. Ten leva go to Bureau Express for shipping to Stara Zagora, so what are we at, six hundred fifty, right? I borrowed four hundred from my father . . . that makes it two hundred fifty. I got two hundred nineteen from going around the newspaper stands like an idiot, I gave thirty-one from my own pocket . . . Oh, I forgot Chipev's wooden box for shipping—another fifty leva. This is just for the regular circulation. Let's compare with the luxury edition. One sheet yields two quires, so for one hundred issues in five quires, we need two hundred fifty sheets. Chipev, that's where I had to go, because he's got better paper than Kotev, and Chipev wants six hundred fifty leva from me. And how I tormented him to cut it down to six hundred. He wouldn't budge! So now one sheet comes out to two-sixty. That's when I gave up and decided not to print a hundred issues from the luxury edition, but fifty, because then we'll need only a hundred twenty-five sheets, which is the same as three hundred twenty-five Bulgarian leva . . ."

Sheytanov heard him out without interrupting, but when the poet turned the sheet over, about to start some other calculation, he politely raised his hand.

"Look, Milev," he said. "How about we don't talk about money right now?"

The poet stuttered and tried to object, but Sheytanov asked:

"If you were a general about to lead your troops into battle, what would your battle cry be?"

"I don't know," he mumbled. "Maybe 'On to battle!' I don't know . . ."

"Most people think that," smiled Sheytanov. "But if you ask me, a general, a military commander, shouldn't have 'On to battle!' as his war cry. I think a real general would tell his people 'After me!'"

The poet shook his finger at him . . . He laughed suddenly, and told Sheytanov his thinking was identical to that of the Bulgarian writer Joseph Herbst. He'd written a similar anecdote . . . In the middle of the night, a young soldier runs away from the bottom trenches—he's looking for a better seat in the *battlefield theater*. An officer stops him, "Where do you think you're running to, soldier?" "Well, I must have gotten lost, Second Lieutenant, sir," the young soldier replies. "What the hell are you talking about boy, I'm a chief corporal major!" And the soldier responds: "Gee, how far did I run?"

Sheytanov erupted in laughter, but Kiril sat silent . . .

"You didn't get it, did you Kiril?" the poet was laughing too. "And how would you, you haven't even been to the barracks, let alone fought in the war . . . The battlefront is like the theater, my dear boy—the best seats are in the back."

He gesticulated and smacked the table triumphantly.

"Sheytanov!" he said, "And do you know, my friend, that I already have a name? *Plamuk*! What do you say? *Plamuk. Flame.*"

Sheytanov looked at him and quickly raised his glass.

"And so," he said in turn, "then what are we waiting for? Let's do this! You'll be in charge of the magazine, I'll get in your hair, and we'll take it as it comes."

[Monday, January 14, 2013]
[Would you look at that, it snowed this afternoon. And it's sticking . . . I hadn't even noticed.]

[Tuesday, January 15, 2013]
"Now we're talking!" the young man from Yambol spoke up—and years later, when he would grow old, proudly, and with the stateliness of a solitary wise man, he would write in his journals about the things that happened on that Wednesday night, the tenth of October, nineteen twenty-three, a day after the authorities had lifted the martial law declaration brought on by the king's eleventh decree, and lasting eighteen miserable days . . .

The poet's wife rose up from her chair, thanked them for their visit, and asked them to come back often, then wished them goodnight with a kind and tired bright smile before disappearing through the dreamlike draperies. The three of them wished her a good night and sat around the table until the first garbage trucks began to roll down the boulevard and the powerful streams from the street cleaners' water-carts pelted the pavement. They thought about everything on that long-forgotten night and made many decisions.

And so it was.

At the end, when he and the young man from Yambol stood up to go, Sheytanov took out a package from his overcoat, wrapped haphazardly in newspaper. He gave it to the poet and said:

"Don't worry, this is just to start things off . . . you decide what you'll do with it, but," he said, "don't go to a cheap printer."

The poet unfolded the newspaper and the young man's

[Wednesday, January 16, 2013]

eyes bulged from their sockets. The package contained money, a lot of it—a pile of hundreds equal to ten, maybe even fifteen thousand leva, according to his lighting-quick estimation.

"Look at that!" he couldn't contain himself. "That's a lot of money!"

"It's a lot for our enslavers, *du lieber Augustin!*" the poet cut him off scornfully. "And if you're going to be appalled, don't do it here."

"Milev," Sheytanov began, grinning at him rakishly, "I hope you understand that I don't want this mountain giving birth to a molehill. I have my name attached to it. I don't want to become a laughing stock."

"Neither do I, Sheytanov," the poet assured him. "Neither do I."

As he said that, he wrapped the money back in the newspaper and dropped it into the pocket of his housecoat,

[Thursday, January 17, 2013]

while the young Kiril, as soon as he got back to his student flat—unexpectedly and surprising even him—turned toward what he thought was the east (he had long lost any sense of direction in the labyrinth of corridors and crooked attic staircases) and whispered excitedly:

"Thank you, dear God, for this day and for giving me these intelligent comrades! Something great's going to happen! Amen!"

Not that he believed in God, but saying a prayer had been a habit he'd developed as a child, when he was chastised anytime he didn't say one, so he said one now, just in case.

Then he got under the covers and fell asleep in an instant.

[Sunday, January 20, 2013]
[How strange . . . it's the twentieth of January and yet it couldn't be more like spring outside. There's not a trace of the dusting of snow that fell last week, and the sand poured on the streets by the sanitation department has gotten into everything, crunching under our feet as we track it into our houses on our shoes . . . Only the sky isn't a spring sky—it's gray and lead-like. Strange indeed.]

2.

[Tuesday, January 22, 2013]

What might have gone through Sheytanov's mind when a handful of unkempt villagers clad in breeches jumped out from the other side of the railroad tracks with their crooked rifles? He knew what they were up to. It was a well known fact the authorities mobilized armed groups in the villages and asked them to patrol the railroads, since killing rebels was still legal—a reality held up by two laws: the Law for the Extermination of Thugs, left over from Alexander Stamboliyski, prime minister and leader of the Agrarian Union until he was ousted in the military coup of June, nineteen twenty-three, brutally tortured, and then murdered; and the Law for the Protection of Bulgaria, with its newly added eleventh article . . .

Sheytanov could have easily escaped the mangy scrags—it wouldn't have been the first time. The wheat had grown tall that spring, and if he were to slip into the surrounding fields he'd have disappeared in minutes and vanished completely into the graying mountains to the north in another hour or two . . . If he had taken off to the east, he would've been back in Yambol by dark and they would have never caught him.

But he could see the villagers in front of him were already jittery, and if he were to take off they would've panicked and fired indiscriminately.

And they would've gotten Mariola . . .

He sighed and stood up.

"Stop, don't move!" the others started screaming. "Don't move! We'll shoot!"

"Relax," he groaned. "Are you blind? I've got my hands up. And put these rifles away before someone gets hurt."

[Wednesday, January 23, 2013]
He looked into Mariola's eyes and his heart broke from anguish and powerlessness: there was no hope in her eyes, only fear.

They'd been on the run for a few days when they'd made a fatal mistake. There was no use in cursing each other out about it now: they'd sent the miller to the Urva neighborhood for provisions, and the grocer would've had to have been an idiot not to figure out what was going on when the customer asked for sixteen packs of cigarettes, *all different brands.* It didn't take long for the search party to come after them—an entire horde of rabid anti-partisan mongrels from Veliko Turnovo. Sheytanov had yelled up at his men to keep running, then sprawled across the mill-stream, shooting at anyone from the enraged mob who showed his head above the trees and bushes—just to make them panic and lose time by having to bury their heads into the piles of last year's leaves. Somewhere behind him, Mariola attempted to take her own life. She grabbed a gun and put it to her head, and were it not for Zhelyo, she may have succeeded. "Mariola!" he hissed in her ear and tore the gun away. "I'll rip your head off, fool! Stop this nonsense!" He then dragged her up in between the trees—away from the forest ambush and into the icy rain, which hadn't stopped for days in that spring of twenty-five, and they were all soaked down to their frozen bones.

[Thursday, January 24, 2013]
He caught up with them all the way up at the Predel. And when he laid eyes on Mariola, drenched like a frightened forest animal and with the same spring coat she'd put on in Kilifarevo on the Monday after Easter, he quickly took off the Poseidon raincoat from his own shoulders and wrapped her up in it. He pushed the wet strands of hair from her forehead, but had no idea what to say to her.

[Friday, January 25, 2013]
Back in Kilifarevo, they couldn't get enough of the story . . . When, on the tenth of June the previous year, a day after the coup, the bells in

Kilifarevo began to toll and the crowd gathered in protest against the coup organizers, it was none other than Mariola's father who came out to talk to the infuriated people in the village square. Whether he did so in his capacity as army reserve captain, or because he had been the former district constable of Turnovo—either way—those currently in power had made him the chair of a three-person committee of the Democratic Alliance, which was created to replace the village administration. But nobody wanted to hear a word of what he had to say. They told him that this fascist committee of his wasn't going to be doing any work here, and announced they were dismantling it and reinstating the village administration.

And there you had it: her father had joined the newly minted fascists, and here she was running away with a band of anarchists. Not with the agrarians, not even with the communists, but with the anarchists . . .

[Saturday, January 26, 2013]
And so it went.

Twelve of them had fled Kilifarevo—and by the time they reached Konyov Roadhouse No. 24, it was only the two of them: him and the girl. Even Zhelyo took off for Turnovo Seimen and Harmanli, looking for Mityo Ganev to lead him into Turkey.

When Sheytanov saw the hopeless fear in Mariola's eyes, he reached out his hand, helped her to her feet, and probably wanted to tell her that everything would be all right . . . but why lie to her? Nothing was going to be all right . . .

"Calm down!" he said to those villagers by the train tracks. "Take it easy with the rifle waving, or you'll do something stupid. . ."

[Sunday, January 27, 2013]
[A long time later, in a completely different time, there would still be those who remembered how in the late afternoon of the twenty-sixth of May, nineteen twenty-five, a whole herd of cops—uniformed and plain-clothes murderers—brought two people, a man and a woman, into the

station in Nova Zagora. They were bound to each other by an awfully short rope—his left hand to her right—and it wasn't until they got them into the muddied yard that they separated them.]

[Monday, January 28, 2013]
Dusk set as king's guards arrived at the police station. They were led by some sort of lieutenant. Darkness had set in completely by the time this lieutenant took out a piece of paper and started walking around the cells, calling out each person on the list. After he called out yet another name, the elite officers dragged the respective person out of the cell and pushed him outside, where the person was then chained up. Each time they hammered down the wedges into the shackles' rings, the yard echoed with a steel clang. They took Sheytanov out last.

3.

[Friday, February 1, 2013]
One Wednesday in November, a little after the National Assembly elections, right on Michaelmas, November eighth, when butchers marched in the streets to celebrate their patron, Sheytanov and Milev had just established a brick-and-mortar location for their *editorial office*: the small apartment of one Marcho from the village of Marcha. The office was located at 145 Rakovski Street, and the poet joked that he worked right across from the Council of Ministers. Marcho's landlord—a civil procedures lawyer, a civil law *specialist*, as the sign outside proclaimed—was an old man completely disinterested in politics, and even less so in literature. He had a son who was studying somewhere in Europe and a paraplegic wife, whom he had to take out for a walk in a wheelchair every day, so keeping track of the comings and goings from his one-story house wasn't a priority. He even ignored the sheet of paper stuck on the brick-colored siding with four drawing pins that read *Plamuk* Magazine . . . The poet went around to all the Sofia presses, waving his hand disdainfully at any mention by the directors of their unreasonable prices, announcing coldly that money was no issue—he wasn't there to haggle. All that mattered was the quality of the publication. Their mouths gaped open and, who knows why, they even started to lower their prices and immediately scattered all sorts of samples on their writing tables: beautiful typographic paper, matte and glossy card stock for the covers and inks and letters made of lead, and antimony for color prints. They sent the workmen to bring artistic jobbing fonts and all sorts of engraving plates: right- and left-pointing arrows; vignettes with grape

leaves or finely engraved fascicules, ornaments with interlaced designs and monograms with Latin letters, anything you could imagine . . . The engraving plates, their precious copper gleaming, weighed no more than a feather because their overlays were made out of hollow cubes from an unknown African tree—light yet resilient. It was reliable and made to last forever . . . They explained all this in great detail, but the poet again gave a disdainful wave of his hand and told them they could put away this garbage. He asked them not to waste his time with unsightly stock imagery, as the magazine would be new and different.

"You can sell this bullshit to Podvurzachov. But not to me. I'm going to work only with original lithographs. The typeface will be Korina and that's that; I'm not discussing this any further."

The printers would quickly agree and begin to imply of even deeper discounts. He responded that he still had to think about it, and then left to go to yet another printer.

And so it went.

[Saturday, February 2, 2013]
Right around that time Geo Milev wrote to five people, inviting them as contributors. He wrote that he was starting a new magazine, which he referred to as "superb" and which would, as its name *Plamuk* suggested, set the literary world ablaze. It would be something entirely different, it would be exactly what everyone had long ago agreed was missing. He wrote that it wouldn't be "expressionistic," it would be nothing like *Vezny,* and that Georgi Bakalov, who thought himself a monopolist of all leftist publications, had already been cut off from it, since he had somehow gotten it in his head that he was going to be *Plamuk*'s guru and use it as a communist pamphlet. New! Every time he got to the part that *Plamuk* would be illustrated, he swelled with pride. *Illustrated,* he wrote. *We have the funding.* And he especially delighted in ending each letter with the following: *Circulation: 3,000. Honorariums: substantial!* He signed off with, *I am eagerly awaiting your response. Yours, Geo Milev.* He was elated and impatient.

It wasn't clear if it was these letters—not yet officially sent—that caused the news of Geo Milev *himself* starting a new magazine to spread so fast and so fiercely around all of Sofia that had turned the tiny room at 145 Rakovski into a veritable madhouse.

Disheveled poets with yellow-tinted lenses flocked from all over with bags bursting with titanic opuses, and Milev read and read and read . . . He read everything, skipping nothing and swearing through it all. "Oh, here's another one!" he roared and recited out loud: "*Poor, pallid Bedouins, wandering desolate deserts, mounted on camels, their legs thin as pins . . .* Unbelievable!" he yelled, and pulled out another piece of paper from the piles of poems. "*When the beak of the wood-pie taps the tired tree . . .* Bravo! You're one dangerous *forgeron*, my friend. Very modernistic, I'm simply speechless. I haven't been privy to such literary crap in quite a while!" and things of that nature. He'd then dress them down even further, address them with a fierce derision and tell one author he didn't know the difference between Thermopylae and Propylaea, or palindrome and palisade; he'd tell another that he wrote madrigals with the exquisite touch of an iron stove; and a third he told to, quite simply, eat shit . . . It was as though he was possessed by a demon of condescension. He threw their folders at them and exclaimed he'd better not see their faces back there again, uniquely giftless as they were, then rudely kicked them out, while they demanded to know the meaning of *forgeron*, and when they did find out—they conceived a hatred for the poet deep within their wounded souls. "Opa!" he would yell after the door slammed shut behind yet another hurt, tearful loser. "Ladies and Gentlemen, yours truly has gained another savage little nemesis! . . . This one here, *zum Beispiel*, I fully expect to become a mighty literary warrior."

And he would laugh darkly, unaware of exactly how right he had been. (Or maybe he had been very aware, who can say.)

[Wednesday, February 6, 2013]

He also cursed those whose essays he did like—but in such a way that they turned scarlet with pride. He alternated between calling them literary heroes and a literary army-supply train, army privates and feebles, demons, waywards and lambs and a literary band of brothers, until they became enraged, suddenly vociferous, taking off and returning before dark, tortured by love and hope and with still more poetry in their hands. Sometimes they materialized wearing two different shoes—let's say one black, one red—and the poet sourly remarked: "Fools! So this is how one becomes a bohemian . . ."

Once, Sheytanov heard him explain writing to a very young man. At first he could barely contain his laughter, but thought better of it and listened—and suddenly the need to mock disappeared.

"Listen to me boy," the poet declared, "here's a little piece of advice from me about what it takes to write. Buy a notebook. Sit down and write something on the first page—write whatever you like. A poem, a story, doesn't matter, just write. The next day, wake up, tear out that first page, rip it up, and throw it in the fire. Or in the garbage, all the same, the important thing is that you throw it out. The next day, write some more—again you'll be on the first page, right? On the third day, wake up, tear it out, crumple it up, and throw it out, then sit back down and write! You follow me? Keep going until you are out of pages in your notebook. Then go and buy a new notebook and start all over again . . . That's it. Somewhere around your tenth notebook you might have something worthwhile."

The young man eyed him with the devotion of a neophyte.

"Do you understand?" Geo Milev asked, but the other kept on staring.

"Well I just don't understand you!" he grew angrier. "Are you dumb, or just an idiot?"

But then he'd get over it.

[*Thursday, February 7, 2013*]
One afternoon, when, for some unknown reason, the whole stable of literary exhibitionists wasn't loitering about and the two men sat alone next to the coal heater in the *editorial offices*, the poet asked Sheytanov

how much of what people were saying was true—that he'd spent time in Paris.

The other gave a dismissive wave.

"I was there long enough to say *bonjour* to the French," he said with a crooked sneer. "Teenage indiscretions . . ."

But then he let out a laugh and admitted that the whole ordeal had actually been a veritable odyssey. He'd only been seventeen when, following a rather puerile attempt to drum up antagonism in Yambol, he'd decided to go off the grid and run away from Bulgaria. Done and done. The antagonizing itself had been quite a good time, too . . . One beautiful summer night, instead of singing songs and pinching the schoolgirls in the city gardens, he and Delyo someone-or-other decided to set fire to the courthouse archives. They bring a demijohn filled with gasoline, enter through an open window, pour out the gas, strike a match and— off they run . . . The archives go up in flames, which is all fine and well, but in the morning, as soon as the constables come to see what's happened, they spot the demijohn's cap right outside the window. And conveniently written on the cap? The name of the store where Delyo had bought the gasoline. The cops go over to the shop to ask the owner a couple of questions and, sure enough, he immediately remembers how Delyo had come in the night before and bought a demijohn filled with gasoline. So, they gather up Delyo, slap him about a couple of times, and Delyo rats out his companion, so the cops gather up Sheytanov too. Then they proceed to spend the entire day idly beating both of them, just so they can't say they got off scot-free; but in the middle of the night, Delyo and Sheytanov kick through the window grating, since, as was customary for those times, the grating was flimsy. Sheytanov grabs a cudgel and runs by the police station, passing right in front of the cop on duty, who, as soon as he spots the cudgel, pretends to be asleep. From there Sheytanov goes home, takes his revolver and his knife, and proudly tucks them into his belt, while his mother watches with fear in her eyes.

"What are you doing?"

"I'm on the lam. There's no other way—I have to go."

And—off he goes!

From Yambol, he takes off for Varna with a stolen passport, boards the cruise liner, and off he goes to Kustendja. From Kustendja, to Bucharest. In Bucharest, some clerk looks at his passport, looks up at him, looks at the passport, back up at him . . . "Now wait a minute *domnul*, sir," he finally says to him in Romanian. "This here says you are thirty years old, but you still look like a student to me. How do you explain that?" "Don't worry about it. I'm an old man, I just can't grow a beard!" The clerk tells him to get lost. So from Bucharest, he hops back to Kustendja, from Kustendja back on another cruise liner into Tsarigrad. But as soon as they catch sight of him in Tsarigrad—disheveled, wrapped in a cape, a wide-brimmed hat on his head—they simply arrest him, without grounds. Two cops start dragging him back to the station, and he thinks to himself, I've barely left home and these two idiots are going to send me right back to Bulgaria—what a waste of gunpowder that would be. As soon as they turn down some crooked street, he just knocks them both down, runs for it, and goes straight to Father Pasterov at the Exarchate. Pasterov, a fellow Yambolian, takes him in and gives him a job, which Sheytanov stays at for an entire month before growing restless and taking off for Jaffa. From Jaffa, to Alexandria, which the Turks still call Iskenderun. From Alexandria, he circles back and this time lands in Jerusalem . . .

"And now you can laugh at me all you want," he added, "but on the twenty-fifth of December, nineteen thirteen, on high Christmas Day, your faithful servant became a Hadji!"

"What?" the poet chortled. "You became a *what?*"

"I became a Hadji!" he laughed back. "I'm dead serious! I leapt into the Jordan River and now—cross my heart—I'm a Hadji, and that's that."

"Would you look at that!" the poet nodded in approval. "I'm speechless! So now you must be Hadji Georgi Hadji Sheytanov!"

"Well, Hadji Georgiev, too!" the other shrugged.

"The first holy devil in the history of civilization!" the poet continued with the same approving tone. "Not bad."

"I'll take it. I even sent my mother a postcard. 'Your son finally became a Hadji, don't cry for me Mother, don't grieve—I'm fine!' And what do you think was on the postcard? The Gethsemane. I thought the postcard was quite nice, too, I sent it to make her happy . . ."

Anyway, once in Jerusalem he started working at a bakery. It could even be said that he almost settled down: he was there a whole ten days before getting thrown out for giving seven loaves of bread to a beggar. Not one loaf—seven. The owner could have parted with one, but seven—never! So the owner starts yelling and shouting . . . "What the hell are you doing, Bulgarian? What do you think this is? How could you waste my bread like that?" "I don't know how you can even call yourself Jewish when you don't know squat about business! It's simple," Sheytanov argued back. "I gave him seven loaves, so that he'll stay away for the whole week, not scaring your customers and getting in the way of your *alush verish*!" The boneheaded owner, obviously failing to live up to his Jewish heritage, reveals himself devoid of even a whiff of humor and promptly throws him out. Sheytanov shrugs and spits in his direction, and curses him out in his mother's name in his trademark Yambolian style. By January—now nineteen fourteen—he winds up in Cairo in all his heroic glory.

Of course everything's great in Cairo—libraries, pyramids, camels, Nubian whores, baklava, dirt-cheap paper bags brimming with dates, Turkish *zaptiehs*, unaware of which god to pray to because it isn't the Turkish Empire anymore, but it's technically still not entirely a British colony, either—peace, quiet, and British tourists with parasols . . . But as for a revolutionary atmosphere? None. He thinks to himself that he just can't justify staying here if there isn't a revolution brewing, so he hops right back to Alexandria, where he sneaks onto a cruise liner with no passport, no money, nothing. And since the Alexandria port is international, there are cruise liners for days. So he hops on one, and it just so happens to be a Russian one. He tucks himself into a lifeboat and the liner takes off for England, with a scheduled stop in France. It had all been very revolutionary up until then, if it weren't for the fact he was starving! . . .

"And you just can't do it," he explained to the poet seriously. "The revolution is a revolution, but you just can't take it on an empty stomach!"

So he crawls out from underneath the awning, cocky, since the liner's already out in the open sea, what're they going to do, take him down to the police station? He tiptoes around the deck to see what's happening, and the first thing he spots is a cabin with its door wide open—and inside it's bright and warm, with plush furniture and a table covered with salamis, cheese, bread, oranges, apple cider . . . perfect for a hungry revolutionary. He sneaks in, takes the salami, the bread, and the bottle of cider—all in the name of the future revolution, of course—and just as he's about to sneak back out, an imposing madame appears. A fat Russian lady, to put it plainly, and she starts screaming: "*Vor! Vor! Pomogite!*" Sailors immediately rush in from all directions, grab hold of him and start pulling him this way and that way. He defends himself, he's not a thief, he says, just hungry, but they keep roughing him up. He gets fed up with the whole ordeal and sacrifices the bottle of cider by breaking it across a sailor's head. The whole deck is now covered in glass and cider. At this point the captain himself storms in, bellowing: "Put your hands up! Put your hands up!" and he's waving his Mauser around. The Mauser looks loaded! Or maybe it's not, but it's still a Mauser, still terrifying. Sheytanov stands fierce. "I," he says "am a Bulgarian revolutionary, and a Bulgarian revolutionary would die before he surrenders! So don't you dare tell me to put my hands up. And as for the salami, I refuse to give it back!" "Would you look at that," the captain shouts, "Revolutionary, you say. You revolutionaries," he says, "I can't stand you! You people," he goes on, "you have nothing better to do than to ask for someone else to feed you, while you wave your flags and give your speeches. Revolutionaries! As though you people today can be compared to the real revolutionaries!" he yells. "Real revolutionaries set off bombs and killed emperors!

You, and your mothers, all you know is how to steal people's salami! How many emperors have you killed?" The captain was fearsome as he asked this and Sheytanov couldn't figure out whether the man was a reactionary associated with the tsar, or simply a buffoon. So he responds that no!—he hadn't yet killed an emperor. "I knew it!" the other shouts, "always the same story! You haven't even killed a single emperor yet, all you've managed is to break this poor sailor's head!"

"He was a buffoon!" the poet said resolutely. "He may have also been a scoundrel, but a buffoon for sure!"

"Well, yes," sighed Sheytanov, "he was a buffoon. But he holsters his Mauser and says, 'Where do you think you're going? Revolutionary or not, show me your ticket!' I'm ready to burst out laughing at this point. I tell him I have no money for a ticket and he tells me, 'Well of course! When have revolutionaries ever had money for a ticket! You've got money for everything *except* a ticket. You think everybody owes you something. Since you're going to be liberating them anyway, why not get a free ride now! Tell me,' he continues, 'Where are you headed?' 'To Paris,' I tell him. 'Because,' I go on, 'Paris is full of revolutionaries.' And he pats me on the shoulder and says, *'Molodets!'* Of course Paris is filled with revolutionaries, and of course they're just sitting there waiting for you to spark the world revolt. As for me,' he goes on, 'I've never been to Paris, but I've been told that it's not only full of revolutionaries, but that the Parisian whores bathe every day, can you believe it? Okay then!' he continues, 'I'll take you to the French shore, and you can go from there. I can't take you all the way to Paris, you understand, but I'll take you to Marseille, I promise you that. I can take you to London too, if you want, but to Paris, never.' 'I don't want to go to London,' I tell him. 'I don't have any business there. That king they've got is a first cousin of your little tsar, and there aren't any revolutionary crowds . . .' 'You and your revolutionary mother!' He tells me. 'If you don't want to go, I won't take you!' The whole thing had turned facetious by this point, the sailors were doubled over with laughter, and the captain, if you can believe it, takes out twenty rubles and hands it to me, to stop stealing salami from the other passengers. I couldn't resist biting back, too. "'My apologies,' I say. 'Mon Capitan! I had no idea the madame was a passenger! I thought she was . . . cargo!'"

"And he didn't hit you?" The poet asked gleefully.

"No. He didn't, but the fat Russian tried. He says to me, 'She might be cargo, but it's paid cargo, whereas you . . . you're just deadwood, aren't you?' And the cargo is about to faint, you see . . . 'Bastard! Bandit! How dare you offend me! I am a noblewoman!' And she's coming at me! The captain stops her. 'Madame,' he says 'I will not tolerate this sort of ruckus on my ship! . . . I can only imagine what sort of noblewoman you are, since you're aboard my gothic piece of shit-tub here . . . Please don't make me sound the alarm and collect everybody's passports! One revolutionary without a passport is enough for one day.' And he turns to the sailors: 'Men, hang on to this fat dragon here and don't let her get too rowdy.' Then he turns to me. 'Now, take these twenty rubles, though just so you know, I'm really giving you twenty-five, but I am deducting five for bandages for the sailor whose head you busted, and for Rivanol! . . . You break it, you buy it,' he says. All in all, a good guy. . ."

[Friday, February 8, 2013]
Despite everything, they get to Marseille, where the captain gives him another twenty rubles, tells him to get in touch with some railway worker friends of his who'd gladly take him to Paris, then sounds the horn and sets their course for London.

Sheytanov stays in Marseille for a couple days, then leaves for Paris.

"Lalyo Marinov* says that you got to Paris on foot," the poet said, "is that true? You weren't yanking his chain, were you? He believes everything you say, you know."

"Oh, I'd never do that to him," Sheytanov responded. "I really did walk it. Remember—puerile antagonism! I've walked the road to Golgotha, you know. I can't take the train to Golgotha!"

"So how long did this crusade take you?" the other sat blown away. "It's pretty far from Marseille to Paris, no?"

"Well, if you've decided to walk it . . . all together probably about two weeks," he said, and suddenly began to laugh. "Forget about how long it takes, it's nothing when you're seventeen. But you should have seen me, soaked to the bone the entire time! I'm telling you, the rain was unbelievable! It didn't stop. I threw on a bunch of waterproof clothes, but I was soaked, miserably wet as a . . . I won't even tell you what."

"Wet as a dog?" The poet watched him.

"Wet as a hen," he clarified. "Just don't tell anybody, I'll lose my heroic nimbus! At least I discovered the meaning of *mistral*. And if someone tries telling you how poetic it is, don't believe him for a second. Seriously. I tasted the mistral's poetry."

On one such night, when the pouring was especially vile, and he swore at the rain and at Paris and its revolutionary masses, but at himself most of all—what the hell had he been thinking setting off to the middle of fucking nowhere—he spotted a faint light on the side of the road. It came from a farmhouse. He was wet and frozen and he immediately went in the direction of the small light. The house was dark, save for a single window, which he peered through. Inside the warm and cozy room was a woman. And a baby. The baby was in a cradle, and it appeared the woman was singing to it—he couldn't hear the song, but he could see that's what she was doing. There was not a soul around in the bitter night, just the window and the woman and her baby in its cradle, and he felt such a devastating nostalgia in his heart that he immediately knew—no matter what, he could not go into the house.

He finally got to Paris, and intent on seeing it right away, the first place he headed to was the teacher and anarchist Sébastien Faure's famous alternative school—La Ruche.* But the *hive* turned out to be nothing more than a school. Different-looking, but still just a school.

Then came the first of May. May Day in Paris! What a grand event. Speakers everywhere—Belgians, French, Germans, Italians, Russians— all inspired like prophets, fists shaking in the air, flags waving . . . He couldn't figure out where to look first: to the speakers on the tribune or to the sea of people. It was the same at every rally he attended—the speakers alternated between French and English, English and Russian, and French again, without a single person protesting this Babylonian Bacchanalia. It possessed far more method than chaos.

Not two months later, news broke that the Archduke Franz Ferdinand and his wife Sophie had been assassinated in Sarajevo. Every newspaper exclaimed: "*Double attentant! Double attentat! L'Archiduc héritier d'Autriche et sa femme assassinés en Bosnie!*" He immediately remembered how the captain had challenged him—what kind of a revolutionary could he have been if he hadn't so much as killed an emperor yet. And he started to hate that Gavrilo Princip fellow! Because he envied him. "How funny life is," he thought to himself, "people are already killing the heirs to the throne, soon they'll move on to the emperors, and me, I'm sitting here at the *patisserie*, listening to speeches and wiping tables after some mollycoddled princesses!" Indeed. He'd become a pastry-shop busboy. "Fuck these revolutionary masses! Fuck Paris!"

"And to top it all off, he's my age," he sighed. "I'm seventeen, he's nineteen. He kills emperors, and I'm waiting hand and foot on these tarts, for God's sake!"

"That's right!" Milev exclaimed. "They couldn't even hang him because he was a minor."

"Anyway," Sheytanov sighed.

He stayed in Paris exactly three months in all. Aside from the pastry shop, he also worked at a furniture factory, and just as he'd been planning to bolt to London—so that he could listen to the famous writer and anarchist Kropotkin* speak against capitalism and feudalism at the gathering of the anarcho-communists—World War I broke out and the gathering hadn't even taken place. He'd then written to his father asking for three hundred leva because he was home sick, then he waved au revoir to the Parisians and was back in Yambol by August.

And that was it . . .

"Mmhmm," Milev said, "By that time I was already in London . . ."

Sheytanov laughed. "But you know what I missed the most? I missed a good old-fashioned *Bulgarian* profanity, that's what. Those Frenchies can't even get a good swear going! Their language may be fine for poetry and rhymes, but if you really want to revile somebody you just can't do it. So the first thing I did when I stepped foot back in Bulgaria was to spit out the biggest, fattest curse I could muster."

"You know what, Sheytanov," the poet exclaimed. "You should write all of this down!"

Sheytanov looked at him carefully and shrugged again.

"What for?" he said. "Life," he said, "is far too serious to be explained away in a book. I say live it, and let whatever happens, happen."

And with that, he took the fire-tongs and stirred up the embers in the heater, prompting sparks to scatter and spray . . .

Just at that moment, the literary barbarians came charging in with their yellow glasses and their student hats, and the poet mumbled: "Church is out, the *Jacquerie* is here!" and everything went back to normal on 145 Rakovski Street, just as it had been in those first months of nineteen twenty-four, when their magazine sold out every month and the subscribers paid on time, when the shadow of a vengeful envy was yet to discompose them and the hell to come was still far.

4.

[Saturday, February 9, 2013]

That January in nineteen twenty-four happened to be very cold—so cold the snow had frozen and the pipes inside the houses burst. Despite the fact it snowed from New Year's until after Christmas,* which was still on January seventh according to the Orthodox calendar, the air did not soften up. Unprecedented storms and blizzards swooped in and trees toppled with the hollow crack of death, and the trains stopped in the middle of nowhere because the snow had seemingly buried the tracks forever. Even the express train from Vienna got derailed somewhere between Tsaribrod and Dragoman, so the minister Dimo Kazasov had to send for a medical train with a snowplow attached to its locomotive to gather up the frozen passengers, who had, for some unknown reason, decided to set off from Europe to Turkey at the worst possible time . . . The snow halted all the trains from Slivnitsa onward; even the buses were stopped throughout the entire country. The Maritsa River froze, the Tundzha froze too—from Yambol all the way down to the border. Even the Danube froze, and *Utro* wrote how Tutrakan filled up with Romanians, who got there by travelling over the ice in horse-drawn sleds and carriages so they could drink chilled, aromatic *pelin* and wine, making the barkeeps quite happy and not at all deploring of the cold. *Dnevnik* wrote about Vidinians going grocery shopping across to Kalafat, but *Zora* said that whole herds of starving Transylvanian wolves had in turn also crossed the benumbed river to cause mischief in the pens . . .

["... these wolves bred around Turnu Magurele, eating maize all summer long, which turned their fur white—and when a wolf that white lies in the snow, you'd never even notice it . . ."]

Still, during that same time—in that very cold winter of nineteen twenty-four—a royal wedding was thrown in Bad Mergentheim, Germany, and Duchess Nadezhda became princess of Württemberg. The old King Ferdinand I had been there too, and for this reason, his firstborn and the heir to the throne, Boris, hadn't shown up, sending instead his younger brother Kiril, so the people would have nothing to whisper about. *Illustrated Week* sent a special correspondent who had later written that his majesty the young prince had shown the happy couple his goodwill and gifted them an automobile. "The automobile," it had been detailed in the gazette, "was a Steyr, 6 cylinder motor 12/40 P.S. – Model 5, manufactured by the renowned Österreichische Waffenfabriksgesellschaft in Steyr. These same automobiles," the article continued, "are widely used in Bulgaria. They are well known for being sturdy, economical, and elegant." And since it had been an *illustrated* newspaper after all, they placed a photograph of the vehicle Boris had given to Nadezhda. Indeed, it had all been very elegant.

Only a day later, in the small town of Chamonix, beneath Mont Blanc, the international week of winter sports began and Sofia hosted the Bakers Association Congress, plus another congress—in Ruse—of traveling salesmen. The first issue of the magazine *Woman* came out, a publication from the association of bachelors, widowers, the abandoned, and the yearning. In Kyustendil, anarchists and police officers had collided—both sides opened fire right in the middle of the day, resulting in one dead policeman and two dead anarchists, a pair of wounded wardens, and an injured passerby. The authorities at the Varna port discovered a whole two people with the plague aboard an Italian cruise liner, and around the same time the HMS L-24—whatever an L-24 is—sank at La Manche. In Germany, communist uprisings marked the anniversary of the death of Karl Liebknecht; in Vienna, three thousand disabled rose in revolt; and in Soviet Russia, on Monday the twenty-first, at exactly six fifty in the evening, the leader of the local Bolsheviks, Vladimir Lenin, died. On the twenty-second in England, Ramsay McDonald became the first Labour Party Prime Minister; on the twenty-fifth in Chamonix, the aforementioned winter games began; on the twenty-sixth in Russia, Petrograd became Leningrad; and on the twenty-seventh the burial procession for Lenin was held at the Red Square in Moscow . . .

[NB! On the twenty-third of January, at nine o'clock in the morning, the body of Lenin, dressed in a paramilitary jacket (a garment he'd never worn while he'd been alive), badly shaven, and with a closely cropped haircut, was placed in his coffin. The nearest train station was four kilometers away, so Lenin was carried from Gorki to Gerasimovo in negative thirty-five degrees Celsius. His body was then loaded up on the ceremonial train—decorated according to the somber occasion and followed by crowds the entire way to Moscow. Lenin's body was then unloaded from the train and again carried until it reached the columns in Pillar Hall inside the House of the Unions. This final journey of Lenin's took six hours.

The wake lasted from seven o'clock at night on January twenty-third until the twenty-seventh. The newspapers were filled with telegrams coming in from all corners of the vast country, but one surpassed all others. It read, "Vladimir Ulyanov died—Lenin lives!" A slogan read: "Lenin's tomb—cradle of the world revolution!"

In any case . . .

It was still so bitterly cold, all the streets and squares were lined with small bonfires: the people squeezed out from between the columns to warm up, then got back into the slow crawling lines.

Lenin's brain had already been removed, as was the heart, along with a bullet lodged in his neck just next to the carotid artery.

The brain and heart were necessary for Lenin's resurrection: they were in fact *certain* it could be done.

The bullet, of course, they did not need.

But the people standing in those endless lines did not suspect that.

They erected a mausoleum in Lenin's honor, deciding to do this on, let's say, the twenty-sixth. The mausoleum, resembling both an Egyptian pyramid and a Babylonian ziggurat, was built on the twenty-seventh.

And since the ground outside the Kremlin was frozen, they thawed it by lighting fires as they dug the foundations. And when the fires weren't enough, they blasted open the earth. One such fougasse tore through a sewer canal. An animal stench spread all around, and it is said that Patriarch Tikhon of Moscow spitefully exclaimed: "These aromas are becoming of Lenin's relics!"

Beneath all that, at six feet under, among the red and black drawings of the theater decorator Ignati Nivinski, lay Lenin himself. People descended along the right-hand staircase, circled the sarcophagus on all three sides, then ascended out through the left-hand staircase. They all wept, and years later, someone would say: "Half of mankind mourned his death, when they should have been mourning his birth!"]

[I really ought to write these things down, they're so easy to forget . . .]

[Oh, and another thing! When, afterward, they built the *third* mausoleum with reinforced concrete and granite, marble, and elvan stone, Moscow became the only capital in the world to measure distance to all corners of the world not from its central post office, but from Lenin's mausoleum.

And that was that.]

[Wednesday, February 13, 2013]
They sent the announcement for the new magazine a little before the New Year in nineteen twenty-four. It was something to behold—magnificent, large-format, luxurious paper, a handsome jobbing font, and unprecedented circulation. Soon after, the poet left an impressive down payment at the royal printers, and two weeks into January, three or four days after Christmas, the nimble printers finally mounted *Plamuk*'s first quire onto the big machine. The poet and Sheytanov stood by on the side, surrounded by the aroma of inks, lead, and glue, and when the machine turned with a groan, the poet grabbed the first sheet that sank softly into the basket.

He folded it and froze, spellbound. He could barely contain the joy he felt at these white pages, big as bed sheets, where the poems swam as if finally free. It was a world away from the orphan pages of *Vezny* . . .

Which is why once the magazine was printed he became irate upon spotting an ugly typo, courtesy of the typesetter, inside his manifesto. "The ivory tower, the refuge of poetry and hiding place of *pieces*, collapses into pitiful ruins."

"What pieces, goddamn it?!" he was imbued with the helpless rage of a duped child. "What *pieces?* The poets," he screamed, "The *poets!* These people are making a mockery of us. They're still piss drunk from Christmas. You have to be a complete imbecile to mistake *poets* with *pieces* . . ."

The boys with the yellow glasses were writing the addresses of the subscribers on the still-warm books, happily licking stamps and sticking them to the covers of the magazine with a slap, but when they heard him screaming—they became dumbfounded and perturbed, put on their raggedy student overcoats, grabbed piles of addressed issues, and bolted from the editorial office.

The poet screamed, swore like an animal, called the typesetter a provocateur, and spit out the most violent profanities he could summon, courtesy of the army reserves in Kniajevo, then he swore a hundred times he wasn't going to pay these incompetents for the magazine and that he was going to shove it up their let's not say where . . . He turned to Sheytanov and told him that when he was a student in Germany before the wars, one of the big papers—the *Frankfurter Allgemeine Zeitung*, which had been published since eighteen fifty-six—always had a special note, set in large letters. It said the newspaper would give ten deutsche marks to the first person who reported a typo . . . There had been maybe one person a month who got the money, if that.

Sheytanov sat and looked at him, and finally spoke:

"Listen Milev," he said, "you want me to go off on that fucking fascist? One word and I'll go shoot them all up—the whole print shop. I'll start with the typesetter and take them all out until the last useless one of them is gone . . ."

Then he laughed, patted Milev on the shoulder and said:

"Enjoy this! Why are you letting it poison you like this? The magazine is out in the world—enjoy it!"

The poet shut up, insulted.

He stood quiet for about a second, then said:

"To Koprivshtitsa, forward march! You're the patron, drinks are on you."

"You got it," said Sheytanov. "But we won't be going to Koprivshtitsa today. Today," he said, "I'll take you someplace else. It's closer."

The poet said he didn't mind, as long as he wasn't the one paying, and not five minutes later they were already inside Benoni on Alabinska Street—it was warm and smoky, and the smell of bean salad and pickled cabbage and wine and rakiya blanketed the air, which was so thick that, if someone had decided to shoot a gun, the bullet would have ricocheted in the air. The tavern was filled with dark men wearing wide-brimmed hats that hid their faces, and the barkeep did absolutely nothing to hide the two revolvers tucked into his belt.

"Come in, come in," said Sheytanov, "it's time you met my people. It's not I who is your patron, my brother. These are your patrons, remember their faces."

5.

[Friday, February 15, 2013]
After that night in Benoni, Sheytanov disappeared for two whole weeks,

[Saturday, February 16, 2013]
and while the poet's father sat in Stara Zagora, incredulous that the new magazine, *Plamuk*, was selling so well, the poet finally decided to legalize the family's Sofia address at the sixth residential commission. He'd delayed it for months and he could tell that Suselov, his landlord, was becoming flustered. The man had thirteen apartments in Sofia alone, a summerhouse in Borovets, villas in several villages in the Plovdiv region, and who knows how many other properties, so it wasn't about their measly rent. But the man was a lawyer, and he was very well aware of the terrible law for residential demand, and what's more, its addendum with those inhumane domicile decrees and registrations, and even his millions weren't going to save him from the merciless and uncompromising residential commission.

The air was weighed down by fear that year; everyone was afraid of something. Mila had been urging him gently, but she grew increasingly persistent—they'd already moved twice and that hadn't been that big of a deal, but now the kids were growing, and they had more possessions, so if their landlord decided to kick them out . . . And, well, she'd been completely right.

The poet let out an annoyed curse over having to stop his work, and got up and went down to the station to fill out a residential housing ticket. Inside the dusty chancery, a young man—the secretary of the commission—leapt toward him and practically fell over himself with exclamations of amazement, invited him to sit, begged him to sit, even, and then, while he anxiously dug through all those files, did not cease to repeat what an honor it was to meet him, that he was a regular subscriber to *Vezny* and how he had read the first issue of *Plamuk* cover to cover and couldn't wait for the second. He had nothing against Teodor Trayanov's *Hyperion*, but it had an air of wilted chrysanthemums, of something threadbare and decaying—people had forgotten about symbolism— while *Plamuk* represented the new and the authentic. He humbly threw in that, as a matter of fact, he too dabbled in poetry, but of course he wouldn't dare mention his own work in the same breath as the poet . . . He truly did have an affinity for serious magazines!

"What can we even call highbrow," he added bitterly. "Bai Atanas Damyanov* at least says it right! Surely you've heard him speak, Mr. Milev? He wasn't trying to start a magazine for the intelligentsia, he said. I'm after the numbers, he said! I need the masses, the worker, the cabby, the villager, the chimney cleaner, the barkeep. In other words, he wants to publish newspapers for people who move their lips while they read. And he's right. How else can you print that many newspapers—*Utro*, *Zarya*, *Illustrated Week*, *Nedelno Utro*, *Dnevnik* and *Kukurigo*—and build that kind of a monopoly!"

The poet grunted impatiently. He had a galley to proof, an article to write on women's poetry, and he possessed little patience for the young man's chitchat, so he gave him instead a sour "sure, sure okay!" and asked him if he'd be so kind as to hurry the whole thing up.

The other mumbled nervously that of course, of course he would, inserting the blank sheet of paper into his *Ideal*—a typewriter big as a threshing machine. He glanced at the application for only a split second before his fingers leapt across the keys. He wrote impressively fast and didn't stop speaking even while he typed. He explained that residential dealings in Sofia were too intense, endlessly unfavorable, rather, and had in fact become calamitous. Sofia was growing vigorously—not so much growing as bloating. Officially, there were around one hundred fifty thousand people, but nobody knew the actual number for certain, it was quite possible the number was closer to two hundred. Too many—a veritable megapolis! In his mind, this was no longer a housing crisis, but a housing *misery*. Austere measures were needed to eliminate this misery, but the state didn't care for rent regulations on housing, because Bulgaria today was a country owned by money-grubbers. The young man knew what had to be done, but he was a nobody, who would listen to him? Nobody asked him, of course, for he was but a speck in the gray mass of archivists, a plankton in an ocean of clerks. What a pity! Had they asked him, he'd tell them the solution at once . . . He went on, and the poet wondered how it was possible that someone could string together newspaper clichés and slogans stolen from poor people's rallies with the groundbreaking conviction of an innovator.

"The answer to the problem, Mr. Milev," he exclaimed, "the answer is in the creation of reasonably-priced housing and affordable rent. And not," he stressed, "in housing market speculation, as the current situation dictates . . ."

He then pulled the sheet of paper out of the typewriter and read it out ceremoniously. Residential housing ticket, station one, located at 23 Maria Luisa Boulevard, owner Susselov, Dimitar . . .

"Geo Milev," he read on in a deep voice, "Eastern Orthodox, Bulgarian citizen, born on such and such date, in such and such month, in such and such year in Stara Zagora, writer, college educated, served conscription duties in such and such infantry regiment, married, spouse—Mila Keranova Mileva, two children—Leda and Bistra, previous residency at 26 Lomska Street. Application for address approved on the twenty-seventh of February, nineteen twenty-four. Applicant: Geo Milev."

The clerk reached over all the folders and papers that covered the writing table, handed him the sheet of paper and announced:

"Congratulations, Mr. Milev! You have nothing to worry about now."

"Is that all?" the poet asked and rose from the chair.

"Oh yes, yes," the young man jumped to his feet too.

Then, just as awkwardly, he took out his business card and handed it to the poet with a sort of pleading smile.

"If there is anything at all," he said, "it would be an honor to help you out as best as I can. Us intellectuals, if we don't stick together . . ."

The poet absentmindedly pushed the card into his overcoat—he would certainly forget it there, as he always did—and attempted to hurry out.

"By the way, Mr. Milev," the clerk suddenly remembered, "do you know that you and I almost served together?"

"What do you mean?" the poet became even more annoyed.

"Well, I too graduated from the Military School for Reserve Officers!" the other declared excitedly. "Quite before you, however. I was there in the summer of nineteen fifteen. So, about two years ahead of you. They got our entire cohort to sign up right after high school, so we could learn to defend the king, the motherland, and the flag. The Great War started right after that, but you, well, you were at the front line, a hero, you were wounded in battle, and I, well, I got placed at the freight battery of the sixth artillery and we hung around Dupnitsa the whole time . . ."

"Well, there's no escaping fate," the poet interrupted, shrugged, and quickly departed with a wave.

He would never learn the name of the young man—this insignificant little clerk in the housing commission: Geshev.

Nikola Geshev.

[Would you look at that . . .

From nineteen twenty-four to nineteen twenty-five, Nikola Geshev is secretary at the fourth and sixth housing commissions of the Ministry of Internal Affairs and National Health, but he leaves when the position is eliminated.

On May twentieth, nineteen twenty-five, he is appointed to a criminal pursuit-party. His salary would be eighty leva a month. Were he to catch a criminal—he'd get at least five thousand. Were he to kill one—up to twenty thousand. And if he was the one killed in the line of duty—fifty thousand leva for his family. Were he to become disabled—another twenty thousand.

And disability pension.

But even before that, in April, actually, immediately following the St. Nedelya Church assault, Pane Bichev—a top cop and the main investigator on the case—personally summons him to help . . .

It is on May fifteenth that Geo Milev disappears.]

[Sunday, February 17, 2013]
Sheytanov finally appeared again on a Thursday at the beginning of February. He arrived frozen and dead tired, but the poet didn't waste time with pleasantries, mumbling instead that he'd come just in time, and proudly pointed to the piles of colored postcards laid out on top of Marcho's table.

"Metzger?" asked Sheytanov.

"Metzger!" the poet answered and spread out his arms. "Who else? Look, just look at this!" he exclaimed. "It's not a vignette, can you believe it? It's a wood engraving! This thing is a modernist icon. What do you think? I commissioned him to do it last night, and he had it ready first thing in the morning. Metzger is unbelievable."

Metzger had, as always, done an excellent job: the illustration resembled an explosion—erupting with large chunks of shattered browns and pale greens, out of which Lenin's brick-red face popped out.

The poet impatiently admitted that he'd already written the caption that would go beneath the photo, grabbed a sheet of paper from the table and read it excitedly, then took one of the January issues and showed him exactly where the note would go and where the color photo would be glued—something he'd only dreamed of with *Vezny*. He then stared at Sheytanov in palpable expectation of praise. Sheytanov was quietly nonchalant, however, and instead the poet recounted going to

Balkan, Ivan Naydenov's chromolithographic printer, with Marcho the day before, how they'd brought the engraving, how the man had cut them off immediately, the shameless skinner.

"No way!" he'd said to them. "It can't be done! I wouldn't be able to get to it even the day after tomorrow." He was in the middle of printing labels for something. Some sort of large order from the Luv cognac factory in Veliko Tarnovo, the poet wasn't paying attention—and besides, they could've been printing "Rooster" soap labels for all he cared, it was all garbage. And yet, one hundred thousand pieces of it! Don't bother me with small-scale jobs, was Naydenov's underlying implication, and the conversation was over. Naydenov turned around and disappeared, and the whole thing would've been over, had it not for one Bai Stoichko, an old printer and secret communist: he went into the chancery, and when he came back out just a few minutes later the machines had stopped! Bai Stoichko took the bullshit labels' typographical cliché off the press, while Marcho did what he did best and got in the way of the whole thing, then they washed the blue ink out and poured in the red, and her printing majesty, the American, started turning again. The poet yelled in Bai Stoichko's ear, wanting to know what had caused this miracle, and the other responded he'd simply explained to Naydenov who Lenin was.

"Would you look at that," he laughed crudely as he remembered the story, "is that what did it for the goddamned printer? And Bai Stoichko is sitting there laughing and he tells me, no, of course it wasn't. 'I told him,' he says, 'that if he doesn't let us do Lenin's portrait right away—we're not working for three days.' 'So you threatened him with a strike?' I say to him, and he's looking at me incredulous. 'What did you think? That they care about Lenin that much? Threaten a strike, though, and it'll work every time.'"

He went on and on, as if he couldn't stop . . .

"Take these, take them!" the poet said and handed Sheytanov about ten postcards. "Take some for your guys . . . Bai Stoichko printed at least two hundred extra!"

[Monday, February 18, 2013]
"Lenin is a vile human being." Sheytanov said calmly.

"What?" the poet bristled. "Sheytanov! Don't do that, I don't want to argue with you. You want to rain on my parade?"

"He's vile," the other shrugged. "You can treat him like an icon, but to me, he's a wretch."

He wanted to tell the poet the first thing this man did was to go after the same anarchists who'd handed him his victory on a silver platter that one horrible month when, while half the world was already in November, Russia was still stranded in October.

But he didn't. He didn't want to argue either.

He'd seen this Lenin.

Not face to face, of course. He'd seen what Lenin was capable of.

But first, he'd met Karl Radek.

[Tuesday, February 19, 2013]
Sheytanov arrived in Moscow one March day in nineteen eighteen, a week or two after the Bolsheviks had established it as the capital of Russia, and who knows why, but the first thing he laid eyes on was a Chaliapin concert placard. He didn't hesitate for a second: using the last kerenka rubles he'd been given by the army council in Odessa, he hopped on a phaeton and went to the theater; he used the rest for a ticket and after, when he walked out of the theater with his head spinning, he had only a couple of copper coins left in his pocket.

He spent a brutally cold night nodding off and then waking up on a bench outside the theatre. In the morning, he saw seven somber geese marching through the muddied theater square. He joked to himself the geese were probably on their way to rescue the Third Rome,* then spent a good amount of time laughing at his own joke.

He bought a paper with the few *copeiki* he had left and spotted an ad inside with a call for agitators. Sheytanov went to the address listed in the paper and found the editorial offices for a gazette called *Revolucija*— a Serbian gazette, Yugoslavian, rather, very much communist. It's there he met Radek.* This Radek had the face of a crook, which he was: much later, Sheytanov would find out the man's real name was actually Karol Sobelsohn—an Austrian and an international swindler who was simply bereft of morals. But there was no way for Sheytanov to know it then.

We digress . . .

Sheytanov told Radek he was a Bulgarian revolutionary, perfectly qualified for the volunteering position they'd advertised. The other had the nerve to ask him for a referral.

"From who?" he asked, incredulous, and Radek responded that he needed to see a letter of recommendation from the Bulgarian Marxist Socialists.

He'd had the urge to leave right then and there, but clenched his jaw and pulled out a memo from the regional police department, stating he was a revolutionary anarchist who'd escaped from the Sofia Central Prison and that he was armed and dangerous.

"Here's my letter of recommendation," he hissed, and Radek let out a laugh.

"Bravo!" he said. "A wanted man! Very clever, but you have to wait my dear, wanted comrade. We'll be in touch!" And he disappeared.

It was Godina the Czech who took him in. At least that's what he claimed—that he was Czech and that his name was Godina. He worked for that same paper, as an editor or God knows what; that year Moscow had been overrun by people with shady pasts: professional revolutionaries, financial wizards wanted by the police, or just common gangsters.

Godina took him in at the former Dresden Hotel on Skobelev Square, precisely where—from the window of room 152—Sheytanov witnessed the enthused Bolsheviks destroy Skobelev's statue. That same Skobelev—the White General. Lenin himself had given the order!

Godina told him that come fall, the Russian Army was preparing to celebrate the anniversary of the revolution, and the government had decreed that monuments erected in honor of the tsars and their servants, generals, and commanders—essentially any monument of no interest from a historical or art history perspective—were to be dismantled and removed from the squares and the streets; some were to be put in storage, others were to be used as scrap metal. They took down all those statues and monuments and who knows why, but Skobelev's Lenin was expressly singled out for demolition. From his hotel window, Sheytanov witnessed how they shattered the fine, white Finnish marble at the base and, using levers, broke off the bas-relief with its images from the war for the liberation of Bulgaria . . . The sight stung. It wasn't so much that he mourned the monument as it was that his mother had taught him at an early age that Bulgaria's liberators deserved respect—Stoletov, our general, Radetzky, who arrived with a bang, and, of course, the White General, that same Skobelev.

They demolished the monument in a day, and on the first of May, a barren spot stood in its place.

[Wednesday, February 20, 2013]

[Hmm, would you look at that, the prime minister resigned . . . "We did all we could!" he said. Actually, it was the government itself that announced its own resignation . . . we did all we could. It's much like that story with the soldiers . . . An old man's two oxen fall into a hole. The old man, this *dyado*, looks around and sees a bunch of young soldiers doing their army exercises. So he asks them to help him get his animals out of the hole. "Of course we'll help!" they say, and tie one end of their wire rope to their tank and the rest around the animals' necks and start pulling. They pull and they pull, until the wire ropes cut off the oxen's heads. Then the soldiers put their ropes away, rub their hands together and declare to the old man: "Well, dyado, we tried our best! No need to thank us, that's just what we're here for . . ."

Resignation . . . what a joke.]

Before that, on the ugly night of the eleventh of April, Dzerzhinsky's Cheka attacked all twenty-five palaces the anarchists had occupied during the previous year's revolution, doing nothing in the time since but partying. They all talked and talked, then drank, danced and sang—reveling with abandon like zombified lunatics until the early morning hours. And they shot a whole lot. The paintings on the walls became targets in the relentless shooting of their Mausers, they used the priceless carpets like army tarpaulin—wrapping the wooden chests filled with bullets in them and barricading the windows with the thick, sturdy covers of rare first-edition books from the lavish libraries.

This was all detailed in the newspapers, and if something was written in the paper, how could you not believe it?

All of Moscow gossiped about the debaucherous life the anarchists led inside the residences they occupied, and the easily repulsed grannies whispered resentfully in each other's ears about the disgusting orgies, the gatherings of bastards maniacal with disenthralment, and the exalted girls, who discarded every bit of clothing off their backs, letting the sailors contort their bodies every which way. The palaces had turned into ribald brothels, places of reprehensible doings and elemental disgrace, and they smelled of smoke, fish, and carrion.

Dzerzhinsky's Chekas, together with Jukums Vācietis*—Chief of Russia's armed forces—and his Latvian gunmen simply burst in.

They shot at everything that moved, indiscriminant at wiping out anarchists and women whose bodies were toxic with vodka and semen, then arrested those who'd somehow survived the massacre. When they took out those they'd detained, they came eye to eye with the same men they'd started a revolution with just half a year prior, but in that April night, the first group decimated the second.

The first door to hell had opened.

Sheytanov asked Godina what happened, but the other bared his teeth and sourly remarked:

"Lenin got 'em!"

He fell silent and then gave a disgusted snort:

"What's more, it was an anarchist who handed him the power, in case you didn't know . . ."

He recounted how, in January, during the founders' assembly, they'd sat around waging their tongues with all sorts of nonsense, and earlier, on the nineteenth of January according to the new calendar, at four twenty in the morning, the head of the military guard, the sailor Jeleznyakov, burst into the shiny hall inside the Tauride Palace where the meeting was supposedly in session, climbed up on the podium, put a hand on chairman Chernov's shoulder and said: "Please adjourn this meeting! The military guard is tired and wants to take a nap . . ."

"So just keep all that in mind, Bulgarian," Godina sighed. "Just keep it in mind . . . By the way," he added, "Zheleznyakov was also arrested by Dzerzhinsky's people. Keep that in mind, too—Lenin does not forgive or forget, Dzerzhinsky even less! . . . As for Vācietis, up until yesterday he was lieutenant colonel in the Imperial Russian Army . . . And that's that!" he said. "Turncoats don't keep their word."

All of Moscow looked over its shoulder and whispered in fear about the *leather men*. At first, Sheytanov had no idea who these men were or what they were about, but two surviving anarchists from that April night explained it to him. The Cheka were referred to as leather men because they wore double-breasted, black leather air force jackets, in actuality the same uniforms worn by British pilots. The new government had discovered a Triple Entente storage depot in Petrograd, and appropriated and gifted the leather jackets to Dzerzhinsky's people. A perfect gift, indeed. Very convenient, too, because leather is the perfect defense against lice—that irrepressible wartime pest.

And so it was.

Sheytanov hissed with disappointment, "Very clever, very clever indeed." And clenched his teeth again . . .

He attended meetings and rallies to look for other Bulgarians with whom to form a unit, but he found no one who'd take him up on it.

One night Godina dampened his revolutionary enthusiasm by elaborating a few points for him. Turns out, the total number of casualties on that October night in Petrograd—the October Revolution!—totaled a mere six people. On both sides.

"Bulgarian," he said. "There are two million in Petrograd. Officially. No one knows the real number. Tell me—was there any way this multimillion city was even aware of what was going down?"

He told him about the coup at the Winter Palace as well—how it had been really taken over. The Winter Palace, was, in actuality, one big, giant wine cellar guarded by barefaced cadets and girls from the women's regiment. The cadets and the women drank what they could and when they got word a bunch of Bolsheviks were headed their way to attack their palace, they filled up their bags with bottles and ran. That's precisely what the attackers were looking for—the wine reserves—and there was still a sea of booze left.

"This great socialist October Revolution was, if you can believe it, history's most bloodless revolution," he said, but Sheytanov had no idea whether to believe him or not.

[Thursday, February 21, 2013]
He met up with Radek a few more times, listened to him tell disparaging jokes about Jews, despite himself being Jewish, and witnessed him ingratiate himself with people who didn't even want to sit at the same table with him; it quickly became apparent what kind of person he was. At the beginning of July he saw Trotsky at a rally inside the Moscow Circus: it was there that Trotsky announced that any and all *parasites* would be tracked down and captured and sent away to unspeakable places to do dreadful, difficult things, and those who dared to oppose this plan of his were guileful windbags. The crowded circus exploded in applause, and Sheytanov enjoyed it too, but afterward, Godina clarified that this Leon Trotsky was in actuality Lev Davidovich Bronstein.

"That's how it is, Bulgarian," he said, "The Trotskys and the Radeks want to start the revolution, and it'll be the *Bronsteins* and the *Sobelzonovs* who will end up paying for it. I've said it before," he added, "don't expect anything good from a turncoat . . ."

A strange fellow this Godina was. During the day he wrote about starting the revolution, but when night fell he spoke against it. Sheytanov couldn't quite understand it, but he didn't argue with the man; instead at night he listened to him with even greater interest alongside the preposterously expensive bottle of Smirnoff he had in his hand. On one such night, Godina told him what Trotsky himself had said to the German ambassador Wilhelm von Mirbach. "I know," Trotsky had said to him, "that we're already dead, but I also know that there's no one left to bury us . . ."

"And it so happened that Blumkin and Andreev put a bullet in that same Mirbach right in the embassy, and to make sure they finished the job they threw in a bomb as well," Godina laughed vengefully. "They shot him barely three months into his ambassadorship! What do you know, Georgi the Bulgarian, what do you even know . . ."

Then he fell quiet, took a disconsolate pull from the bottle and informed him he was heading to bed, but that beforehand, he wanted Sheytanov to know something.

"Lenin," he said, "is a very sick man. Lenin might live another five, six years, or he might not. He'll be gone, but someone else will come to replace him. I don't know who that'll be yet, but whoever it is, I'm willing to bet that he'll be even more terrifying. It's inertia, Bulgarian, once it starts it won't stop. The only thing inertia does is gather speed downhill . . ."

Anyway.

Sheytanov did in fact see Lenin once. He didn't remember when or where. He resembled your average-looking, haughty university professor with his hat, his tattered jacket, and wrinkled vest underneath. When, a few years later, he saw Alexander Tsankov for the first time, he immediately thought of Lenin. They could've been the same person.

And when, on the last day of August, the news flew threw Moscow that a woman named Fanny Kaplan had waited at the Hammer and Sickle factory for Lenin after one of his rallies, and had emptied the contents of her Browning into him, Sheytanov felt only one thing.

Malicious joy.

"Not Fanny, Bulgarian," Godina kept on with his poisonous midnight diatribes. "Not Fanny, but Fanya. An anarchist, allegedly, but somehow, suddenly an SR, a socialist revolutionary. What did I tell you about apostates? No one really knows who sent her there, either," he went on, "or if she was the one who really shot him, so let us drink to the revolution!"

Anyway.

The summer of nineteen eighteen had been unbearably hot. Even the animals fainted from the Moscow heat. *Revolucija* was now called *World Revolution* and Sheytanov contributed four or five articles, but had no idea how many people actually read them, if at all.

Two women, whose beauty had long been washed off their faces, lived two doors down from them. The women's names were Raisa and Hriseida, but Sheytanov couldn't say which was which. They fought and insulted each other to death, like the time Raisa accused Hriseida of being Mikhail Lomonosov's lover, and Hriseida responded that indeed she had been, and before he died in seventeen sixty-five, he had personally told her Raisa had been just too damn old for him. Things of that nature. Then they'd get at each other's blue hairs and end up coming over to Godina's, who made them calming tea and amused them with tales about the water spirit in Vltava. Or he recited poetry. Sheytanov remembered how one night he recited Alexandr Blok's* "A Girl Sang A Song": *A girl sang a song in the temple's chorus, / About men, tired in alien lands, / About the ships that left native shores, / And all who forgot their joy to the end* . . . And Raisa and Hriseida wept. Actually, they always cried after the tea and the Czech's stories and usually went home arm in arm, while Godina shrugged and said to Sheytanov, see how easy it is . . .

But that same night he didn't say that; instead he went to the window, stared at the fires burning in the space where the monument had been, and hollowly recited the rest of the poem: *Thus sang her clean voice, and flew up to the highness / And sunbeams shined on her shoulder's white— / And everyone saw and heard from the darkness / The white and airy gown, singing in the light. / And all of them were sure, that joy would burst out: / The ships have arrived at their beach, / The people, in the land of the aliens tired, / Regaining their bearing, are happy and reach. / And sweet was her voice and the sun's beams around . . . / And only, by Caesar's Gates—high on the vault, / The baby, versed into mysteries, mourned, / Because none of them will be ever returned.*

And Sheytanov could have sworn he heard Godina choke up.

[Friday, February 22, 2013]
By the end of August, another monument—an ugly imitation of an Egyptian obelisk without engravings—was already protruding in place of the one that had been demolished. They called it the Monument of Soviet Constitution. By the end of September, he knew there was nothing to stay for.

And so he left.

As he sat on the train and watched the disappearing domes glisten under the autumn sun, he thought of those seven geese he'd seen that first day in Moscow, and it occurred to him it wasn't some Third Rome they were en route to liberating—it was simply that they hadn't yet been eaten by the Bolsheviks.

He crossed a country enveloped in a war with no front line, but with many armies and commanders, where they'd long stopped keeping track of sides, yet none surrendered, and they fought on like beasts. They flew rumbling and tumbling on their horses and companies as uncontrollable drays rolled over—horse-drawn machine-gun platforms, so to speak—and they all fired nonstop at everything in sight, echelons crammed to the brim carried army supplies and weapons to and from unknown locations, and the smell of mud, dust, gunpowder, and sulfur permeated everything. With their hooded cloaks and their waving flags, the armies resembled flocks of Devil Birds.

He reached Ukraine, but the hetman Pavlo Skoropadskyi's soldiers got hold of him on the border. They took him to Kiev and put him in a cell with some Bolsheviks scheduled to face the firing squad the very next morning—and him with them. He didn't feel like dying just yet and he announced loudly that he was a Bulgarian soldier. An officer from the German occupational command overheard him and told the Ukrainians: *"Bulgarien ist mit uns!"* Bulgaria's with us! And Sheytanov was off the hook. In October, when dirty clouds the color of bathwater lazily floated in the sky, Sheytanov set foot on the white, stone-paved quay of Varna's port. And he realized that everything was still exactly the same. Even the cops were the same—so what if they no longer worked for Ferdinand, but for his feeble son, Boris.

He went into a canteen, and when he saw his reflection in the mirror, he spotted a graying lock against his otherwise black hair. He wasn't yet twenty-three. He wouldn't turn twenty-three until February the following year, nineteen nineteen . . .

[*Friday night, February 22, 2013*]
[A cold and tedious rain falls outside—an autumn rain. How strange. It's February twenty-second, but the rain is a lonesome, November rain . . .

Truly strange . . .]

[*Sunday, February 24, 2013*]
Sheytanov told the poet nothing of all this. They'd long since ceased to stand on ceremony with each other, but they hadn't yet become "comrades" either, so he kept it to himself. He looked at the drawing again and suddenly thought that Metzger had really captured the soured disdain and hate pouring out of Lenin's very sick person's eyes. He felt the poet was unnerved and, unsure whether the abyss behind the darkened right lens hid anger or insult, sighed and shrugged.

"I take back my words," he said calmly. "I don't want to argue, either."

He even put a bunch of the cards in his coat pocket, but the tension in the air remained . . .

"Wait, did you see this?" the poet asked quickly and dug out a wrinkled newspaper. "Look what Peev wrote in *Pravda*!" He began to read, "'After *Thought* magazine, published by Dr. Krastev, our meager literature is lacking another publication of similar amplitude and a comparable richness in its literary thought . . .' Well said, bravo! We showed that impudent Vladko Vasillev how it's done, didn't we? There's no beating us now. We have a hundred twenty issues in that Yambol of yours alone. We had one of *Vezny*, and a hundred twenty of *Plamuk*!

[Sunday, March 3, 2013]
Just then the Pechenegs with the yellow glasses stormed in and brought the proofs—the printer was already putting the second issue together. They must have run the whole way, because when they threw off their hats and scarves, their heads were practically steaming. The poet snarled that *the jacquerie is here*! Then forgot everything and lowered his head to the pages, and the others first tried to rummage through the cupboard of Marcho from Marcha but upon discovering it was as empty as it always had been, began to spar with each other.

And so it was.

After he read everything from beginning to end,

[Monday, March 4, 2013]
the poet spread out the galley proofs of the covers.

On the front cover he added in pencil: "Add color photograph: Lenin's portrait, two-color print engraved on wood by M. Metzger."

On the back cover he wrote:

"Correction: Issue 1, p. 44, the first line of the article 'A Light Shines in the World' should read: 'The ivory tower where the poets reside.'"

He wasn't rancorous, but he didn't forget,

[Tuesday, March 5, 2013]
[Hmm, there was a hurricane in Gabrovo. They've announced a state of emergency—many wounded and one killed . . . No electricity or bread . . . Yet Yambol is quiet, quiet and spring-like. Strange. Gabrovo is 106.037 km from here, but Dryanovo is even closer, and there are hurricanes there too, but not a thing here!]

and he didn't let these things slide.

But the second issue came out late as well, just as the first one had—a week or so after the date stated on the subscription. In January he let the delay slide, but when it happened again in February, he couldn't. He barked this wasn't going to work. He stormed into the printer's and raised hell. He told them he wasn't going to let them embarrass him in front of the subscribers, that they didn't know whom they were dealing with, after which he left and returned home, where god knows why he took it out on Mila (after which he couldn't stop thinking of ways to apologize), while the cover of the third issue now read:

"Due to the inadequacies of the printing shop, issues 1 and 2 came out after they were supposed to—on the fifteenth of the month. Because of this mistake, we have been forced to delay the publication date of PLAMUK to the twenty-fifth of every month."

And beneath that, the poet wrote: "Rhodope Printing shop, owner— Todor L. Klisarov, Sofia, 29 Exarch Josif, tel. 575—making it very clear who was right and who was wrong, goddamn it.

But they barely stayed at that press for another two issues before moving yet again, this time to Balkan chromolithography, owned by one Ivan Ts. Naydenov.

Everything was repeating all over again and the whole thing had become personal. The same thing had happened with *Vezny*. The second to last issue was printed at Vitosha, and the last—at the Elit printing house; the almanac—at the royal printers, and every book published by *Vezny* was printed in a different place.

Anguish! Anguish and lots of darting from printer to printer—that's what it meant to publish a magazine in Bulgaria.

[Two]

Свиня е влязла въ храма
на живота — убийте я.

"A swine has breached the temple of life—kill it."

—Written by Georgi Sheytanov in 1919

[Wednesday, March 6, 2013]

. . . Mariola had a strange attitude toward Death in general. She'd seen Death once and there was nothing enlightened about her. Death wasn't how she was described in books. Death was ugly; ugly and repulsive. Death reeked of sweating, snorting men who sprayed their scorching seed wherever they pleased. Mariola had already wished for death—the real and instant kind—instead of the fear and helplessness slowly wasting her since that June day in nineteen twenty-three, when they'd come to her school and arrested her following the coup. The policemen then took turns raping her at the Pleven police station, as ten paramilitary volunteers from Sofia looked on and snickered, shamefaced and squeamish. She had wanted to die then, but she hadn't been *able to*: her young woman's body, broken and destroyed by the beatings and the men's vulgarities, never completely gave up during the twelve months she spent locked up inside a cell in the Pleven prison, and after the amnesty of twenty-four, she came back to Kilifarevo, the small town in central-northern Bulgaria she called home. She now loathed men, and Georgi Sheytanov had had to gradually and relentlessly resuscitate her for weeks on end: slowly, gently, with tender words and soft caresses, until he finally managed to pull her out of the vortex of melancholy and bring her back to life, and she had felt like a woman again.

Mariola and Sheytanov had been close back before her father sent her the hundred thirty kilometers away to Pleven—far from her wanton, anarchist-leaning friends in Kilifarevo. She'd been a diligent high school student until the day they brought her to a shack behind the vineyards over Tarnovo and she'd first laid eyes on him. She still remembered the talk he gave that night—eloquent words on Kropotkin, Senkevich, and Chernyshevsky—but what exactly it was he'd said she couldn't recall. She'd listened to him speak just as everyone else in the shack had, but heard only the irreparable gravel of his voice, caused by drinking caustic soda as a child, and the words passed through her without meaning. She was hypnotized by him. The same thing happened every time someone brought him to a tiny student dorm room somewhere in Tarnovo so he could speak on Tolstoy or Dostoevsky, whether high up in the forests or under the Kilifarevo poplars where, during the spectacular, quiet nights, he lectured them on future uprisings and battles and the enlightenment of the masses . . . He spoke of these future uprisings and battles, and the enlightenment of the masses, but Mariola stared at him, and what she felt had nothing to do with an impulse to grab a gun and fight for social justice and universal human rights. What she felt was something else entirely, and Mariola flushed, embarrassed, and all the while Sheytanov's black eyes glimmered in the rusty half-light.

He never read from a piece of paper when he spoke. Instead, he asked his audience for what it was they wanted to hear. "My friends," he'd say, "I'm simply not interested in reading you my words off a piece of paper. May I suggest you name the topic of discussion, and we can begin. And if and when I'm ignorant of a particular subject matter, I'll let you know upfront, you have my word." He'd then speak as if he'd spent days in libraries and reading rooms, preparing. They all aahed; how was it possible for him to possess this knowledge? But Mariola just stood there, transfixed by his eyes.

Following his discourses he would, without exception, disappear for weeks and months on end, leaving Mariola to agonize . . . At first the price on his head was a hundred thousand Bulgarian leva, then it went up to two hundred and she'd open her father's newspapers dreading she'd find out how the most dangerous criminal in the kingdom—the most wanted man in the land—had been captured and killed unceremoniously. Rumors flew that a young woman named Mara Bargazova from Ruse—also Mariola's age—had, after being questioned by police on

Sheytanov's whereabouts and refusing to give him away, undressed by the bank of the Danube and diligently folded her clothes before drowning herself. Mariola locked herself in her room and wept for a long time . . . She cried until she realized that she wasn't crying out of sadness for Mara Bargazova, but out of pure, helpless jealousy. She cried even more when someone gloatingly whispered in her ear that a girl named Stoyana had her stomach out to here—also Sheytanov's doing. Mariola had no way of knowing whether it was true, but her jealousy only became fiercer. She had difficulty going to sleep, and when she did, she dreamt dark and sad dreams. And when she woke up, she wept again.

[Thursday, March 7, 2013]
They released Mariola from the Pleven prison with the late-summer amnesty in nineteen twenty-four, and she took off back to Kilifarevo. The thing that scared her most was running into him. Which she did. Yet he was terribly attentive; he did not question or interrogate her—not about Pleven or anything else, he only stroked her hair and took her to a movie. They had just started showing Chaplin's *The Kid* at the Modern Theater on Samovodska Charshia, whose very first subtitle revealed this was to be *a picture with a smile, and perhaps a tear*, and in the dark salon fragranced by a hint of wood, amid the periodical bursts of laughter from the audience, she managed not a single smile. Pleven had made her incapable of it. She cried for the little boy, whom Charlie Chaplin had taken in, and whom the government was trying to take away. The little boy stretched out his little arms toward Charlie Chaplin, and then toward God, and Mariola wept. She wept even when Charlie Chaplin ran and ran on the rooftops, jumped into the truck taking the kid away and beat up the government official as the kid clung to him. She wept even as everything ended happily. The white sheet in front of them flickered and blurred inside her tears, and as she sobbed and swallowed the lump in her throat, she knew she was crying from indignity and from relief. After the film ended, Sheytanov got a taxi and took her back to Kilifarevo.

And so it was.

Mariola took her final eighth grade exams in Turnovo, but without the right to ever attend university. She was already twenty years old.

Once Mariola came back from Pleven, her father, Mitko Sirakov's, two-story house in Kilifarevo became a field hospital for the local band of communists and anarchists. Mitko Sirakov, humiliated by having to head a three-person committee in Kilifarevo, had otherwise been a decent man: he saw what his daughter was up to and nagged her, but Mariola let his criticisms wash over her; he'd been more afraid for her than he was interested in political loyalty. She walked past him with clenched teeth, silent as the moon, and he withered behind her—the powerful bureaucrat and fascist, now nothing more than a crestfallen and dumbstruck old man. Mariola hurried back and forth between Kilifarevo and Tarnovo, where she went every other day to buy medicine and gauze, becoming a charitable nurse and ward maid in the process, constantly hiding or bandaging someone new.

That's how it went that entire fall of twenty-four when the tattered, gloomy fog smoked and drifted down the valley. After that, right on the first of January, nineteen twenty-five, Norway renamed its capital from Christiania to Oslo, and lighting struck the colossal statue of Jesus Christ in some forgotten little town in Guidaliolo, Italy, somewhere close to Rome, shattering it from its pedestal up, resulting in the prophesies of all sorts of bad things and cataclysms. As it happened, not long after, gale-force winds ripped the English airship R33 from her mooring mast at Pulham, tearing and shattering her bow and sending her adrift, yet she hovered in the air for 28 hours before landing safely, a wild explosion inside the Magirus automobile factories took four lives and critically wounded around fifteen, the rebels continued to destroy the Spanish armies in Morocco, and Italy's metropolises (where Mussolini had just recently and abruptly abandoned his longstanding plans to become a founding father and supreme leader of a future Fascist International) were now host to loud quarrels and gory encounters between the indignant fascists and their most bitter enemies from the opposing parties. All of Europe sat under a rising smoke, and even before the old one could be forgotten, the smell of a new war began to permeate.

Such was that rainy spring of twenty-five, all the way up to that Easter, the sixteenth of April, when the terrorist attack on the St. Nedelya Church in Sofia's city center unleashed a merciless war on anyone who was suspected of siding with the opposition, and the doors of hell finally burst wide open . . .

Bulgaria was no different. It was barely February when a band of hoodlums crossed from the Serbian border and attacked the village of Godech. About a hundred of them split up into three groups: one group broke into the postal and telegraph station, another into the municipal offices, and the third into the police station. They cut the telephone and telegraph lines, killed one cop and wounded another, then retreated back into Serbia scot-free. Only after that, like an umbrella after the rain, did the police and some troops finally show up in Godech. The cold spring showers followed, the surrounding hills turned black and ugly, and the trees awoke in a cautious, scant green. Mityo Ganev's band suddenly took off, pillaging anything and everything from Haskovo on out—through Kavakliisko, Karabunar and Malko Tarnovo. The story went that they were all armed to the teeth, that they even had a Hiram Maxim machine gun, as well as another, medium sized one—a Schwarzlose—and long-range carbines from the arms factories of one Paul Mauser in Oberndorf, good French automatic rifles, piles of bombs, and excellent semi-automatic Nagants, prototypes from the now phantom-like eighteen ninety. Some wrote that all these weapons were brought to them by Soviet Russia, others explained how they got the shipments by sea from the Turkish sailors, while others arrogantly declared that smugglers of tobacco paper bootlegged the weapons for them on donkeys via Strandzha and Sakara.

"Don't believe a word of it," Sheytanov assured Mariola. "It's bullshit! As if Mityo Ganev needs machine guns in those thorn bushes and in that mud . . ."

Such was that rainy spring of twenty-five, all the way up to that sixteenth of April, when the gates of hell truly, finally opened . . .

[Friday, March 8, 2013]
On the Monday after Easter, Sheytanov told her softly, "It's time to clear out." He took her to his twelve-man partisan crew, the Kilifarevo Pack, and they went on the run. Death followed Mariola here, too, together with the rain, which was incessant even during April, and then May. Death was constantly at their heels: she screamed commands and orders hysterically from behind the trees and bushes, she thundered behind them while the bullets hissed and snapped at twigs just above their heads. They escaped Death, but she would catch up to them in another place and with another ambush.

Once more Mariola wished to die, and when the search party caught up to them yet again by the Urva neighborhood and Sheytanov stayed back to guard them, she ducked into some bushes and raised a gun to her head to end it all. But Zhelyo saw her in time, tore the gun from her hand and dragged her through the forest. And when he saw she was limping, he threw her over his shoulder and carried her. He was a large man, Zhelyo. And strong. It's probably why everyone called him *Bolshoi*.

Sheytanov caught up to them, and they all headed toward the Predel Pass—the mountain passageway between the Pirin and Rila mountains, over a kilometer above sea level. They climbed over the Balkan Mountains, scraping up their faces and hands, and slid down last year's blackened leaves and into the precipices. At Borushtitsa they crossed the tracks only a second before the troop train carrying soldiers and gendarmerie thundered by, and a thick black rain pelted them again, continuing even as they split up near the riotous village of Enina, each group taking off on its own way. When they reached Nova Zagora, only three of them remained—Mariola, Sheytanov, and Zhelyo.

In Nova Zagora the three hid at the house of a woman named Minka, whom Zhelyo and Sheytanov addressed as *kaka*, like an older sister, and who lived only with her daughter, Mariika—a student in her last year at the local high school.

Every bone in Mariola's body ached from the endless eighty-kilometer trek from Kilifarevo to Nova Zagora. She was soaked and scared, shivering pitifully in her drenched city coat and deeply grateful when kaka Minka cleaned the scratches on her face and brought her some of Mariika's dry clothes to try on. They fit.

Kaka Minka did odd jobs at the train station and informed them about the mobilized thugs—murderers—who had been guarding the railroads for the third week in a row. Stay away, she warned, those idiots were armed and jumpy and something bad was bound to happen. She'd also seen the groups of armed fascist gangs that had been brought in on two covered trucks—one from Stara Zagora, one from Sliven. Kaka Minka gave Mariola her daughter's ID card, made the beds for them, and went into the other room.

Zhelyo looked at Mariola, huddled into Sheytanov, and again attempted to convince him to head south and cross into Turkey.

"Sheytanov," he said, "It's nothing—just a short walk—for Mityo Ganev to take us into Turkey!"

But Sheytanov refused again. He likely harbored a different idea: to take Mariola into Yambol where they could both vanish into the Second District's maze of blind alleys until the storm subsided. All of this had to end sometime.

Mariola did not sleep a wink all night. She lay nestled in Sheytanov's arms, listening to the deep, even breathing of his slumber, and looked out toward the scattered shadows on the wooden ceiling, alternating between a paralyzing desperation and mystifying bursts of energy borne out of blurred hopes and possibility of a new life.

They went their separate ways in the early dawn: Zhelyo embraced Sheytanov, promising to have Mityo Ganev wait for them at Sakar Mountain, on the other side of the Maritsa River, while Zhelyo himself would meet them both in Odrin, if it so happened that Sheytanov changed his mind. He then turned to Mariola and muttered: "Mariola, don't you dare get scared! And don't think for one second about shooting yourself again, because I'll kill you myself, you got it! . . ." And he disappeared to the south.

The two of them, Mariola Sirakova and Georgi Sheytanov—the most wanted man in the kingdom—left the town, and the gray dawn on that twenty-sixth of May, nineteen twenty-five, found them on their way to the Workman's Lodge, No. 24. As they walked, Sheytanov told her the story of a monk from the Order of Friars Minor Capuchin, who died a hundred and fifty years ago. They had recently discovered a manuscript of his written on parchment paper, and what do you know, when they deciphered it, it turned out it contained prophesies from seventeen sixty-three—all the way up until the year two thousand. All the newspapers in Rome were falling over themselves to publish every single little detail; the whole thing had become a spectacle.

"And as you probably know," said Sheytanov, "*all* of the old prophecies come true."

Mariola couldn't tell if he was serious, but he kept going. It also turned out that the monk foretold the French Revolution, and the manuscript also detailed a new machine that was going to be used to behead the king and queen. The monk predicted the revolts and mutinies of eighteen forty-eight, the Polish uprising from eighteen fifty, and even the Great War of this century, which devastated all of Europe and caused the famine that spread throughout the world.

"For this year," he went on, "for nineteen twenty-five, he predicted earthquakes, floods, and all types of natural disasters. But the most important thing he said, is that three suns will appear, can you imagine that?"

"No!" she laughed.

"Neither can I," he said. "But that's what the man said! And if he wrote it, it must be true. Just wait till you hear what else is going to happen in this century."

In nineteen sixty, he told her, the island of Sicily would sink; France and Spain would be destroyed by an earthquake in the seventies; and in nineteen ninety—the guy did his prophesies by the decade—there would be a big solar eclipse.

"How big?" Mariola kept laughing.

"Huge," Sheytanov said. "It'll cover the earth in darkness and it will be six whole days before a single star will appear in the sky. Death will devastate the world and people will leave the cities en masse."

"How is that going to happen?" she protested. "You're making it up. If death devastates the world, who's going to be left to leave the cities? I don't buy it."

"That's what it said in the paper!" Sheytanov defended himself. "Have you ever known a newspaper to lie?! So let's see, with everything bound to happen in the nineties, the world will end by the year two thousand. And that's it."

"That's terrible!" Mariola exclaimed. "I'm only going to be ninety-six . . ."

It was likely around lunchtime by now, so the two stopped to rest by a water fountain near the workman's lodge, taking a seat near the stone basin. Sheytanov covered her shoulders with his raincoat and out of nowhere said:

"One shouldn't get old. It's ugly and disparaging." Mariola looked at him, stunned, because she'd had the same thought at the precise moment.

"We had this really old woman in my old neighborhood," he went on, "all of Yambol knew her, she was something of a midwife, constantly surrounded by people: women she'd raised, almost as old as her, people whose children she'd delivered once upon a time, piles of relatives, children, grandchildren, great-grandchildren . . . They didn't let her out of their sight for even a minute, despite the fact she was a tough old granny who had no issue taking care of herself. When she topped ninety, she turned to my mother and said, 'You know, sister, all these people around me all the time make me feel so wonderfully superfluous. God gave me too long a life: what a cruel blessing!'"

Just then, the handful of ragged murderers in breeches jumped out from the other side of the tracks with their crooked rifles, screaming that no one move. But their faces betrayed a primal fear. Mariola was certain Sheytanov would dash into the waist-high cornfields and vanish; after an hour or two, he'd be up in the mountains across from them, or, if he headed east, he could disappear into the streets of his native Yambol by nighttime. She imagined this and grew numb.

But Sheytanov only stood up, raised his arms, and yelled at the panicked scarecrows to put down their guns before someone got hurt.

They took Mariola and Sheytanov to nearby Mladovo, where something no one could have predicted happened: at the municipal office, when they looked at their identification, someone remembered to send for an officer to bring the local high school teacher.

She told them that yes, indeed, she knew the student on the ID card, Mariika Vassileva, but as soon as she laid eyes on Mariola, she confirmed *hers* was not the face of *their* Mariika . . .

[*Saturday, March 9, 2013*]
[Many years later, in another time, Sheytanov's brother Ivan, having never gotten over his batko's death, and having pieced together his life scrap by scrap to write about it, attempted to find this same high school teacher. He found her in Sliven. When he looked her in the eyes—he suddenly realized there was nothing to be said.

He turned and left, and she exclaimed to his back:

"Don't hold it against me!"

"I don't," he answered.

And that was that.]

6.

[Monday, March 11, 2013]

On March fourth, nineteen twenty-four, a Tuesday, Sheytanov went to Zheko "Gerginata" Gerginov's funeral. He took the bus from Turnovo to Stara Zagora, and then the train to Haskovo, where the funeral procession had already stretched from the Turkish baths in the center of town all the way to the Kenana Cemetery. While he strode through the mobs of people, Sheytanov looked on darkly as Ignes told him how it had gone down.

Two days prior, on the second, on the eve of the forthcoming amnesty set to release everyone detained in connection with the June uprising, a couple of guards pulled Gerginata aside for some bullshit reason and separated him from everyone—out of the communal cell and into a completely isolated part of the prison. In the middle of the night, three non-coms from the Haskovo garrison burst in screaming, "Freeze! Don't move!" as though they'd caught someone making a break or inciting a riot, and shot up the cell, riddling Zheko Gerginov with bullets before he'd even managed to sit up in his plank-bed. The three non-coms then disappeared and left the man to agonize all night. He did not breathe his last breath until the morning, at the precise hour the guards went down their lists and freed the inmates.

Sheytanov listened to all of this in silence and, when Ignes added that, according to someone he was close to, it had been Russev himself who had called up the director of the prison from Sofia and personally ordered him to do whatever was necessary to keep Gerginov from getting out alive, the anarchist spat with the kind of somber decisiveness borne out of suppressed rage:

"They want war. We'll give them war."

[Tuesday, March 12, 2013]

Before the dirt on Zheko's grave had even settled, five men entered the army barracks at the Tenth Rhodope Polk and took out ten Austrian Steyr Mannlicher carbines, two dozen nine-millimeter automatic pistols with wooden holsters, fifteen cases of bullets for the aforementioned guns, and a whole lot of trusty, club-shaped, Bulgarian-made hand grenades. They loaded all of this into the car of one of their guys, a White Guard, and took it to Mityo Ganev on the other side of Harmanli—in the Sakar Mountains. Mityo Ganev was even more furious than they were, because he loved Zheko and considered him more than a brother, and he hadn't even been able to say goodbye. Now, as his fellow rebels found themselves armed to the teeth, they ran wild in the surrounding areas— devilishly deft and elusive—like angels of darkness. They kidnapped the famous tobacco businessman from Haskovo—Smochevksy—a majority stakeholder of Nikoteya, and gave him a good beating; they occupied the Momkovo and Malko Popovo City Halls, which were lacking in any resistance (who could stage any sort of defense with those feckless, pre-war rifles anyway?); they blocked the wrecked, muddy road between Malko Gradishte and Ortakyoi and took a captain and his ten startled little soldiers captive. They didn't hurt them; they confiscated their guns and their bullets and immediately brought them to Mityo Ganev, who demanded to know the names of the three men who'd murdered his friend Gerginata in prison, and when he got what he needed, he gave them all a good kick in the ass and let them go. Except for their weapons, of course. He stole those.

But even before that, Mityo Ganev made sure word spread in Haskovo: Gerginata's killers were as good as dead; he had personally sentenced them, and whomever they were, they could expect visitors in the unknown hour of vengeance.

But the poor souls already sensed what was coming their way.

[Wednesday, March 13, 2013]
[That had all happened in March—during the limbo between winter and spring—when people prayed for the first green buds to appear.

One night in the middle of summer, on the twenty-sixth of July, two days after the government finally acquitted everyone who'd been convicted following the June uprising of nineteen twenty-three, the air was thick and tense as it is right before a thunderstorm. Mityo Ganev shouted: "Now!" and pointed to two of his best *haidoukhs* to go into Haskovo with him to take the three killers by complete surprise.

In the now almost four months since the murder, the poor wretches had not so much as left each other's side in a lame attempt to keep from falling apart. They drank endlessly in the hope of numbing the horror of the inevitable, knowing very well who Mityo Ganev was and what he was capable of doing. Everyone knew—songs were sung in the man's honor from Kavaklii all the way to Koprivshtitsa. Tense and jumpy, the three were quick to reach for their guns and hassled everyone they came into contact with in Haskovo. Even their commanders were at their wits' end. They understood their situation, sympathized with it even, but the whole thing had gotten out of hand. So they wrote to their superiors, pleading with them to release the three from duty and send them off.

That night, the three were together as they left the summer masquerade ball at the officer's hall, where they'd already rolled three cigarettes with tobacco mixed with hash and apple blossom, which is perhaps why they pissed their pants the instant Mityo Ganev and his merciless harbingers of death came out of the shadows on that lilac eve and surrounded them. They appeared in all their splendor: black-bearded and long-haired, girded with leashes, cartridge belts, and scabbards. The vaivode surveyed each of the three lowlifes, personally swore at each in an even, coldblooded manner as if he were reading him his verdict, and informed all three they had no idea what kind of man they'd killed, that they didn't deserve to live themselves, that they were better off dead, in fact, because even the chicken—that brainless creature—still looked up to God when it drank water, but they, they didn't even have the fear of God in them. He swore at them again, this time invoking their mothers—and that was the last thing those three heard in their ratty little lives. The rebels then shattered their skulls point-blank and dissipated into the shadows of that July evening, leaving the three corpses to lie soaked in their own urine and feces in a remote alley of the city gardens. The three bloodstains the color of overboiled, strewed, dried fruit hardened overnight, until a spring shower came around midday the next day to wash it all away.

That's how it went down.]

[The evening of Thursday, March 14, 2013]
[Back in the spring of nineteen nineteen, Mityo Ganev went delirious with the legends of Vaivode Angel's untold treasures, and, stubborn as a mule, dug around for days in the places where Angel and his gang had once roamed. He wasn't afraid of digging—he was young, barely nineteen, and strong as two men—and when he started digging, he dug and dug—with a map no less!—from Kozlek all the way to Karakolyova Dupka on the other side of Kavaklii. He lingered for a while around Kavaklii and punctured the earth around Paleokastro, then went all the way back from Kavaklii to Harmanlii. He'd become a spectacle. "What in God's name are you doing?" they mocked him. "What are you now, a treasure hunter?" But he just kept on digging. He dug for one month, then two, and in the third month a miracle happened! One June morning in that same nineteen nineteen, in a ravine by Bryastovo, amid the prickly blackberry bushes and the milk thistle, in between two wizened, wild plum trees, Mityo dug out five *delvi*, earthenware pots, each brimming with hundreds of old gold Turkish *mahmudiye*, handfuls of heavy Napoléons and Austrian *münze*s, strings of gold coins and gold and silver necklaces, rings and bracelets with diamonds cast in precious metalwork . . . Spellbound by their sheen, Mityo sat and stared at the jewels. For three days and three nights he took pleasure in the fortune before he buried it back in the ground—this time in the hellish, barren lands around Dragoina . . .

Mityo Ganev met Zheko Gerginov inside Haskovo prison three years later. Gerginata taught him to read and write and made him learn all of Hristo Botev's* poems by heart. And in November of twenty-two, just a little before he got bored of prison and decided to split, Mityo Ganev pulled Zheko aside and told him the incredible story of Vaivode Angel's treasure. He had a plan:

"You," he told Zheko, "have become more dear to me than a brother. As soon as we get out of here, we're splitting the haidoukh's treasure, you have my word!"

But Zheko replied, "Mityo, Mityo . . . Do you understand what you're suggesting? You want us to act like those goons and miscreants, like some rich wannabes? . . . It's not who we are. Give some of what you found to the poor and stockpile the rest for the revolution. Got it?"

"Got it!" Mityo yelled out. A week later he jumped off the train taking him to Sliven for his trial.

He returned to his kingdom amid the oak forests of Sakar Mountain, where his men had already gotten word of the treasure and eyed him in hungry anticipation. But there would be no talk of dividing up anything; he told his men loud and clear he had given his word to Gerginata.

"The only way you'll ever get your hands on a single gold coin or jewel is over my dead body," he said.

In Mityo's mind, Gerginata's plea may as well have come from God himself. The rebels grumbled for a while, but they couldn't break Mityo's word any more than he could go against Gerginata and let it go. And when, in nineteen twenty-five, he sensed with his entire being—the way a cornered animal might—that he was about to be wiped out, he dug up those same five *delvi* and brought them to a man named Dimko in Haskovo.

"I am entrusting you with all this," he said. "Hide it and protect it for better times. And don't for even a second think about touching it. Or I'm personally going rise from the grave and cut off your arm myself!"

Dimko was flabbergasted by the bitter threat—he couldn't imagine ever laying a hand on the treasure. He really did keep it hidden, for seven years. Until one day several unidentified men showed up, claimed they'd been sent by the communists, and coaxed him into giving them everything for the "cause."

It was the last time he saw either—the emissaries or the gold. And that was that.]

7.

[*Monday, March 18, 2013*]

Sheytanov caught the express train to Sofia that night after Gerginata's funeral. He pressed a large bill into the ostensibly snooty conductor's palm and sat inside an empty first-class compartment. He turned the key and sank into the velvet seat; by the time the train reached Pazardzhik, he'd written the article he'd promised the poet for the April issue. He titled the piece "Inception" and signed it Georgi Vassilev instead of Georgi Sheytanov: no need to pull the devil by the tail and destroy the magazine prematurely—his name had long been considered a path to blitheness anyway. The snow had not yet melted from Pazardzhik on out, and he caught glimpses of snowdrifts underneath the reflections of the train lights—small squares of light that ran and jumped, and then spun and disappeared into the jet-black nothingness beneath, pierced only by the orange sparks from the locomotive. It was the darkest hour of night. Inside the warm compartment, with the hollow pulse of the iron beneath his feet, and engulfed by the comfort of the velvet, mahogany, and polished brass detail, Sheytanov closed his eyes and slept all the way to Sofia.

He began to dream. He was walking down Turgovska Street in Yambol, and at the corner of the town's cloth mill and the bus depot, he came across a fallen horse. A fallen, white horse. It lay there, breathing heavily, and yet no one else stopped by it—the people passed the animal at Sheytanov's feet as though they didn't even care the creature wasn't long for this world. He continued on up toward the Federation Club on Coburg Square when another horse jumped out from behind a street gate. This one was sorrel. The animal then somehow lifted both of its right legs and tipped, collapsing onto the white pavement. In his dream,

Sheytanov stared in disbelief. He turned back toward the intersection where the small white horse had fallen and froze: behind him, the entire street was covered with toppled horses . . . white, black, sorrel: healthy animals with powerful muscles visible underneath their shiny hair, and yet unable to stand up, convulsing as if they'd been struck down by something horrifying. Sheytanov tore away and ran off, suddenly flying. It had been a while since he dreamt of *flying*. A long time ago, when he was a little boy, he'd often dream he was flying, and he still recalled the joy of roaming above the trees. He remembered these youthful reveries well—when he squeezed in between the cables and whirled around the bell tower of St. George, the church right next to their old house and the highest point in Yambol's entire Second District, visible from every part of town . . . But this was different. There was no joy in this dream, no freedom in this deceitful flight. It was something terrifying and agonizing, as if he were freefalling into a black abyss—like a stone plummeting into a bottomless pit. The dream became more chilling: the bottom of the hole was now visible and blanketed by lifeless birds with shiny feathers, yet warped and withered bodies. And he was falling into them . . .

He startled awake, sweating heavily. The sweat beneath his collar stank of fear. He feared nothing when awake—he could always find a way out. But dreams were far from nothing, and he felt helpless once he fell asleep. Oftentimes he'd jolt awake, sweating and shaking, unable to recall even a fragment of the dream that had caused the distress. But it made no difference even when he could remember—superstitions and interpretations weren't his thing, and he wasn't about to go digging around dream books. What was the point? He'd been terrorized already anyway.

Now the train swayed softly atop the dispersing tracks, the orange lights of the station slowly drawing closer, and the pearl March dawn of the Wednesday grayed somewhere behind . . . he'd arrived in Sofia.

[Wednesday, April 10, 2013]
The first thing he did in Sofia was buy *Utro*, where he read that only a day earlier the government had gone after the Macedonian factions

everywhere it could find them. Numerous people had been arrested, close to five hundred according to the newspaper . . . But there were no names mentioned, and he tucked the paper into his pocket.

Instead of taking the tram, he decided to walk down Maria Louisa. Police patrols were at every step, and when he passed each of them by, he tilted his hat and greeted them. Trams gathered and filed out for their daily routes, milk carts rattled, carriages carried vegetables in from the greenhouses at the outskirts of Sofia, the shop shutters rolled up with a bang, cafés and shops opened their doors, and the apprentice boys swept the sidewalks in front; and the air was sweet with *mekitsi* and *burek* and fresh bread . . . The first shoe-shiners were already clattering with their brushes on Banski Square; Sheytanov stopped at one. The man first scraped yesterday's mud off his shoes, then shined them until they sparkled, dandified . . . Then Sheytanov stopped at a barber's somewhere on Turgovska and got a shave. And after the barber was finished and sprayed him twice with eau de cologne, and had brushed the crisp one-leva bills bearing Stamboliyski's face on his beard for good luck—for it was the first money to come in that day—he went so far as to walk him out to the door, and Sheytanov had felt as good as new. He didn't even sense the foul odor of horseradish and vinegar still lingering beneath his shirt . . .

He entered the Macedonia Hotel café, ordered a German coffee and reached over for the bamboo stick holding Krapchev's newspaper, *Zora*. Its first page was also dedicated to the Macedonian factions' arrests, but again no mention of any names, so Sheytanov turned to the third page. There he saw the photograph of three men seated at a table, with a caption underneath that read: "A Bulgarian record! Three jolly fellows from Pazardzhik, the first of whom (from the left) drinks 30 liters of wine, the second (standing) 25, and the third—40 liters, every single day!"

"*Ashkolsun!*" he thought to himself. "Well done, champions! That's how you build a strong country."

The fourth page, however, was entirely dedicated to Henry Ford and how Henry Ford raised his workers' wages, how he cut their workday from nine hours to eight, and how he even made the workweek five days instead of six—even before the war. Now everybody who worked for him in his factories could buy a car with his salary after only four months. Everyone was happy, the workers were loyal down to the last one, and Ford had completely squashed the competition—and now, in nineteen twenty-three, was already producing around two million automobiles a year. It also said that Ford slashed his prices, so now one of his vehicles cost only four hundred dollars, and he still managed annual revenues of eight hundred million dollars, or eighty billion leva. Ford raised his workers' salaries once again, and now nobody even thought about labor unions anymore. It occurred to Sheytanov that you can't liberate such a person—what would you be liberating him from? How would you be able to convince this person that co-ops were the future of the working class, he thought, when no co-op can give this person tomorrow what Henry Ford can give him today? The paper even cited Ford himself—and luckily Zafirovi Brothers Press had just published a translation of Ford's *My Life and Work*. In it, he wrote that if you want someone to dedicate himself entirely to his work, you must pay him enough to eradicate his financial worries. And that, he said, is a good thing. According to him, there were two reasons men worked: one was for wages, and the other for fear of losing their jobs.

"And he's right, too, that scoundrel!" thought Sheytanov. "He's happy and they're happy. Everyone's satisfied."

He tossed the paper on the table and stepped out onto Banski Square—filled with rumbling vehicles, many indeed Fords, imported by the international automobile trading company Strela. "We need to have Effi and Bae give this Strela the once over," he thought to himself.

And so it was.

[Thursday, April 11, 2013]
The cold silver sun glimmered through tall windows as Sheytanov entered the David and Mois Aronovi brothers' shop. He went straight to the confectionary counter and bought two chocolate bonbons. One

was from the chocolate factory of the famous chocolatier Velizar Peev in Svoge, and the other—from the commercial and industrial house for tahini and confectionaries owned by Avram Chalyovski; both bonbons were packed in exquisite little boxes lined with velvet. He only bought the chocolates for the boxes anyway: the bonbons were for Leda and Bistra, but the boxes—for the poet. The poet had a strange affinity for these little boxes; he collected them passionately and guarded them jealously, and had amassed a whole lot of them. Sheytanov wouldn't forget how the man had once made an unfortunate waiter run around for thirty minutes in the confectionary of the Grand Hotel Panah, making the poor guy bring down various boxes until he was finally satisfied. The people standing around weren't sure if they should get angry or just assume he was crazy, but the poet paid them no mind. He was possessed. If someone had burst in to rob the place in that half hour, he'd have yelled at him to get out of his way.

So it went . . . He arranged the prettiest boxes on his display shelf, together with the wooden house he had brought some time ago from England—an exact replica of Shakespeare's house—behind whose miniature door you could see the chestnut the poet had taken from Shakespeare's yard in Stratford. This shelf was not to be touched by anyone else—not even the children—it could only be admired from afar. The poet had a strange affinity for miniature memorabilia, he thought it terribly important: he didn't let anyone get near it and the things just stood there, where he left them, seemingly because of their importance, but they slowly sank into the dust of oblivion.

[Friday, April 12, 2013]
That morning the poet had, of course, already been working for some time—he was neither disturbed by the hollow rumble of the boulevard outside, nor by the children's ruckus behind the curtains, nor by Mila's voice as she tutored them. The ashtray in front of him was overflowing and the entire table was covered in galleys, various notebooks, sheets of paper, books and dictionaries, and his brand new typewriter, which

stood out amid everything else. He was very happy to see the funny *armagan*, the amusing gift from afar, but he quickly got to business and let Sheytanov know he was just the man he needed!

"I'm selecting this and that from the Sinclair anthology," he said, "so have a seat and tell me what you think."

Sheytanov shrugged and politely said that advice was something he'd be happy to give—as long as it wasn't money he wanted.

"Very funny!" the poet guffawed. "Very funny indeed! Now listen. I'm still of two minds as to whether this should go in: 'If my soldiers were to begin to reflect, not one of them would remain in the ranks.' What do you think of the translation? Do you think it's too literal?"

"Kaiser Wilhelm?" asked Sheytanov.

"Frederick the Great!" the poet answered impatiently.

"That works too," Sheytanov responded. "Just don't omit his name, you wouldn't want General Vulkov thinking you were mocking him."

"You think he'd think that?" the poet stood up, on edge. "Does he even speak English?"

"No. I don't know." Sheytanov shrugged again. "Lighten up, I was joking."

"I don't have a sense of humor on Wednesdays," the poet replied. "Just take a look at this though, it's also from Sinclair's book . . ."

He dug out a new sheet of paper, held it up high in front of his good eye and read:

"'Recruits! Before the altar and the servant of God you have given me the oath of allegiance. You are too young to know the full meaning of what you have said, but your first care must be to obey implicitly all orders and directions. You have sworn fidelity to me, you are the children of my guard, you are my soldiers, you have surrendered yourselves to me, body and soul. Only one enemy can exist for you—my enemy.'"

The poet threw his guest a scornful look, mumbled and continued:

"'With the present Socialist machinations, it may happen that I shall order you to shoot your own relatives, your brothers, or even your parents—which God forbid—and then you are bound in duty implicitly to obey my orders.' Well? How is it?"

"Frederick?" Sheytanov asked seriously.

"No," the other laughed. "Wilhelm! But it may as well have been General Goose himself who said it, intellectual that he is! Or any general, for that matter. They all take themselves for generals over there."

"There you have it," Sheytanov sighed. "The state is an antisocial institution, defended only by the lowly . . . what I'm trying to say is—you must strangle the state!"

The poet cut him off and asked him not to agitate and rattled off the translated sentence on his brand new little Adler typewriter.

"I'm not agitating," Sheytanov grinned, "I'm only encouraging you."

Then he added:

"I know a saying, too. 'More comfort leads to less bravery.' What do you think?"

"Frederick?" the poet asked absent-mindedly.

"Suvorov!" Sheytanov laughed again.

"Yeah right," the other responded and pulled the sheet of paper out of the typewriter. "Like one villager at the Kniajevo Military Academy liked to say: 'He who laughs last shoots first.'"

He took a look at what he'd written, liked it, and sighed.

"You know, sometimes I get the urge to go somewhere where there're lots of people, let's say the St. Nedelya altar, for instance, get up on a soapbox and yell out: 'People! Read smart books today, so you won't have to read banned ones tomorrow!'"

8.

[Saturday, April 20, 2013]

That year on April first, someone named Hitler—and his friends along with him—were convicted for attempting to incite a social and national putsch, a coup, in other words, a revolution, inside a Munich beer hall the previous November. The trial had started back in February in the main reading room of the Munich infantry's military academy. There had been three hundred sixty-eight witnesses, correspondents had flocked in from all corners of the world, shooting nonstop with their magnesium lamps and buzzing with their cameras, and what's more, the court let hundreds more into the courtroom to watch, while two battalions from the province's national guard were guarded behind the barbed wire and barricades outside. A true clusterfuck and hullabaloo. When the smoke cleared, some were let go, Hitler and two others were allegedly given five-year prison sentences and a fine of two hundred gold deutschemarks (the new ones), but the men had time taken off for having served in the war and ended up doing just six months. Everyone assumed that after such a disdainful and insulting sentence, this guy Hitler was done with: in a month or two, no one would remember who he was and what exactly he'd fought for . . .

In any case.

In April of that year in Bulgaria, the snow melted and caused terrible flooding. The high water deluged a mass of villages around the Danube and sunk the Pleven-Somovit train line; the torrents washed out the train tracks between Kyustendil and Rujdavitsa, as well as the sleeper cars, gravel—everything. Brutal hail followed, the evil fly befell the villages in the Kulsko region, and hordes of ticks crawled out, bringing with them all sorts of terrible illnesses for the cattle—scabies, tuberculosis, glanders, foot and mouth disease, swine flu . . . all severely damaging and harmful afflictions that everyone had long hoped had disappeared once and for all. The authorities set up sanitary-control posts, put up barricades all over to guard the roads, and the people in the villages wailed while they slaughtered their own cattle befallen by this scourge, then threw out and buried mounds of bloated animals. Destitute times had come. And to top it all off, locusts took over the regions of Karnobat and Yambol, reaching all the way to Malko Turnovo, and the evil fly had traveled through the entire country and gotten all the way up to the northwestern town of Belogradchik.

Right around that time, a whole lot of congresses, conferences, and annual assemblies began to take place. On the second of March, the congress for the Starini Association of Retirees started up. On the fourth, the Union of Cyclists gathered in Lom. On the ninth, it was the annual assembly for peace through allying that came together, suspiciously under the auspices of the masons . . . And after that, on the twenty-third of March, the annual gathering of the Association of Sofia Journalists took place. The Sofia journalists did what they could and once again elected their man Nikola Mitev chairman, since he was a notable mason and quite close to the government, and aside from that had access to the palace and did not have to beg for an audience beforehand. The papers feared him and gave money for the insurance fund without too much whining, despite rumors that half of their installments went to the so-called Macedonian factions—rebels who claimed to fight for Macedonia's liberation, but more often than not were quite simply brutal killers for hire. Nikola Mitev then became guest of honor at the First Regular Congress of the Union of Bulgarian Provincial Journalists. (This guy just loved to be invited as a guest of honor to all sorts of events. And he loved it when they made him boss. The second the masons founded the union of intellectuals, they voted for him to chair the permanent presence of the supreme counsel.) The Union of the Provincial Journalists was founded in January, so the congress in May was a big deal: his royal highness Ferdinand himself sent a congratulatory telegram, Nikola Milev spoke of the debt journalists owed to pacifism, and everyone yelled hooray for a long time.

And so it was.

[Sunday, April 21 2013]

Just then, amid all that proud national appeasement and out of nowhere, a fighting pack of anarchists descended into Sofia. They called themselves "Heroes of the Night"—and it was how they signed the threatening letters they sent to the more affluent politicians and the rich. They were here to combat the new government, their leaflets said. The newspapers regularly published these letters and leaflets, but the Heroes of the Night were about far more than just the written word. One Tuesday, they boldly robbed the offices of the Haim Benaroya bank located at 1 Drin Street; three days later they somehow carried out entire bags of revenue stamps from the national bank, after which they attacked some insurance offices with their Mausers and Parabellums, shooting so wildly all over the place they even hit a student: Vulchev someone or other. Then they shot a Public Safety agent, Stefanov, and they shot up the boss of the second police station, Karamfilov. They shot at Paskalev too—the mayor of Sofia—although, true, he did manage to escape without a scratch, but who would put it past these Heroes of the Night to try a second time? The newspapers *Zarya*, *Dnevnik*, and *Utro* shocked the already cowed people with macabre details from the thugs' raids, and *Free Speech* and the Democratic Alliance called for the government to uncross its arms and be merciless with these people.

The secretary, Razsukanov, really did get the entire Sofia police up in arms, and the head of Public Safety sent entire hordes of secret agents out on the streets, but those Heroes were elusive. They'd hit up a place and vanish in an instant: scuttling into the nearest building and quickly kicking through the back door, then from one basement to another, from one courtyard to another, jumping over little iron gates, dashing through a hole in a stone wall or straight over them, then up a tree and onto someone's roof, and then they'd come down the balconies, the window grates, or simply by the gutters . . . and straight into the neighbor's garden. In Sofia, you could

[Monday, April 22, 2013]
cross entire neighborhoods, even in the city center with its passages and bedestens reeking of plaster and lime, with its new multiple front-entry and multiple back-exit structures built of stone; the skylights were also perfect for one to disappear through, and to reappear completely nonchalantly somewhere else entirely, somewhere far away, where even the cop's whistles faded to nothing. And so it was. Anyone could disappear into the night without so much as sticking his head out into the street—and how were you supposed to catch such a person?

[Tuesday, April 23, 2013]
Also that May, the politician and philosopher Dimitar "The Grandfather" Blagoev died. They buried him on the eleventh, a Sunday, and the streets through which the funeral procession was to pass filled up with cops and secret agents early on.

Milev made it to the house on Debar Street precisely as six mourning pallbearers carried out the coffin. He knew the man standing up at the front—he'd been a friend of Smirnenski's and could recite his poems perfectly. Valko someone or other, Chervenkov.

But he saw another familiar face on the other side of the coffin. He couldn't recall exactly where he'd seen it before, but when the other looked straight at him, the poet immediately remembered. It was the same chatty young man, big boned and dark as a corner, the clerk at the sixth residential commission, that same pseudo-intellectual who'd approved his address registration inside his dusty chancery at the station some months ago. Nikola Geshev. But the poet had long forgotten his name because he'd immediately tucked the man's business card into some pocket somewhere and had put the whole thing out of his mind.

[Wednesday, April 24, 2013]
He strode among crowds unmatched in size since the grand funeral of Ivan Vazov three years earlier, he listened to all the eulogies, he sang when the people sang "You fell in battle," and fell to his knees when someone yelled "On your knees for the Grandfather!" and the undertakers lowered the coffin into the grave. Afterward, he didn't go home, but went straight to Balkan press, which was kind of on his way because it was located on Maria Louisa Boulevard, the same one he lived on, just a little farther down, right next to the train station. Anyway. He burst into the room where the typesetters were, tore a piece of paper from some galleys laying on the wayside and wrote the Grandfather's obituary in one go, without so much as lifting the pencil from the paper once. From there he threw himself onto the already printed pages of the May issue of *Plamuk*, called for the form-setter, and showed him exactly where he needed to fit in the obituary—right after "The Stones Speak" by Hadjiliev and above "The Procession" by Ivan Gol. There was a poem in the space already, but he told them to cut it, disregarding the fact it was already typeset; they could do without it for this issue, but they couldn't do without the obituary. The poem could wait until June, of course, whereas the obituary would look pitiful and useless then. The head typesetter mumbled something, but the poet had already flown out of the production room.

He didn't feel any sense of mourning while this was all happening: he felt only elation and contentment. He was happy that he'd made it to the printer's on time and that the obit would come out in May, not a month after, or something like that.

That's how it was.

[Thursday, April 25, 2013]
Then he went home because he and Mila had to get Bistra and Leda ready for Stara Zagora.

[Friday, April 26, 2013]
Leda loved being in Stara Zagora better than in Sofia. In Stara Zagora there were no trams to watch out for and due to which you had to hold your mother's hand without exception when crossing the boulevard. And they had a big house in Stara Zagora, with many rooms and many doors and many windows, a cellar, an attic, a yard, a boxwood, an oak, and flowers, planted not inside pots, but just like that, right in the ground. In Stara Zagora there was a garden, and a hedge between the yard and the garden, and a big wooden gate out front you could swing back and forth on without getting yelled at to come down; there was a water basin, cats, and two turtles, but the real bliss—even better than all of these things—was Grandpa Milyo's bookstore. The bookstore was filled with magical drawings *from Berlin,* and the best part were the pencils and wonderful paper on which Leda could write as many letters as she wanted and her dyado would never say: "Don't waste the paper, kiddo!" the way her old *baba* Gena, her grandmother Anastasia's mother, always chided her. And she could draw. Just like her father did, always drawing them, her and her sister Bistra. She started by diligently drawing some letters, then she'd quickly do a picture, then she'd write out some more letters and then another picture, and when a piece of paper got folded, it became a little *book,* just like the one she got as a gift from the stunningly beautiful Dora Gabe Peneva. Leda could recite Dora Gabe's poem *Baba,* Grandma, just as expressively as her mother could. "Mommy said that baba too was once so very small, that she too could not dress herself, not even at all." What a funny poem! Even Bistra laughed at the line "Babo dear, Babo sweet!" at the end, even though she was still little—that's how funny the poem was. Leda also knew that every book had to have a *title* (just as Mrs. Gabe Peneva's book *Little Songs,* had) and it had to be

written in bigger letters, and that cover of the book most certainly had to bear the name of the *author.*

So each time she finished another little book, she very clearly wrote on its front: LƎDA.

[Saturday, April 27, 2013]
You had to take the train to get to Stara Zagora. Leda loved the train, too; it was filled with people and luggage and baskets and suitcases and bundles and bags, sometimes even hens and ducks, and it was always bustling and yet *composed,* full of smoke and grime on the other side of the windows and wooden separators on the backs of the wooden seats—but you could easily see the people on the other side if someone lifted you up just a little bit.

Starting this year, she would travel with her very own ticket. True, a half-priced kid's ticket, but still a ticket! She was four now and she could say her age with words, not with fingers, like Bistra, who was still little, did. That's why Bistra wouldn't have a ticket, but Leda would.

Leda knew everything and she was a good kid. Everyone said so. She already knew she was going to an American daycare. Starting next year. Her father said so to her mother—his daughters absolutely had to learn English, had to know it so well in fact, that they *would dream in English.* She heard that and started to wonder what it might be like to dream in English. But it would be years and years before she would understand what that actually meant.

[Sunday, April 28, 2013]
[A bat in the apartment entryway. Strange.]

[Monday, April 29, 2013]
The poet took Mila and the kids to Stara Zagora, stayed a day, just long enough to teach Leda how to lie next to the trimmed boxwood, just as her aunt Maria had done when she'd been the same age, and on the

second day, he took the train back to Sofia to put together the sixth issue of *Plamuk*. Sheytanov was in Sofia as well, so at dusk one June day in nineteen twenty-four, as they finished whatever they had yet to finish with the new issue, the two men sat down at the St. George rotunda on Battenberg Square to drink beer and to eat *kebapcheta*. The poet ate ten. When he saw Sheytanov's incredulous eyes, he nonchalantly told him ten kebapcheta was nothing—he'd eaten seventy fried-dough cakes, *mekitsi*, at the Kniajevo Military Academy.

"Come on," Sheytanov laughed. "Play it down a little bit. Nobody can eat seventy mekitsi."

"I beg to differ!" the poet seemed insulted. "The entire academy is my witness. Whoever's left, anyway. I made a bet with one of the villagers that I could eat seventy mekitsi, but they—like you—did not believe me. I only had one condition—I also had to have a big washbasin of yogurt."

"And?" Sheytanov couldn't stop laughing.

"A whole crowd gathered," the poet laughed, too. "The whole company lined up to form a square. In the middle—a table. On the table? A paper bag. Inside the paper bag? Seventy mekitsi, personally counted by the sergeant major, because, well, he's the mother of the whole group, who else would do it. Next to the paper bag? A washbasin filled with yogurt. Next to the table? Your humble servant. And so the séance beings! Thirty-two mekitsi with no yogurt whatsoever. From the thirty-second one on, I had a whole system set up: one mekitsa, two spoonfuls of yogurt. This was in July. The sun is brutal and the heat unbearable. God damn, the whole thing was a pain in the ass. One mekitsa, two spoons of yogurt, one mekitsa, two spoons of yogurt. You don't believe me, but at the end, all the troops applauded and yelled 'Hooray!' Even the platoon leader congratulated me—for the first and last time, and even the sergeant major said to me, 'Well done, klutz! I know you as the biggest lout at this school. There was always something bothering you, you never lined up in formation on time, yet here you turn out to be a bona fide Balkan hero, cadet Kassabov!'"

[Tuesday, April 30, 2013]
"You're lying!" said Sheytanov.

"I swear to you on my life!" the other did not let up. "I wrote a whole poem about it. *I am a man / the man wonder who prevailed / a whole cassole of yogurt I inhaled.* The others thought it went with the poem 'Maritza Runs,' can you imagine that? I think it did go with it. Go on, try it out. They even tricked me into writing the refrain, and well, who am I to refuse? I wrote it on the spot: *Eat! Eat! Eat! Beans and rice and milk! / First into the food we'll tuck / and then we'd like some girls to . . .* you can figure out the rest yourself. It nearly got me thrown into the cooler after all those hoorays. Complete bullshit, but what can you do? Military school is military school, not boarding school. Nineteen-year-old lads—barely out of high school, can't even swear properly—get told by some old guys in caps that they're men now. So they do their best to act like men—they swear and spit out vile curses. And you know what, the sergeant major was right. I *was* always bedraggled and unbuttoned, my breeches—wrinkled, my cap—ragged. When everyone lined up for formation, I always ran out last. When we went to eat in the cafeteria—I was late again, and everyone got angry with me for that too. You know what I loved the most? The individual exercises. Of course, you haven't so much as smelled a military school—you have no idea what I'm talking about. Individual exercise means every man gives himself orders. You command yourself to: "Pull out the knife!" and then you follow your own command. You yell, "Fire!" and you get down and shoot. Guess what I told myself to do."

"I have no idea! What?"

"I told myself to 'Freeze! As you were!' All the time."

"What?!" Sheytanov spit out his drink.

"There's no what. 'Freeze! As you were! Excellent, cadet!' Things like that. What's more, I'd tell myself 'at ease!' I came up with that all by myself, and the sergeant major went blue in the face."

[Wednesday, May 1, 2013]

He sighed, then they both laughed, and only then spotted the young man with a too timid disposition standing next to their table, nervously shifting from one foot to another.

The poet scowled and snapped at him to stop sticking out like that and to sit, if he's going to sit.

"Listen to me now, young man," he said, when the other sat down wimpishly, barely on the corner of the chair. "Obviously I read your notebook, and what can I say . . . Apropos," he growled, "I had a damn hard time with your handwriting. You have the handwriting of a genius, goddamn it. No matter, I read them all. Now, your poems are meant to be erected with the leitmotifs of social discontent, and yet you deck out your constructing mechanisms with the style of the symbolists and the decadents. Well? How could you think you could get away with that, my boy? After the wars, nothing is as it was. Think about that! Before the wars women still walked around with crinolines and hats like birdcages, and just look at them now. They don't just put make up on, they smear it on with a distempering brush, as if they're applying war paint. They threw away their corsets and now what? Two little rags in the front, two little *urkuzuncheta* in the back."

"Urkuzunche?" the other's face reddened from ear to ear.

"Ties, strings," the poet clarified, "Don't you know what *urkuzun* means? They founded some international women's league for peace and freedom, invented some kind of hula-hooping dance and look at them now—they've got us wrapped around their little finger."

He shut up long enough to light a cigarette and went on.

"And us," he went on, "we came back from the battlefronts excoriated. If you ask me, the twentieth century didn't start in nineteen and one, it started in nineteen fourteen, that's what I think! Europe today has nothing to do with Europe then—just look at the map: brimming with new nation states. There are four or even five new countries popping up out of Austro-Hungary, and I haven't even counted how many came out of Russia. After all that hell, you need to break the mold! All the molds. Anywhere you see a mold, you have to destroy it and obliterate it. Because what should you want from life?"

"What?" the young man whispered, intimidated.

"Nothing if not everything, my boy!" the poet banged the table. "Only that!"

Georgi Sheytanov looked on curiously as the poet's demeanor transformed right in front of him: he straightened up his posture where he sat in the black Viennese chair, raised his finger triumphantly, and brought his voice to the same timbre he used for his lectures in those small, dark community-center salons. The only difference being that while he tried not to smoke during his lectures, here he chain-smoked and the cigarettes hissed and crackled like lit bomb fuses, and the ash scattered all around him. A drop the color of wax crawled down his cheek, but he paid no mind to it—not yet. The usual bustle of restaurant clamor encompassed them, with all those plates clattering, the ringing of glasses and the shouts of the waiters—"Right now, please!" and "We're bringing it!" and "Coming up!" Instead of the dim and buzzing lamps in those salons and reading rooms, here the electric globes shone fiercely high above the high ceiling, but the poet was far from being discomforted by the fact, just as he was completely nonplussed by the fact he wasn't speaking to twenty or thirty people, but just a lone, sweaty young man. Bewitched by those prideful demons of haughtiness, he spoke to him as though he were speaking to a sea of one hundred.

Indeed. After the short introduction about the wars and the changing times, the poet confidently spat out that it was here that expressionism truly burst into life, powerful and unyielding. Because what was expressionism if not a rebellion?! Why? Because it rose up against the old and broke the cliché of the patriarchal literary comfort—and in search of what? In search of the new form, of course. He raised his hand and clarified that yes, symbolism was adept at that as well—the visual resources of symbolism taught man how to use beautiful symbols to illustrate his thoughts, to give them a deeper perspective.

"Symbolism," he said, "is far too young for us to label it and lock it up inside the archives of human misconceptions."

He added that so far, so good! But, what happens now?

"Alright, let's see," he said. "You take the words "night" and "death" for instance. What will the symbolist do with them? The night is preternaturally sorrowful, the night is more Stygian than death. Beautiful? Beautiful. That 'more Stygian than death' is simply magnificent, no doubt. I could kill a man for one simple 'more Stygian than death,' but let's move on! What would the expressionist do with those same elements?" He snapped his fingers, "let's see if I can improvise something."

He lowered his head, thought for a second, and began tapping a beat on the table:

"Something like this. The night gives birth . . . the night births from its dead womb . . . you see it, right? Something is born out of something dead! Death gives birth, and that which is born is alive. That's it. *From the dead womb of night*, but what comes out of that damned and intrusive night? Let's keep going. From the dead womb of night, the legendary spite of the slave is born! Let's see, what would come after. No, wait a minute! Legendary won't work. It's too persnickety, too melodramatic and vulgar. We need something raw here. Age-old. Yes! *From the dead womb of night, the age-old venom of the slave is spawned!* Now let's add a couple of things from what we know of symbolism, something like: *His crimson spite, so mighty.*

"Incredible!" the young man exclaimed. "It's great! Powerful!"

"Precisely." The poet agreed.

He then turned cheerfully toward Sheytanov and cried:

"What do you say, Sheytanov? *From the dead womb of night, the age-old venom of the slave has spawned! His crimson spite, so mighty.* I just came up with that on the

[Wednesday night, May 1, 2013]

spot. I could gift it to the young man, but he'll only ruin it. Like Lalyo. For some reason I said to him that the faces of our modern-day saints should be imprinted on iron icons, so I told him: Here! Take it. I'm giving you the iron icons. And he couldn't stop. Now they're a dime a dozen. I can probably make better use of it. *From the dead womb of night, the age-old venom of the slave has spawned!* I'm thinking of a poem about Prince Marko and Musa Kesedžija, we'll see how it turns out."

He then turned his chair back toward the young man and added that the futurists would take it even further. The futurist would never be content with "the night spawns from its dead womb"—the futurist would by all means add something like Zang tumb tuuum . . .—but that was going too far.

"Zang tumb tuuum is gluttonous," he declared, "but yours too is far from being ripe for a revolution. You need fire to spark a revolt, you don't go to war with wilted chrysanthemums. And let us quit while we're ahead, because we're risking stepping into the barbed wires of the big question of style versus substance, if you catch my drift!"

The young man attempted a flaccid defense, but the poet cut him off, asking him not to defend himself like some old lady, but to write!

"I want you," he ordered him, "to bring me new material by the time we get to the twenty-fourth of May, the day of letters, got it? Either new stuff, or you edit these ones. Wait, wait. Did I say the twenty-fourth of May? That's too late. Can you get them to me by Saturday?"

The young man went scarlet and mumbled fervently, that, well, but the poet cut him off once more.

"Done, then. Let me ask you something else. You," he said, "what did you study in Vienna?"

"Business," the other responded in despair.

"Would you look at that Sheytanov!" the poet exclaimed. "Look at what the kids are studying these days, not like you and me."

"Don't look at me!" Sheytanov said defensively. "I'm innocent. I didn't even graduate high school."

The poet didn't even hear him—he was already saying something else to the confused youth.

"Very practical," he said "Business. Extraordinarily practical, that profession! And since you're not lacking in imagination or wit, I think you'll make an excellent millionaire. Just cure yourself of the desire to write poetry. I'm serious!" he exclaimed enthused, "Why aren't you a bank director yet? Literature?! *Basta*! Literature is a blighted endeavor in this country, haven't you figured that out yet?"

He tapped him on the shoulder, told him to run along, and that he was expecting him on Saturday with the poems. The young man jumped up and flew away through the tables. Sheytanov cracked a smile.

....

....

....

9.

[May 2, 2013, Holy Thursday]

Around midday on April sixteenth, nineteen twenty-five—on Holy Thursday before Easter—Sofia's city center resembled a fairground: all of the capital's streets and squares and boulevards—Maria Louisa Boulevard, Banski Square, and across it on both sides of Turgovska and Dondukov Streets—brimmed with quickly-erected stands and tables filled with sweet Easter cakes, popcorn, sunflower seeds, chickpeas, bonbons, Turkish delight, red rooster-shaped lollipops, caramelized apples, cotton candy, bobbles and all kinds of knickknacks for the *Shopki* girls—rings, bracelets, necklaces, earrings, combs, and mirrors . . . Watches with painted dials and cloth straps for the kids and miniature flags and high-pitched clay whistles shaped like tiny birds and water pitchers; marionettes that jumped and twisted like gymnasts when you gripped the crisscrossed sticks holding up their strings; beautifully decorated Easter eggs made of wood, and postcards depicting the resurrected Jesus, glassworks of all sorts and endless trinkets. Crowds flooded from all directions with a mighty stomp and clamor. Only the mournful din of the brass music up the street in front of the St. Nedelya Church, where the funeral service for the Army Reserve General Konstantin Georgiev—assassinated by a communist terrorist two days prior—threatened to destroy the jubilant mood. But only in part.

Mila stood at the staircase beating the dust out of her husband's books. She knew there was no housework to be done on a holiday, but the books gathered dust so quickly inside their house above the busy Maria Louisa Boulevard that she had to constantly clean them because of the children, holiday or not.

She had no idea what time it was when a fearsome explosion shook the windows and a whirl of wind blew her hair back. She screamed, dropped the books, and rushed into the room where her children and her sister's daughter, Anna, had been. The little girls hadn't even been frightened; they appeared more curious by what had happened, and Lili rushed to tell her how, right after the explosion, the poet threw himself on Bistra and Leda, stroking their hair and calming them down, and he'd even asked Lili if she'd gotten scared. They all got up and leaned out the windows to look outside. They saw people—covered in debris, red brick dust, and glistening shards of glass—screaming, terrorized, running from the cathedral down toward the Bania Bashi Mosque and trampling the street stands as they went.

Above St. Nedelya, still Holy King to many, the stern creation by the architect Lazarov, puffs of black smoke and ash slowly rose up from the tattered roof of the church as if straight from the devil's furnace. The black cloud cast its heavy shadow over the entire square, imbuing the air with the smell of brimstone and sulfur.

As if suddenly sensing what lie in store for them, Mila whispered: "Dear God, please no."

[May 3, 2013, Good Friday]
Then the check-ins started. Two agents appeared at their doorstep around midnight about seven days after the attack. Everyone at the house was asleep except for the poet, up reading galleys, which was why he was the one to answer the door.

He soured at having his work interrupted, but the two agents were exceptionally courteous—apologizing profusely when they heard the children wake from the strange voices in their house, sleepily protesting as their mother whispered, anxious but gentle, not to worry. They were simply checking the address registrations of everyone in Sofia, nothing more, they said. The poet brought them his documents. As one of them checked the papers, the other, still so very politely asked whether the poet minded if he lit a cigarette. He spoke mutedly, almost whispering so as not to wake up the children on the other side of the thin curtains dividing the living room from their bedroom. The poet answered that he could, of course, and the agent took a box of Tomasyan cigarettes out of his coat pocket. He offered one to the poet, but the latter preferred his own Sultans, which he kept inside his army brass tin.

"You have a trial coming up soon," the agent smiled at him, "isn't that right, Mr. Milev?"

The poet cracked his mouth into something resembling a smile and mumbled that yes, there was something like that coming soon.

"I can tell you didn't recognize me!" The other kept smiling.

The poet looked closer. The man did seem vaguely familiar. But he couldn't recall where he'd seen him, let alone what his name was.

"I had the honor of personally validating your address registration," the man kept on, "last February. You were a little late getting it registered, but I let it slide, didn't I! *Geshev*," he reminded him warmly. "Nikola Geshev!"

"Oh yes, of course. I remember you."

"I'm not there anymore," the other went on. "I'm not at the housing commission! Archiving is such tedious work . . . See, even you couldn't remember who I was. No one remembers a clerk!"

He waved his hand dismissively.

As he spoke, the agent's fingers leapt between the sheets of paper, galleys and books scattered on the poet's desk—his eyes seemed calm and his gaze affable, but his fingers were searching for something.

The poet clenched his jaw, there was nothing he detested more than having someone go through his things, but he held his tongue because his kids were right there.

"Ha!" the other exclaimed. "May I?"

Before the poet could answer, the agent picked up a yellowed copy of *Reflections on the Revolution in France*.

"Edmund Burke?" he said surprised. "Incredible! Is this a first edition, too?"

The poet responded that yes, it was a first edition; he'd picked it up from a bouquiniste's in London. He then reached over to take his book back, but Geshev absentmindedly pulled his hand away.

"You never cease to surprise me, Mr. Milev," he said. "You're reading an author who writes *against* the social revolution. Very interesting!"

The other agent had finished looking through the poet's documents, as well as those of Mila and her sister, and looked at him with tired eyes, but Geshev hissed for him to wait outside and began to recount being a student in Italy, where he too read a lot about the French Revolution. Which is how he had come across Edmund Burke's *reactionary theories*.

He put the book down and whispered confidingly that, out of everything connected with the French Revolution, most fascinating to him was the fact a revolution could birth that perfect executioner's tool, the guillotine! He'd read everything he could find about the guillotine, and he was most struck by the concern of the revolution's leaders that death sentences could be carried out . . . humanely. They sentenced hundreds of people to death, yet they wanted that death to happen quickly! They had wanted to improve on hanging, which was long and torturous for the condemned . . . not to mention the horror of being burned at the stake, or the barbarianism of being drawn and quartered—up until then, the only three ways death sentences were carried out. Only those in high standing had their heads cut off with an ax! Mercy for the highest bidder.

The poet discerned a cold covetousness in the other's whispers.

"The irony here of course being that Dr. Guillotin himself was utterly opposed to the death penalty. But one day they called him in and ordered him to devise a new way to kill. And I'm not sure whether you know this or not, Mr. Milev, but the guillotine as we know it was not actually built by Dr. Guillotin. It was someone else, also a doctor, a surgeon perhaps . . . Antoine Louis, yes. And he in turn asked someone else—a harpsichord maker, a German guy, I'm forgetting his name now . . ."

"Schmidt," the poet interrupted.

"Say again?" Geshev was caught off-guard.

"His name was Tobias Schmidt," the poet replied edgily, "and he built pianos, not harpsichords."

"Oh, is that how it was?" the other raised his eyebrows. "True, pianos and harpsichords are indeed different, aren't they? See, I'm starting to forget things. Anyway, on the seventeenth of April, seventeen ninety-two, at ten o'clock in the morning, they tested the new machine for the first time. The first guillotining took place, so to speak! I don't know if you know this, but that first test run was attended by Paris's chief executioner, Charles-Henri Sanson, so that he could personally approve the apparatus, give the go ahead, so to speak. And, well, he obviously did, because not a week later it was already put into operation. The first to have his head cut off was just an apache, a vagabond, not even a bandit in the real sense of the word, a pickpocket. And do you know how the story goes, Mr. Milev? The crowd, if you can believe it, was terribly disappointed! The people had gotten so used to executions taking at least an hour, and for the condemned to be tortured, frenzied, twitching, eyes popping out, biting their tongue, even, pardon me, shitting themselves as they were being hanged . . . And here was this guillotine—shhhing!—and it was all over."

"Very interesting," the poet tensed up, "now if you'll excuse me . . ."

"One second," the other stopped him. "May I just finish my thought? I beg your pardon, it's just been so long since I've spoken to an intelligent man. By the way, after Dr. Guillotin died, his family petitioned the state to change the name of the guillotine! They didn't want executions referred to as "guillotining," either. Moreover, people already referred to the guillotine as the *Louisetta*, assuming it was Louis who'd actually invented it, not the doctor. But the government refused. So do you know what the family did?"

"No," the poet groaned. "What?"

"Very simple!" Geshev exclaimed with affected nonchalance and dead, soulless eyes. "*They* changed their name. And guillotine stayed! Life, what are you going to do? But there was something else I was going to tell you. After they tested the guillotine with that lowlife apache, they moved on to the aristocrats. Louis XVI, his wife Marie Antoinette, and so on, and after that, they went after their own people. And it was then the industrialization of beheadings truly began!

"But, not long after, word spread the guillotine wasn't that humane after all. Doctors claimed the head lived for at least fifteen minutes after it was cut off! Even now, the books I read in Italy were filled with eyewitness accounts of detached heads' eyelids opening and closing, blinking, mouths moving their lips, things of that nature. I even read that when they cut off Charlotte Corday's head, her face expressed in no uncertain terms her absolute indignation at what had been done. This was written somewhere by the executioner Sanson himself . . . I'm only telling you what I've read on the subject, of course—I haven't witnessed a guillotining personally, I'm only interested in it theoretically."

"I know something else," the poet couldn't resist. "This same Charlotte Corday was Pierre Corneille's great-granddaughter."

"Is that right?" Geshev lit up. "*That* same Corneille, the poet?! Would you look at that. It *will* turn out the world really is a small place, won't it?"

He shrugged, relishing a drag from his cigarette, and asked after the poet and his new magazine, *Zhar—Ember*—and would the first issue come out soon because he was awaiting it with great anticipation. He missed the now defunct *Plamuk* terribly. He said it just like that—*he missed it terribly.* He could hardly wait for *Zhar* to come out.

"I hope," he remarked buoyantly, "that it is exactly like *Plamuk.* After your articles," he stressed, "I liked Georgi Vassilev's articles best. A great polemicist! I am assuming that he will continue contributing to *Zhar* as well? I wonder if you might one day introduce me to this *contributor.* He goes by Shaytov as well, doesn't he? I am dying to have a chat with him sometime!"

The poet started, but hid it and only hmmed in agreement.

"And here you are, awaiting trial," Geshev added solicitously. "I'm probably the last thing you need right now. The trial is set for the fourteenth of May, if I remember correctly? I personally find it rather unfair that you are on trial for writing 'September.' How absurd that you wrote a poem in 1924, *after* the article incriminating literary works for inciting class hatred was removed from the Law for the Protection of Bulgaria! It just isn't right. I promise you, I will be in the courtroom that day to listen to what you have to say! It's sure to be riveting."

"Riveting, yes, no doubt," the poet groaned. "Better that it wasn't happening at all. But we'll see, we'll see."

"We will most certainly!" Geshev said energetically as he surveyed the room for an ashtray. "By the way, I do have a copy of 'September.' It's inside an issue of *Flame* some friends of mine brought over. I might even recall a line or two . . .

> "The people's voice
> > is the voice of God"
> The people,
> Pricked
> By a thousand knives,
> Dulled,
> Degraded,
> Poorer than beggars,
> Deprived
> Of brain
> And nerve
> Arose
> From the darkness and fear
> Of their lives
> —And wrote with their blood
> > FREEDOM!"

He pinned the poet with a zealous gaze.

"When that ridiculous trial is over, Mr. Milev, I'll stop by so you can autograph the booklet for me . . . and then perhaps introduce me to Georgi Vassilev, I hope . . ."

Now Geshev really seemed as though he was leaving, but he suddenly thought of something again and turned around.

"Apropos, Mr. Milev," he whispered, "the Industrial Revolution, in turn, gave birth to the electric chair! Doesn't it seem as though every revolution first invents a new way to kill, and only then gets around to thinking up new laws?"

He tipped his hat and left.

The poet locked the door behind him and stepped back into his office, where books, papers, and proofs shrouded the small writing table and his typewriter. He went to open the window, and felt the crispness of the cool April night, but he also caught the smell of something else. A heavy, cloying scent. It wasn't coming from the viridescent trees in the garden across from their bathroom.

It was reminiscent of carrion.

Not exactly carrion, but rather burning flesh.

The Gospel of Herod the Great

On the fourteenth of May, nineteen twenty-three, they murdered former Prime Minister Aleksandar Stamboliyski. Velichko "the Uncle" Velyanov did the deed. The Minister of War Ivan Valkov personally ordered Captain Harlakov to do it, and the whole operation was led by retired Colonel Slaveiko Vassilev.

Ivan Valkov lived to be eighty-seven, and claimed it wasn't he who ordered the murder, but Aleksandar Tsankov. And so he said, "Slaveiko Vassilev turned Stamboliyski over to Harlakov, who carried out the murder, personally ordered by Tsankov, as a way to implement the decision of the Military Union."

Aleksandar Tsankov lived to be eighty years old and said that it had all happened on the order of Ivan Valkov. He said, "Ivan Valkov and the people around him were cleansing Bulgaria from any and all traitors, spies, and saboteurs."

Ivan Harlakov lived to be fifty-seven and said that both of the others ordered him to do it. But he added: "It is my deep conviction that out of everything done on the ninth of June, this murder was carried out with the king's knowledge and consent."

Velichko Velyanov lived to be sixty-nine and said nothing.

Slaveiko Vassilev lived to fifty-five and killed himself on September ninth, nineteen forty-four.

Etcetera.

On August twenty-sixth, nineteen twenty-three, they killed the politician Rayko Daskalov. He was thirty-five, and they detested him almost as much as they detested Stamboliyski. He had decided not to return to Sofia and instead stay in Prague—maybe the whole thing would blow over and they'd forget about him. But they found him in Prague anyway and killed him there. Yordan Tsitsonkov, an agent of IMRO, the Internal Macedonian Revolutionary Organization, was behind the murder, and they caught him at the scene of the crime. First they acquitted him, then they sentenced him to twenty years, and in the end he hung himself in jail. This happened on January twenty-fifth, nineteen twenty-five. Yordan Tsitskonkov had just turned twenty-six.

On September twelfth, nineteen twenty-three, the police arrested dozens of communists based on reports of informants that revolts were imminent. They even arrested Dimitar Blagoev, but he had just turned eighty-seven, so they put him under house arrest.

On September fourteenth, nineteen twenty-three, the communists caused a big stir at the Sofia outdoor market and the deputy of the local police station, Konstantinov, fell dead to the ground in the hullabaloo. An anarchist from Aytos by the name of Anton Kutev killed him.

The intelligence that the communists were cooking up a revolt ended up being true. The authorities put an end to it, but not without numerous victims—it's doubtful anyone could ever confirm how many died. Some say this many, others say that many, and the truth about death is never somewhere in the middle. The leaders of the revolt—Georgi Dimitrov, who would go on to become Bulgaria's first communist leader, and Vasil Kolarov, future deputy prime minister of Dimitrov's government—ran away to the Serbia, and Dimitar Blagoev cursed them from his house arrest.

On October seventeenth, nineteen twenty-three, at eight thirty in the evening, they killed Nikola Genadiev. They ambushed him at the corner of Krakra and Shipka Streets and shot him several times. The killers were never found. The parliamentary opposition proposed Milan Grashev be assigned as special investigator to the case with unrestricted rights. Milan Grashev was born in Prilep and his real name was Mihail, Mihail Grashev. He had lived in Sofia for twenty years and was a well-known attorney. He authored a leaflet declaring the IMRO a mafia, Todor Aleksandrov and Aleksandar Protogerov mobsters, and the king's court: their main patron.

On April thirtieth, nineteen twenty-four, they shot down the deputy of the Second Police Precinct, P. Karamfilov, at the Bodega beer hall on the corner of Nishka and Osogovo Streets. The man had sat down to drink with his friends Dimo and Konstantin Antonov, but around eight o'clock, a middle-aged stranger enters, hat pulled down low, and heads straight for their table. He approaches, pulls out his revolver and fires three bullets into Karamfilov, who falls dead on the spot. One of the bullets shattered his jaw, knocking out several teeth, while the other two bullets pierced straight through his heart and kill him instantly. Mayhem ensues, and the killer disappears into the night. Some said it was that same Anton Kutev from Aytos, others claimed that no, it wasn't him at all, it was Hristo the Hare from Dupnitsa, but either way, he was never caught.

They killed Milan Grashev on the twenty-sixth of May, nineteen twenty-four. He was twenty-four, and his killers were never found.

On November tenth, nineteen twenty-three, they killed Spas Douparinov. They were allegedly taking him to Sofia to stand trial, but they killed him on the way there. Then they buried him around Cheshmadinovo, where he was born. He wasn't even thirty years old.

On the fourteenth of June, nineteen twenty-four, on the corner of Moskovska and Rakovski Streets, the plainclothes police officer Stefan Karkalashev fired three bullets into Petko D. Petkov, killing him. Karkalashev was from IMRO. They caught him at the scene, but he showed them his badge and they let him go. They arrested him again and sentenced him to death, then changed it to life. He was out in three months. Petko D. Petkov had been only thirty-three.

They killed Mihail Dashin in Samokov on the eighteenth of August. He'd barely qualified for amnesty and returned to Samokov, where he'd briefly acted as mayor during the second local commune. It wasn't clear who killed him and why—too many people had it out for him already for leading the June uprising.

On the thirty-first of August, they killed Todor Aleksandrov up in the Pirin Mountains as he traveled to the congress of the Serski Revolutionary Region. He was killed by Shteryo Vlahov and Dincho Vretenarov. They, in turn, killed themselves on the fifteenth of September in some shack by Pripechene, and when their bodies were found, they were thrown into the Struma River. Todor Aleksandrov was forty-three, Shteryo Vlahov had just turned forty, and Dincho Vretenarov couldn't remember when he'd been born.

On the twelfth of September, Kiril Drangov killed Aleko Pasha in Gorna Dzhumaya.

On the thirteenth of September in Sofia, Vladislav Kovachev from Štip was killed by Mircho Kikiritkov. Kikiritkov was forty years old when they killed him in Yugoslavia.

On the same day, the thirteenth of September, they killed Dimo Hadzhidimov from the communist party. He was forty-nine. He was killed by Velichko Kerin, aka Vlado Chernozemski, from IMRO.

[Let it be said! Vlado Chernozemski lived to be thirty-seven, becoming Vanche Mihailov's right-hand man. Vanche Mihailov personally referred him to Ante Pavelić, who then made him a terrorist instructor for the Croatian Ustashas. On October ninth, nineteen thirty-four, now going by the name Peter Kelemen, with a Czechoslovakian passport in his pocket, two guns—a Parabellum and a Mauser—and a bomb beneath his blue blazer, Vlado stood together with the crowds lining Marseille's lakeshore boulevard, La Canebière, to greet the King of Yugoslavia, Alexander I Karađorđević. The king had arrived in France to discuss a joint action regarding the problem with Macedonia. The king and the French Foreign Minister, that old fox Louis Barthou—seventy-two at the time—sat in the back seat, with the top down, making what little security there was—two mounted policemen and one civil agent, someone named Gale—completely useless. Vlado Chernozemski jumped out of the crowd and apparently yelled "*Vive le roi!*" But as he tore through the street and threw himself onto the step of the black Delage, he screamed, in Serbian, "Death to the tyrant!" He then withdrew the barrel of the perfect killing tool—his Mauser—and shot once, then again, and then again straight into the king's heart, and the latter slid down the car seat. The third bullet pierced Barthou's arm, four others were fired at General Alfonse George, who had attempted to stop Vlado, and also gunned down the unlucky Gale. Only then did one of the pair of mounted police finally get to the automobile and twice hit Chernozemski with his sabre as the assassin clung to the vehicle's door. Vlado Chernozemski collapsed on the pavement, but continued to shoot. The policemen swarmed him and jumped on top of him, and the bystanders went delirious: people tore through the cordon and stampeded toward the car, trampling Vlado. King Alexander I Karađorđević died on the spot, having not yet turned forty-six. Louis Barthou died as well, but later: in the commotion someone attempted to stop the bleeding from his wounded arm, but did an amateur job tying it up, instead of stopping it making the bleeding even worse. An ambulance arrived and took them both—him and the killer—to the nearest hospital, but Barthou had lost too much blood and lost consciousness. He died in the doctors' arms. He was seventy-two. And General George? He lived and survived World War II, even with four bullet wounds in his chest. He died in nineteen fifty-one—just a little short of his seventy-sixth birthday. Vlad Chernozemski, slain by the policemen and trampled by the rabid crowd, died that same evening at eight o'clock. He would have turned thirty-seven ten days later.

But this would be another gospel altogether.]

On December fifteenth, nineteen twenty-four, around six thirty in the evening, after darkness had set, they killed the prosecutor Joakim Dim-chev—thirty-six, French-educated, pretty as a rosebud and spiteful as a widow. He had been the one who ordered the prison directors to keep political prisoners chained up at all times and to deny them newspaper reading privileges, and as for newspapers in general, he ordered that they be confiscated at his whim—he really was spiteful as a widow, this guy. But he was gunned down on the doorstep of his home with a single bullet to the heart. That was it for prosecutor Dimchev!

On January second, nineteen twenty-five, about two weeks after Joakim Dimchev's murder, they got Nikola Kuzinchev. He was Pane Bichev's personal agent. His murder was identical to that of Dimchev: both men were taken down in the same way, and in both cases the murderer—or perhaps murderers—left a trilby hat next to the corpse. *Utro* was having a field day with the police. "Maybe next time the killer ought to leave a business card too, so that the Police Department can know for sure who the perpetrator was."

On the eleventh of February, nineteen twenty-five, they killed Vulcho Ivanov. They strangled him and hung a note on him, "Go to court with prosecutor Dimchev!" and dumped his body right below journalist Joseph Herbst's windows, knowing he'd write about it the very next day in his newspaper *Ek Vecheren*. And he did. "They took him," he wrote, "and with no court or trial, strangled him and dumped his body out on the street—in the capital of a democratic Bulgaria, lead by the most enlightened government in the world." Vulcho Ivanov was killed by Kocho Stoyanov's men. They didn't even know which side they were on, they just liked to kill—regardless of who—and couldn't care less how they did it: rope, bludgeon or dagger. That year, however, they felt as though they were government executioners—they killed with righteousness, they did important work, for which they weren't reprimanded, but paid off. Kocho Stoyanov, their captain, was the police commandant of Sofia. He was fifty-one years old when he killed himself on September ninth, nineteen forty-four, the day of Bulgaria's communist coup d'état.

On February thirteenth, they killed Nikola Milev, who was from the village of Mokreni, on Dondoukov Boulevard. He was a history professor and chair of the Union of Sofia Journalists, and also director of the newspaper *Slovo*, a member of the alliance board of the Grand Mason Lodge of Bulgaria, and God knows what else: he would kill for status. He perpetually attacked Stamboliyski any which way he could, but it didn't stop him from accompanying the latter to the conference in Lozana. He had a hand in drafting the Bulgarian Law for the Protection of the Nation, and was even being groomed as an ambassador to the United States. He took advantage of every single perk Bulgaria had to offer, yet persistently referred to the country as a *foreign constituent.* Many took credit for his murder, but officially it was attributed to Milan Manolev from Kukush, a statistics clerk. He in turn was killed on the fourteenth of April. When they killed Manolev, they also dumped the body where Nikola Milev was killed. Nikola Milev was from the Democratic Alliance, and Milan Manolev was an anarchist and a member of IMRO. The thirteenth of April that year was on a Friday. Friday the thirteenth.

On the seventeenth of February, at seven thirty in the evening, they killed Todor Strashimirov with a single shot to the back of the neck. His killer was never found. His brother, Anton Strashimirov, wrote an obituary that read, "They've murdered my brother, Todor! May God save us all!" A rumor began to circulate that the authorities ordered the dead man's corpse be driven to the cemetery while it was still dark out—seven thirty in the morning—and that Todor Strashimirov was buried with only four or five people as witnesses. But it wasn't a rumor; it was the sad truth.

On March sixth, while the amendments to the Law for the Protection of Bulgaria were being voted on, Haralampi Stoyanov walked out of the National Assembly. Haralampi Stoyanov had started off as a member of the Communist Parliamentary Group, then became one of the six who left the group almost immediately and formed his own, called the Independent Labor Parliament Group, and then abandoned that, too, and proclaimed himself a communist. But never mind all that. He stopped by the Army Club to buy some newspapers. They killed him with a single shot to the temple. The killer never did surface: the newspapers wrote that a Ipokrat Razvigorov from Štip had done it, but he never did confess to anything of the sort.

On the fourteenth of April, around eight o'clock in the evening, they killed the reserve general Konstantin Georgiev—also a member of parliament, but from the Democratic Alliance—in the garden in front of Sveti Sedmochislenitsi Church. He was quite young for a general—not yet fifty-two. The two killers were from Petar Abadjiev's Six. Their names were Atanas Todovichin and Jivko Dinov. Three shell casings from a Luger pistol were found next to the body.

[Petar Abadjiev lived a long life; he even became a colonel in the Red Army, after which he came back to Bulgaria and was appointed lieutenant commander in the Air Forces. In April of forty-six, during military exercises, his commander's automobile crashed and his head was decapitated by the front windshield. They found the head eight meters away on the side of the road.]

The general's wake was scheduled for three o'clock in the afternoon on the sixteenth of April, Holy Thursday, in the St. Nedelya Church.

[Sure enough! It was a time of casting stones and a time of gathering stones, a time to kill and a time to die.

A time of silence and a time to speak.

Life for life, eye for eye, tooth for tooth, arm for arm, foot for foot, burn for burn, wound for wound. Stripe for stripe.

It was a time for war, but not a time for peace . . .

After that, there was lightning and voices, thunder and quakes, and a great hail.

That's how it was.]

On April sixteenth, Holy Thursday, at precisely twenty-three minutes after three o'clock in the afternoon, fifty kilograms of melinite and pyroxylin erupted beneath St. Nedelya's main dome. Five fuses were used to detonate the bomb. The tails of the fuses were dipped inside a tin filled with rubbing alcohol, so that when the rubbing alcohol was lit— the fuses would light up alongside it, burn together, and blow up the entire devil's apparatus in synchronicity. That's how it happened—it all blew up. And the man behind it all was Nikola Petrov. On that particular day, Nikola Petrov had not yet turned nineteen years old, but it was he who lit the match and ran out of the church, revealing the inferno in his wake. One hundred thirty-four people died instantly from the blast—twelve generals, fifteen colonels, seven lieutenant colonels, three majors, nine captains, three members of parliament and the head of the Office of the National Assembly, Krastev, mayor Paskal Paskalev, district governor Nedelchev, three masons, a whole lot of other people, one baby, and four Jews. Some died from asphyxiation due to the poisonous gas from the fuming sulfuric acid, which the attackers had placed right underneath the bomb. Those wounded inside the church and around it numbered over five hundred, and since some died later from their injuries, the total number of victims reached two hundred and thirteen.

But not a single priest!

And not a single minister!

The king did not step foot inside the temple that entire day. Some said that he and his retinue were attending the funeral of their chief huntsman Petar Kotev in Beli Iskar.

That's the story of how God turned his back on Bulgaria, how the gates of hell opened once more, and how in the weeks following, this same hell claimed victims who would forever remain uncounted.

Tsar Boris said: *thousands perished.*

The Minister of War, General Ivan Valkov, said: twenty-five people, in total.

Amen!

10.

[May 5, 2013, Easter]
But all this would happen lat

....
....
....

He'd heard the poet was worshipped by the younger generation, that a considerable number of them knew all his poems by heart, and that just as many simply emulated him. Many even adopted his moniker, shortening their own Georgi to Geo, but the pinnacle of it all was witnessing no fewer than three young men with the same lock of hair over one eye at 145 Rakovski Street.

"Say now, Bai Milev," said Sheytanov as that same young man flew between the tables at Battenberg Square, "these lads, these young poets, fear you more than wealthy men fear me! Are you beating them or slaughtering them or chasing them with a gun . . . what exactly are you doing to have that effect on them?"

"What can I say," the poet sighed conceitedly. "I give them a beating here and there. But here's the thing! When you're young, you look at the geranium on the windowsill and you think it is the pinnacle of creation, and you can't wait to piss on it and mark your territory. And there's talent there, and lots of it—for the growing poet, I mean, not for the geranium. The young poet needs to aim for the poplars beyond the stone wall, not for his daddy's backyard hedge. But until you give him a good slap on the back of the head, he won't get it."

"I get it now," Sheytanov nodded.

"Sure you do," the poet sighed. "Look, to be honest, today's youth really trouble me. They're full of rapturous Salieris and maybe a Mozart meandering here and there, like a thorn in your fucking side. See what I mean? These people are no longer writing in the name of literature. Not at all! They're not even thinking about their readers when they're writing. All they're looking for is the three snobs aahing and wringing their hands in the reading salon . . ."

"So what *are* they thinking about, then?" Sheytanov interrupted him.

"The literary awards!" the other yelled and angrily slammed his fist on the table. "Because they know very well just what the awards juries like, and they've learned to mold it exactly to their taste. These juries don't have an ounce of literary consciousness, so you can imagine how literary their awards are. 'The awards were given precisely to the right people!' says Dr. Galubov. He was apparently feeling just like Buridan's ass—the donkey that died of thirst *and* hunger because it couldn't figure out whether to go for the pail of water or the stack of hay placed at an equal distance before him—*all* of the books were so wonderful, he just didn't know which one to pick. And accordingly, the writers take out their arsenal of stock phrases and check the boxes: here a rhyme, there a rhythm—a little rain here, snow, yellow leaves, fall, wilted roses, and crestfallen damsels, night, moon, the desolate flame of a candle inside an abandoned house, a forgotten love letter, the melancholy curls of the smoke rising from my cigarette, tearful eyes, strange accords, broken strings . . . 'Inside the poky hovel, at dawn I'll spin a loom, at night, alone, I'll snivel, a necklace of black gloom' or 'That's how I will pass life by, insatiate and malcontent. And when I die alone, abroad, a cuckoo-wanderer I'll be.' And behold the flood of awards! The epigones scratch their amateur vulgarities onto the paper knowing full well who likes what and how, and who sits on what awards jury and where. Everything's been thought out. Because now—the writers must choose between *Vae Victis* and *Winners Are Never Judged!* And they always choose right. So they win their awards and the following spectacle ensues: first the winners get awarded, then the same people who gave out the awards praise the ones who've won them, then the ones who've won them praise those who have awarded them in the first place! A truly awesome thing! They award them, then praise them, then award them again, and all the while, they claim to be doing it all in the name of inspiring the budding poets. The awards go to their heads and they become regulars at Bai Ilia Yugrev's confectionary on Tsar Osvoboditel Boulevard, the unawarded raise hell because they don't want to be left out of the confectionary and they come out to fight with their little canes, so then they're awarded so they'll keep quiet, and in the end, they all get into the Writer's Union together. Poets with pomade in their hair and cologne in their moustaches. That's the poetry scene of today—misters decked out in smooth, dark suits, so many with pale foreheads, a miner's disposition, and sorrowful smiles. It is a scary thing, I'm telling you! Don't even ask me how many people now despise each other because of these literary bursaries. Young people, my ass! So what does it all come out to then, Sheytanov? If you sell your body, we call that being a whore, but when you sell your talent—we call that stardom, right? That's why I've always said: we need to do like Hungary's Béla Kun. The man knew what he was doing. All burgeoning, hardworking and worthwhile poets, he said, would receive two-thousand-krone subsidies—so they can sit on their asses and write. The epigones—eight-hundred-krone lifetime pensions, on the condition that they—under the threat of death—don't write! But what happened here in Bulgaria? Just the opposite! The Ministry of Popular Enlightenment gave a bursary to Lisa Belcheva! Can you imagine that? How does that even work? She's written three, maybe four poems in her life, and it's not even clear if she's going to write anything ever again. Some Gergi from Ruse took the last name Polyanov, and this year the Writers' Union, when it accepted him as a regular member, did so because half the writers

voting thought they were voting for the old Polyanov, for Dimitar Polyanov, for Alana! It's a dangerous thing, I'm telling you. When did these
people get so goddamn savvy—I just don't get it! *Malcontent* . . . there's
another word that comes to mind, but let's not go there."

Sheytanov gave a short laugh and told the poet he really ought to be
a little more careful.

"What for?" the poet bristled. "Am I wrong?"

"I'm not one to judge if you're right or wrong," Sheytanov said, "but
what I do know is that once a person begins his sentences with 'when I
was their age,' he's done for."

"You do have a point," the poet agreed. "But do you know what I was
doing when I was their age? Get us a cognac and I'll tell you."

Sheytanov snickered again and waved to the waiter. The poet was
already leaning over the table, recounting how, in nineteen fifteen, a year
before the man's death in the war, he'd proposed to the poet Dimcho
Debelyanov* the following: as a way to protest the habitual philistine
logic of society—which is always standing in the way of literature's high
tides, clipping her wings—in rebellion and in opposition to all of that,
all the young poets should come out of their houses and hang themselves
along the streetlights of the boulevard.

"What now?" Sheytanov's eyes widened. "Come again?"

"You heard right!" the other slapped the table again. "We should
all come out and hang ourselves, one after the other. Can you picture
that? A young, misunderstood poet hanging from every street light, jazz
playing, the tram headed to the Military Academy rattles mournfully by
the streetlights, and the whole of society wails and pulls out its hair. Just
imagine the beauty of the picture! With the legions of poets that would've
swarmed the place—we'd have hung for miles. And if we'd run out of
streetlights, we'd have doubled up on each one. And if we'd have run out
of those too, we could've started with Dondoukov Boulevard. I'm being
facetious, of course, but when I said all this to Dimcho Debelyanov, I
was dead serious. How did you put it before? Puerile antagonism? Well,

mine was the same thing—puerile *antagonism*."

He sank back into his chair, overcome by the guffaws Sheytanov so enjoyed hearing.

"Wait till you hear what Dimcho wrote back," he said, "I know his letter by heart, more or less, because it was memorable. 'I didn't write you back right away,' he wrote, 'because I was busy with something very important—torturing myself by trying to convince myself and the others that it's high time we acquiesced to our own impotence and take your advice to contrive a never-before-seen spectacle: hang ourselves on the electric streetlights along Tsar Osvoboditel Boulevard . . . but!' he wrote, 'what do you know, all my efforts were for naught. Neither I, nor the others, it turns out, were ready to perish, so young, so green. The reasons being literary,' he wrote, which was of course the funniest part about the whole thing. That's exactly what he wrote! 'For reasons steeped entirely in literature!' What a refined human being he was, he would never smack you across the back of the head, he would only give you a teasing tap on the nose, and if you felt like getting it, you would."

"And then what did you do?" Sheytanov asked as he took two glasses from the waiter.

"What do you mean what did I do?" the poet raised his eyebrows. "I became very distressed, I read the letter a thousand times, I pulled out my hair, traitors, I yelled, apostates, and the like, but . . . you as my witness, I'm sitting here and drinking my beer with you. Ergo, I didn't hang myself."

"True," Sheytanov affirmed, serious. "You did not."

[Saturday, May 11, 2013, a day for reflection]
[Every television channel is bursting with scandal, some news bulletins have apparently been found in some printing press . . . I must have missed something, because I understood nothing. Everybody's giving press conferences, the hubbub is brutal.

Piss on this day of reflection!]

[Sunday, May 12, 2013, Election Day]

"Where was I?" the poet asked, "Oh yes, the young people. Today's youth is ready to gouge their eyes out, they're dying to compete with each other. I saw it the other day in *Hyperion's* last issue—Luydmil took a little bite out of Lalyo Marinov. In short, he says, Troyan's Lalyo Marinov is threatening Europe! He who has ears, let him see, he says, *he who has ears, let him see.* A jokester, too! He who has *ears*, let him see. Very clever! Now Lalyo wants to shoot him. Earlier, Boyan Penev called Luydmil a literary Plutus. Very dishonorable. You can prove anything you want that way, but that's another story. And Vladko the timeserver? Straight to the journal *Zlatorog* that very second! Because he and Boyan Penev are Zeus, the Thunderer of literary impertinence. Lyudmil goes to Lalyo and says: 'Let's go get rid of Boyan Penev!' Lalyo didn't ask too many questions, he just went along, and now Luydmil judges Lalyo from the position of Apollonius, of the muses, of the Dryads. Tombs he calls mounds, anchors—mudhooks, paddles he calls blades, fingers he calls thumbs. Not words, but passcodes for entering the kingdom of immortality. He prattles left and right about some *international symbolism.* You can't find a more senile aesthetic, my dear man! I just don't understand, when did this guy grow so hopelessly old? He's become yet another dreadful *deadbone* in the corpse of literature."

"Dreadful *what?*" asked Sheytanov.

"Deadbone!" the poet repeated. "From a dead bone—deadbone. I just came up with it. But it could be as though *bacho* Anton said it, couldn't it? It'll come in handy, I should remember it and write it down somewhere because I'm starting to forget things."

[Friday, May 24, 2013, holiday; St. Ivan Rilski Clinic]

[This is of course, a well-known fact, but I'll say it again: May twenty-fourth will always bring a beautiful rain, with raindrops like gems. Always. It always rains on May twenty-fourth. I don't know what this means, but thank God it always happens this way.]

[Saturday, May 25, 2013]

....
....
....
....

[Monday, July 1, 2013]
[I've never known what to expect from a month that starts on a Monday. June came and went in a rainstorm, now July comes, cold.]

[Monday, July 1, 2013]
[Outside, they're protesting again—beating their drums and blowing their whistles and horns and yelling: "Resignation!"]

[Three]

Аз съм независим писател.

"I am an independent writer."

—From Geo Milev's notes
in his written summation
from January, 1925

[Monday, July 1, 2013]

Sheytanov would likely have been back in Kilifarevo by the time the prosecution drafted the accusation against the poet on the twenty-fifth of March, nineteen twenty-five, thus establishing criminal case No. 249 at the third capital ward of the Justice of the Peace Court in Sofia against one Georgi Milev Kassabov. The case was accompanied by a single piece of evidence as to the poet's crime: the double issue of *Plamuk* with two brick-red numbers, seven and eight, on its cover, and "September" on the first page.

They handed the accusation to the poet on the second of April, a Wednesday, and he became furious. His rage was not borne out of fear; he was angry he'd have to interrupt his work and sit down to write a defense, when he had so many other things to do—all of them important, all urgent.

"Idiots!" he yelled, strewing the ashes from his cigarette all over himself. "Total idiots! Shoving the masses into the prisons and tying their hands, and now, trying to shut their mouths too, with this law. And who's deciding my case?" he yelled. "The *barbers!*"

The barbers, indeed. The judges from that third capital ward looking over all the print-related cases and the excise duties, the same ones who decided on forest law fines, had to look at fifty to sixty cases in one sitting: half-assedly *shaving* yet another poor wretch in record time, as the bailiff already called for the next person. Hence barbers, and the department—the barbershop.

All of the famed Sofia attorneys had either raised their arms helplessly, "No, no this'll only bring me a great deal of harassment!" or were already in jail, or simply hid as soon as they saw him, so the poet's defense was eventually taken up by one Stefan Rashenov, who'd just arrived from Rousse and contributed to newspapers here and there under the byline Stanimir Lilyanov. This Stefan was a sensible man and when he heard the kind of speech the poet had drawn up to read inside the courtroom, he told him to ease up.

"Look here," he said. "Your best bet is to fall ill! I'm serious. Get sick, hide somewhere where you can write, and I'll take the medical evaluation to the court and get the trial postponed by a month or two. And who knows how things will play out then—we might not even have anything to worry about."

The poet spat back that that was simply not going to happen, and if he suggested something of the sort again, he'd relieve him from his services at once.

"Get ready to fight, goddamn it!" he snorted, and lit yet another cigarette. "The poetry will come later."

[Tuesday, July 2, 2013]

Meanwhile, sitting behind the colorful drapery sectioning off the tiny kitchen, Mila and her sister-in-law quietly whispered to each other. The poet's sister recalled him pacing the rose garden outside their house in Stara Zagora when he returned from the war—one-eyed and disfigured.

"He'd lean forward," she recounted, "and he'd smell the flowers, then he'd lean again and smell them again, then he'd turn to Mother and tell her: 'Plant roses, many roses! Only roses,' he would say. 'I want the whole garden to be filled with only roses.'"

And she recalled how she overheard their mother tell their father: "What must this boy have gone through that he can't get enough of roses?"

Another time he came back home around ten o'clock in the evening, elated at having a small puppy follow him all the way from the center of Stara Zagora—it didn't want to leave his sight.

"He was so joyous, so alive . . ." the poet's sister recalled. "He said, so excited, 'Here I am shooing it away, trying to shut the gate, but it's going in circles through my legs, whimpering. There it still is, right in the yard! Come on, give me the lamp so I can show you!' Dad's heart just melts and he made us all get up and go out of the house, looking at the little dog, which had rolled up into a ball under the awning, and when it saw my brother, it began to crawl on its belly, just crawling toward him, whimpering, going all around him, jumping, trying to bark, and it sounded all baby-like."

Her brother began to convince their father to keep the little thing! Look how sweet it is, the poor little one, how pretty, look, he said, all white, with only one little black ear. We'll call her Bella. Well, if Maeterlinck's got a sheep, I'll have a little dog.

Everyone exclaimed there was no way they could leave it now, and later she heard her mother say to her father, "What must the boy have been through at the front, that he's this happy to see a little puppy!"

Mila listened for a while then suddenly whispered back:

"What must this young man have been through at the front that he's this happy to play with his children!" and she thought about the poet's impatient yearning for a son.

11.

Sheytanov, in turn, went up into the Troyan Mountains to visit Vassil the Hero. All of Bulgaria was talking about how this man had shot at the king in Arabakonak, but had missed, and he wanted to hear it straight from the horse's mouth. Hesitation wasn't part of Vassil's makeup. And Sheytanov wasn't about to buy the whole 'shot and missed' scenario when, just a year prior, the Hero had shot the local superintendent, Serbezov, at the park in broad daylight.

Vassil confirmed he didn't shoot and miss.

"Sheytanov," he began tiredly. "Tell me, do *you* also think that this dynastic spawn could run not two meters in front of me and that I would *miss*, had I wanted to kill him?"

Sheytanov responded that he was wondering precisely the same thing, so Vassil asked him whether he really wanted to know what'd happened, or if he just wanted to start an argument.

Sheytanov shrugged.

"As you wish," he answered.

Vassil told him how the other Vasil—Ikonomov—got him and five or six other men to go hit up the post office in Orhaniye. They didn't bring rifles, just pistols and bombs. At first they didn't even consider going to Orhaniye—they set off for Gulubets to rob the passing cars, but they were spotted, and only then went in the direction of Arabakonak. Funny thing was, while they walked that way, Vassil told them how, since the king loved to play hunter right around these parts, wouldn't it be funny if they ran into him. He was being facetious, in other words, but anyway. As they walked, they suddenly heard the buzzing of a motorized vehicle.

They all knelt down behind the trees and didn't have to wait long—not a minute later a car approached from around the bend. It was a big, black, and shiny car—expensive, in other words—so it was worth the wait to see who exactly was driving it. Vassil stepped out in front of the vehicle with his hand raised, holding an empty matchbox, as if he'd run out of matches and needed more. Only then did he see who was the driving the car—the king himself, Boris! They all saw it. Ikonomov hissed from behind the trees that they'd really hit the big time now, and all the men lay down on the ground, pistols loaded, fingers on triggers, as Vassil threw the empty matchbox on the ground and pulled out his automatic pistol. He yelled, "Freeze!" and shot in the air, but the uniformed driver sitting next to the king raised his own carbine and opened fire, that idiot. He had no choice, Vassil had to kill him. Another idiot stood up behind him with his own firearm, attempting to be heroic. Vassil shot that man, too. It wasn't until later, when he read the newspapers, that he realized whom he'd shot: the entomologist Ilchev. He still had no idea who the man was. Right then, the regularly scheduled bus from Orhaniye to Sofia rounded the corner. Boris had apparently recovered from the shock of what had happened because he grabbed the steering wheel to turn the car around, but instead crashed it into the telegraph pole on the side of the road—then he sprang through the gaping car door and took off for the bus. Ikonomov screamed at the men to hold their fire and yelled up at the Hero: "Run and get him! But don't shoot him. Bring him back so we can settle the matter." And Vassil really did take off after his majesty. "Slow down, slow down, man," he yelled, "stop, we gotta tell you something! Stop!" But Boris did not oblige; he only ran and ran. He reached the bus, jumped in, and pushed the panicked driver away, took over the wheel and turned the bus around. Vassil the Hero swore, and yes, he admitted it—raised his pistol—but he refrained from shooting. The other, naturally, was not about to wait for anything else: he put the pedal to the metal and tore away to Orhaniye. That's how it had all gone down. And in the whole pandemonium, his majesty had forgotten his binoculars and his blunderbuss inside the car, so Ikonomov took the former and Vassil took the gun. He was sorry about Ilchev, naturally: he'd been a decent man who'd fought for the cause.

The Hero relayed all this, and Sheytanov listened without interrupting.

"You see, Sheytanov?" he said at the end. "I hope you of all people get it. We had no idea the king was going to pass through there, and now Ikonomov's saying I fucked up the whole thing, that I'd somehow known who was coming, and that I purposely came out before anyone else and shot into the air—to warn him! 'You,' he said, 'did it on purpose because the king pardoned your father in nineteen nineteen and let him out of jail, and now you're returning the favor.' Can you believe that fucking story?"

Sheytanov was reminded of that Russian captain on the ship to Marseille, how he'd been certain revolutionaries were only worthy of that name after they've killed an emperor. He smiled bitterly. Vassil the Hero looked at him suspiciously, but he only shrugged, got up and left for Kilifarevo, but it was as though a shadow hovered over him.

A cold and bristling shadow.

[Friday, July 5, 2013]
He walked back, same as he'd done coming in. Every once in a while he stopped horse-carriages whose owners froze with fear, and even before they could acquiesce or refuse to let him on, he'd jump in and ask to be taken to wherever he was going. He just sat in the back and yelled: "They've really put the fear in you, haven't they? Come on, let's go!" and he tucked himself into the driver's goods.

He'd then jump from the carriage, wave goodbye to the man driving it, and take off walking again. His Poseidon raincoat now only got in the way when he walked briskly through the overgrown paths, or when he slid into the thickets surrounding the muddy roads, but he couldn't do without it in that unrelenting rain.

His gun and his bombs were uncomfortable too, but he couldn't leave them, either.

[Saturday, July 6, 2013]

Sheytanov felt strangely about Death. He'd inflicted Death on many, more than once, but that spring she'd begun to repulse him, for he, like many others, had become convinced that he should leave behind the days he would not leave the house without a gun under his belt; the times he shot his pistol at night at the poor policemen, and scared the field-keepers just for kicks. It was true—he'd shot dead plenty in those past years.

But one day he suddenly asked himself: What had the policemen actually done to him, personally? He'd been surprised by his own question, and twice as surprised by the realization—nothing. They hadn't done anything to him. It was then he decided he was done with guns and bombs, and people couldn't figure out how he—the fearsome Sheytanov, the most wanted man in the land—could walk around without so much as a pocket knife. People asked him what was wrong with him, was he giving up or what? And if he saw those posing the questions were actually interested in the answer, he'd take the time to tell them.

Once, he got word that some local boys from Nova Zagora were whispering that he wasn't the same Sheytanov anymore. That he'd buried his guns, that maybe he'd gotten the jitters, and so forth. So he hopped over the Balkan Mountains to Nova Zagora, where twenty scowling men waited for him in a room. He took out his automatic pistol and slammed it on the table.

"I've come," he said, "to straighten some things out."

"Don't let that smooth-tongue speak! He'll only wheedle you in," one of the young men yelled pitifully from across the table.

"Shut up for a second," said Sheytanov and put down a freshly printed copy of *Ethics* by Kropotkin right next to the gun.

"One of these will kill a man, and one of these will make him come with you," he said.

"So what?" the same man yelled out again.

"So nothing. You can either go it alone, or you can inspire someone to come with you. There's strength in numbers."

"I told you he'd try to wheedle you in," the other objected again, but Sheytanov simply put away his gun and the book and told them that he wasn't there to convince them of anything. Better that he tell them a story . . .

During the Yoke, a vaivode sends his men down to the village to do some of their warlord things. They grab their guns, girdle their swords, wave their flag, and set off. Suddenly, they spot two policemen headed toward them. The haidouks immediately run back through the shrubs. The vaivode intercepts them at the top of the hill and asks why they're already coming back, empty-handed to boot. They start explaining themselves and the man cannot believe his ears. "What could we have possibly done, vaivode," they say. "There were two of them and we were just by ourselves!"

"I knew he'd try to trick you!" the same man called out again, yet was the first to laugh.

He may have won them over, but Vasil Ikonomov he couldn't. They stopped speaking to each other for a long time, even though it pained both of them tremendously.

And so it went.

Another time, he told the writer Mosko Moskov:

"Mosko, Mosko my dear man . . . the way we're going, by the time we liberate these people, we'll have killed them all!"

Mosko replied that he'd shoot him too, right on the spot, if he ever saw him in a cop's cap.

"Wouldn't you do the same to me?" Mosko added.

Mosko loved to act like a foolish country boy, walking around with his worn-out vest and his tattered hat and a pouch over his shoulder, all of which he could pull off because he was wide-eyed and round-faced.

He took everything in jest, even his own reputation as a ladies' man with many lovers. He told a story once—his new lady friend had a twin sister, and upon being asked whether he had any trouble keeping track of the ladies' identities, his round face had lit up triumphantly and he happily responded that *they* should be the ones keeping track of *him*. Or he'd say, "In the words of Chekhov, 'People should be beautiful in every way. Especially in their guns!'" And he'd convulse with the innocent laughter of a street urchin.

But he was sharp as a razor.

Sheytanov knew it and asked him to drop the act.

"Do you mean that anytime someone looks at me sideways I should shoot him? Don't agree with someone? Let's get out our guns and shoot each other. Don't like how someone looks at me? Get my sword and stab him. Is that how you see it? Leave that thinking alone, boy."

Mosko gave him a look and responded:

"What am I supposed to do instead? Let the wolves eat me?"

"Mosko," he said, "you're asking for trouble, my friend. Are you seriously unable to differentiate between bravery and idiocy?" He couldn't tell if Mosko'd heard him, and if he had, if he'd understood him.

The young man feigned ignorance yet again, putting his hand on his heart and went on:

"Sheytanov," he said, "wait a second and hear me out! This is how it all happened—I was walking, I wasn't bothering anyone, they stop me. Why, they couldn't tell you, either. If they'd only stopped me, I would've been fine with that, but, no, they have to ask for my identification card. I say fine, I'll show you my identification card, if that's what you want. I'm keeping the peace! I go into my bag and get out my gun . . . So I ask you, what right do they have to ask me for identification? Me . . . with an identification card? Are they out of their minds or what? So I ask you again—which one of us is looking for trouble?"

"I just want to remind you," Sheytanov interrupted him, "that you're an anarchist, not a malefactor. Don't forget that."

Mosko suddenly grinned and said:

"Sheytanov, funny thing is, even if it were you in an officer's cap, I'd still blow your brains out."

His laugh sounded like a young wolf's howl.

Sheytanov sighed.

"No, Mosko. The funny thing is that I believe you . . ."

He was serious. Both he and Mosko Moskov were very serious. That's how it was. But anyway . . .

[Sunday, July 7, 2013]

He was soaked to death when he got back to the Kilifarevo Monastery. Zhelyo awaited him, as did Mariola, frightened with bad presentiments. Sheytanov flopped down wearily on the bench and relayed what the Hero had told him. Zhelyo grinned darkly and let cursed, relieved that at least he needn't think about Vassil shooting and missing, which had been truly worrisome. He took a look at Mariola huddled into Sheytanov and said it was time to clear out.

"Sheytanov," he said, "My men are in Harmanli. They're just waiting for my signal. One snap of my fingers and we're in Turkey, brother. Tell me, what are we doing?"

But Sheytanov sighed.

"It's not that simple. We didn't start this circus, brother, but we're in neck deep, we have to play it till the end . . ."

"Like hell we do. And when they kill us like dogs, we'll really show them what's what! I'm not telling you to run like a coward. I'm offering you a common sense option."

Then he groaned and punched the wall with his enormous fist.

"Think about her!" he said, meaning Mariola. "She hasn't even tasted life and you're leading her to slaughter. Didn't she suffer enough in Pleven?

Sheytanov didn't respond. He only held the girl closer to him and told her: "Don't listen to him. It's going to be fine," and then he went quiet, while that same shadow rose up behind the monastery walls, rustled past the trees, and dissipated in between the bristling hills . . .

12.

[*Monday, July 8, 2013*]

May fourteenth, nineteen twenty-five—the day of the Holy Prophet Jeremiah, the day the village folk chase away the snakes—happened to be gloomy. The rain came down in a soft drizzle, and as they walked to court, the poet made a big deal of seeming fine—he went so far as to attempt a joke.

"Just look at this day!" he said to his wife, Mila, and to his sister Mika. "Byronic gloom! Byronic judgment . . . Byronic peace and love. I shan't be sentenced on such a day, you'll see with your own eyes. You," he said, "just sit and watch!"

He then remembered, and relayed just as joyously that, on top of that, the Orphan had given his word the previous night to show up as a witness.

"The Orphan," he said, "drinks his rakiya with the judge at the Wild Roosters, he'll come sort things out, there's no way he won't! We may have had our disagreements at the theater, but that's a different thing all together. The Orphan is my guy. It's not like I'm asking him to do a whole lot, either—all he needs to do is show up, give a furtive nod to the judge without the stenographer noticing and spreading it all over town, and we've got this."

Mila and Mika nodded and responded that yes, exactly, exactly, and they laughed nervously, but he couldn't even entertain the thought their laughter might be disingenuous.

Case No. 249 was eighteenth in line on this particular day, and the three of them sat down in the crammed hallway.

Nine o'clock came, but the Orphan was nowhere to be found. The poet leafed through the papers containing his summation, adding a word here, crossing out another there, raising his head expectantly every time the door cracked open and the smell of rain and spring rushed into the corridor.

At ten, the Orphan was still nowhere to be found. At fifteen minutes after ten, the poet could no longer bear it and told his sister the man had probably overslept—she should run and get him!—and in all her long and lonely years as a widow, Mika would never forget how she ran and ran and rang the doorbell with all her might . . .

[Before I forget! Maria Kassabova, or Mika, whom everyone agreed was the most beautiful of Milyo Kassabov's four daughters, wed the talented sculptor Vladimir Vladimirov from Ruse in nineteen thirty-four. But they lived together only a few months; he died a young man, that very same year. Milyo Kassabov attended his funeral, and later sent a telegram to his wife. "It was as though I buried my son a second time!" he wrote.

After she was widowed, Penka Kassabova, who had already become the director of the American daycare in Sofia, sent her sister to America. In the United States, Mika, as she was now called, studied pedagogy. In forty-two or forty-three, she tried to come back to Bulgaria—but the war made it impossible, and then . . .

In any case. In New York, she worked as a teacher in a large daycare, and New York was also where she died in nineteen ninety, when she was eighty-six years old.

Childless.

Life!]

Mika would never forget how, instead of the Orphan, it was his wife, Olga, whom all of Sofia knew as the *Orphaness*, who opened the door. She would also never forget what the woman said to her then.

"Oh, he went to his studio to stretch his canvases," she told her. "He must have completely forgotten about your brother's trial, Miss."

"Never mind that!" Mika threw out impatiently. "Where is he stretching his canvases, so I can go and remind him?"

"Well, in his studio, miss," the Orphaness responded, "his studio in Dragalevtsi."

Mika would also forever remember how she had been stunned speechless, how she was unable to utter a single word. "What do you mean in Dragalevtsi!" she had wanted to scream. "How is he in Dragalevtsi? It's at least an hour there, another back!" But she couldn't speak. She only watched, terror-struck, as the face of the woman began to fade, disappear, melt away, how her phlegmatic eyes also dematerialized, leaving only her blonde hair—a spurious halo lit by a vestibule lamp doing its best to offset the late morning gloom.

Mika returned to court worried sick with the news the Orphan was stretching his canvases in Dragalevtsi, but the poet only smiled and brushed it off.

"No worries," he said, "I'll get on fine without him. These people can't even imagine the kind of speech I've got for them."

He said as much, but his smile was now disingenuous as well.

When the attendant called them in the courtroom at noon, it wasn't just the Orphan who was missing. Stefan Rashenov, the lawyer, was also absent.

He simply did not show up.

Actually, he did show up, at the end—when everything had already been settled and the only thing that remained was for the judge to read the verdict and yell a tedious "Next!" to the same attendant.

That's how it was.

13.

As the poet finished his plea in the dusty courtroom, Mila squeezed his elbow hopefully despite her utter despair and whispered:

"When you spoke, we could feel the beating of angels' wings!"

As soon as the words left her mouth, she bit her lip, for they immediately felt like a gruesome prophesy, an omen, a summoning of something wretched, like a subterranean echo.

But the poet was so content with the speech he'd given, it didn't even occur to him how ghastly the vision of angels' wings was.

"I don't know," he whispered excitedly, "I don't know about that, but I gave the judges one hell of a lecture on art and life!"

"Absolutely!" his sister exclaimed. "Did you see how the stenographer was staring at you as you spoke, the chairman had to remind him to keep up with recording the proceedings and to pay attention!"

So it had been. The poet's voice had been loud and thunderous: "Your honors, in the name of Bulgarian justice, do not come down with a guilty verdict! If you," he said to the judges, "give me a guilty verdict, you would be punishing, wounding, and staining the entirety of Bulgarian art! And its development. Because," he said, "art can blossom only when it is planted in freedom. If you censor the writer," he said, "you would be killing art itself!"

But they still came down with their guilty verdict, and the poet lost it. He jumped to defend himself, but the judge only banged his gavel and yelled: "Next!"

They left the room and the poet, seeing his beautiful wife destroyed by what had happened, attempted to calm her down.

"Don't worry, it's nothing! This way I can work in peace in prison, I'll even make more money. The state will feed me for free."

Such were the words that came out of his mouth, and his sister could not fathom how her brother was able to summon the courage to joke about it.

[Years and years later, far beyond continents and oceans and those times, as she lay alone in her apartment in the vastness of New York, she would remember with the clarity one remembers a bad dream, how, as they strode toward the ugly building on Maria Louisa Boulevard, she suggested to her brother that the poet ought to gather the writers and march up to the palace to ask for a pardon since the king was going to celebrate his name day the following day.

"We must immediately go to the chairman of the Writers' Union, Vlaykov! He," she said, "is part of the Democratic Alliance, there's no way they won't hear him out at the king's court."

She tottered at her brother's side, pulled on his sleeve and declared, convinced, that if the writers weren't going to defend their own artistic freedom, who would do it for them? They should at once go to the confectionary on Tsar Osbovoditel, instead of home. Things of that manner.

But she'd been young, so young.

She also remembered how her brother had stopped dead in his tracks and looked her up and down, then waved his hand and hissed something dismissive.

"Right, they'll practically break their legs running to defend me. Writers! Mika, Mika," he asked her, "did you already forget how they all ran to city hall to ask for *permission to protest* the fact I was arrested for literary crimes? We're drowning in their courage."

He walked ahead once more, and she remembered about the Orphan and how he'd chosen precisely this day to go stretch his canvases, all the way in Dragalevtsi.

Every time she remembered all of it, regardless of how much time had passed from that foggy fourteenth of May, nineteen twenty-five—the day of the Holy Prophet Jeremiah, who'd been told by wise men and princes he could never be sentenced to death, because he spoke directly from God, our Lord—every time she remembered all of this, the blood drained from her face.]

14.

[Thursday, July 11, 2013]

Sheytanov was in Arbanasi when, toward the end of June, nineteen twenty-four, he heard the sixth issue of the magazine had been confiscated. He was surprised to hear this, because he knew the contents well and there was nothing that different in this book from the first five, and so decided it'd been yet another dirty attempt to impede them. He realized how right he'd been when the poet sent a young man with a quickly scribbled note. City hall had not only confiscated the entire issue's circulation, he wrote, but had also posted two policemen at 145 Rakovski, where a special police envoy had already come to collect all of *Plamuk*'s past issues and every single book from the archives. And then they arrested everyone! They'd all been loaded up and taken to the fourth police precinct—no letter, no explanation. The poet was livid—he'd written as much in the note—and he was intent on getting to the bottom of this vandalism. He asked about it at city hall, at Public Safety—and nothing, they would not say a word to him. He wrote to the district attorney in protest, but expecting a response was akin to waiting for a letter from a dead person.

"All of this has to be just a misunderstanding!" Sheytanov thought and felt himself boil up into a helpless rage.

He went back to Yambol, but he felt strange there. He walked the streets and although cops recognized him, they passed him by. He thought it might be from fear, or because of the still-fresh memory of the previous year's pointless carnage on March twenty-sixth, nineteen twenty-three. Everyone remembered it and everyone was still on edge about it—including the cops. As early as the previous summer, Tsankov's government had trumpeted the fact it had already, in the name of something—not clear what, exactly—punished those responsible, despite the fact the punishment itself was no punishment at all: several army commanders were moved to different garrisons, a couple of higher-ranking officers who'd really outdone themselves in their efforts were sent out of sight, and Aleksandar Tsankov personally held back some upper classmen at the pedagogical high school (because in his efforts to get them to settle down and keep them from going astray with their penchant for anarchism, the minister of education, Omarchevski, had already sent them away to Burgas and Kazanlak in April). That was the extent of the punishment. Meanwhile, the interior minister, Stoyanov, who'd sent the following preposterous telegram to the district police chief, Spassov: "We can do without a Yambol, but the anarchists must be squashed at any cost!" just sat around in jail, where he was treated like a precious treasure and they couldn't figure out how to get rid of him fast enough.

[Before I forget! Only the chief of police, B., got what was coming to him. First they tried to shoot him down in Yambol, but they only wounded his legs. The new government very helpfully drove him all the way to Sofia to be saved by the greatest medical luminaries. Someone from Yambol sent him a care package—cakes sprinkled with strychnine. He bit into one, but sensed the poison and spit it out, the swine. He dodged that bullet and only threw up. That's when Zhelyo really got pissed off and took the train to Sofia. He waited for B. outside the hospital and saw him taking a stroll along the sidewalk with a young lady. He took him out with a single shot—B. sprawled out on the leaf-covered sidewalk and his crutches clanked against the pavement, and just as the woman opened her mouth to scream, Zhelyo told her: "Not a sound. Count to 100 before you start squealing again." Then he hopped onto a passing tram. And that was that.]

Anyway, during those couple of weeks when Sheytanov was back home in Yambol, the cops turned the other way when they passed him on the street, and he didn't have to keep his hand on the gun inside his pocket the entire time.

He loved Yambol in summer. It didn't matter where he was, at dusk he still listened for the short, whip-sharp whistles of the pigeoners, that pulsating flutter of the pigeons crossing the trees and over the rooftops; he even missed the fumes emanating from the tanneries by the river.

In the evenings he went out, crossing the river over the Balahurski Bridge, past the pedagogical school and the bathhouse, and arrived at the public gardens, still alive with loud crowds and brass music. The young people looked at him the way one looked at a legend, but he just smiled to himself and disappeared into the shadows.

One evening, Kiril, the bookshop owner Vassil Krastev's boy, took him to visit the home of David Krispin, Tasko Gigov's partner at the gutter-tile factory. Krispin's daughter, Esther, was a friend of those modernist literary mules, which was perhaps why her parents invited him so courteously into their big house in the Jewish neighborhood by the river. Inside the guestroom lit up by an electric chandelier and the calming clink of the floor-to-ceiling crystal bookcases, Esther sat down at the piano and began to play something by Chopin. She was an excellent pianist. In the middle of a nocturne, Sheytanov's gun tumbled onto the carpet: he'd let himself relax into a long forgotten and perpetually ignored repose and hadn't even felt the pistol slip out of his summer jacket. Esther hadn't even heard the telltale tumble, but Kiril Krastev saw everything and paled greatly, while Krispin just looked at Sheytanov with sad reproach.

Sheytanov apologized and put away the damned weapon, swearing to never again step foot inside the good people's home while armed.

[Friday, July 12, 2013]
He left Yambol at the end of summer when the army and the police were once again on edge because of the organized groups roaming about. The partial amnesties from the previous summer meant some of the old ruffians came crawling out of the jails—infamous scoundrels, deft, uncatchable, armed to the teeth. They planted ambushes and stopped

passengers, businessmen, and the first impatient wheat-brokers on the side of the road, pulling all of them down from their horse carriages and their cabriolets, first robbing them, then beating them, and finally abandoning them in the middle of the road without a cent, terrorizing the people in the surrounding areas. Not a week went by without bloodshed. They killed the local German, Anton Karden, who'd moved into these parts as far back as nineteen and one—they jumped him as he came back from the Government Cattle and Stallion Depot in Kaya Burun: they put a bullet in his head and disappeared with the money. Plenty fell dead, so the district authorities fortified the police in the city and put up army posts in the waiting room and the platform at the train station, where the mixed patrols greedily seized every piece of luggage they deemed suspicious.

Sheytanov started to travel with a leather bag, the contents of which included: three automatic pistols, several boxes of bullets, and five bombs from Mityo Ganev's arsenal. He buried all of it under paper bags filled with two kilograms of oranges and one kilogram of lemons from Pasko Kulov's new store, Svezda. At the train station, he went right up to the guard in the waiting room and amicably asked him to watch his bag while he bought his ticket. The patrols inspected every single bag, weaved basket, and bundle *but* his bag, which they did not touch, even going so far as to yell at the soldier to move it out of the way. All the while, Sheytanov took his time at the ticket counter.

When the train from Bourgas arrived, Sheytanov came up to the soldier and said, "God bless you brother, for keeping my fruit safe, it's for a little kid, an orphan, ill for two Sundays now!" but the soldier didn't realize the joke was on him.

In Sofia, he handed the bag to Zhelyo Grozev to give to Efi and Bae, and to warn them to be careful because Pane Bichev himself was onto the elusive *heroes of the night* and had woven a nasty trap for them.

The oranges and lemons he took to Mila and the kids.

He and the poet were in Alkazar when they happened upon a sting operation. The cops descended on small trucks and blocked the streets and exits while an entire horde of uniformed and plainclothes officers stomped through the tables, searching and checking the clientele at random. The orchestra broke off mid-note as havoc engulfed the crowd. The women yelped from fear and the men shouted in protest, threatening inquiries and escalations.

The poet looked at Sheytanov anxiously, but the latter simply stood up and yelled out for everyone to keep calm.

"Gentlemen, gentlemen!" he shouted. "Calm down, please. Let the officers of the law do their checks, our police are here to protect us, you know this. These people are here for our own good."

The cops threw him hateful looks and passed him by, and the poet cackled:

"You're quite the psychologist, eh?"

Before that, in August, they arrested Zhelyo in Sofia. They took him to the police directorate and interrogated him for three hours, but he just looked at them, insulted, and alternated between exclaiming "Yes, for God's sake!" and "No, goddamn it!" They searched him and when they found nothing—they told him to get the hell out of there. So when, soon after, Sheytanov met up with Mosko Moskov at the Petropavlov Monastery, he did not miss the opportunity to remind him that if Zhelyo had had his Mauser on him at the time of his arrest, where would he be now?

"Think about it, my friend," he said. "Just imagine how bad things would've been, and stop reaching for your gun every other second."

But Mosko made light of it:

"I love it when I hear a bullet hiss by! When I hear a bullet, that's when I know: it's not my bullet. If I hear it whistle by, it means I'm still standing, my friend."

He and Zhelyo had decided to carry their guns into town only when they were a hundred percent certain they would need to use them. Good thing they did, too.

While he was still in Turnovo, he was asked to speak in front of some people. One night in Dolna Oryahovitsa he stayed out too late, there was no way to get back into town, so someone offered him a place to stay, but that someone's house was right next door to the village police station. And who knows why, they decided to get back to the house in a horse carriage. He told the men: "Get in, I'll rein in the horses." The sentry standing outside the station even yelled at him and called him a clod, hadn't anyone taught him to rein horses? "Who gave you the reins, goddamn it?" the cop yelled at Sheytanov, who did not miss the opportunity to show his teeth and snarled back: "The horses are mine, and I'll do with them as I please! You," he said, "what are you going to do? Arrest me or straight up shoot me? Or are you just bored from standing at that post for hours?" The cop swore at him sourly and told him to get lost, that he could barely stand to look at him, let alone fight him.

Another time in Turnovo, while the police left no rock unturned looking for him, he sat inside the hippest barbershop on Bajdarlak Square, dressed like a prince from an American film. Across the street at the confectionary, Zhelyo and Mosko ate cakes and grinned through the glass: Zhelyo dressed like he ought to be in a movie, too, Mosko with his rubber *tsarvuli* and his village idiot's cap, and there's Sheytanov getting a shave and listening to the barber's jabber. A pretty picture—they couldn't get enough of it.

[Saturday, July 13, 2013]

Right around then, someone called Petko arrived in Turnovo from the village of Duskot. He'd been all over Sofia, treating his tuberculosis of the bone, and he came back deformed, limping, with swollen knees, a cane, and a statement in his pocket, written by six enraged Sofia men. The statement was filled with bitter accusations against Sheytanov—that he'd joined forces with the communists, that he'd come to an agreement with them to present a united front with the agrarians, so that after the revolution it would be the communists who ruled the whole country, with a small piece for the agrarians, and Kyustendil and Turnovo for the anarchists. The rumor made its way through dorms and clubs, it spread like kerosene fire, and the statement changed many hands and was read by everyone, and all of Turnovo was in goose bumps. "This Sheytanov," they yelled, "he's in bed with the Bolsheviks, the dog! Moscow must be paying him in dollars."

He was hurt by the words, but what most weighed on him was how he and Vasil Ikonomov parted as enemies. At one time, the two men planned to blow up the Council of Ministers, precisely when Stamboliyski would've been there with all of his ministers at yet another of their endless sessions. It would have been the perfectly gruesome payback for the Yambol massacre on March twenty-sixth. They were planning to dig a tunnel to the basement of the building and stuff it with dynamite. Then out of nowhere, it occurred to them that this would not only be payback for the slaughter in Yambol—blowing up the Council of Ministers building would also honor the young people who died exactly twenty years prior, on April nineteen and three, when there wasn't a stone left standing at the Ottoman Bank in Solon. They'd realized this at the same time and they both exclaimed: "Just like the motherfucking sailors in Solon!" They even shook hands, the way people who've said the same thing at the same time do. The anniversary may have been a coincidence, but it felt like a perfect foretoken. They immediately looked around for a small, empty storefront on Rakovski, something close by and facing the Council of Ministers building, so they could lease it and start digging, just as the Solon bombers had done. They calculated exactly how many people should enter, pretending to shop, and leave with paper bags filled with dirt from the tunnel, because that's exactly how Yordan "Orce" Popyordanov and Kosta Kirkov had done it. They even arranged for the dynamite—nearly two hundred kilograms of it—as well as two demi-johns of nitroglycerin: both were taken care of by three reserve captains, seething with hatred for Stamboliyski for having fired them from the army at the prime of their might. Ikonomov and Sheytanov even tracked down a guy, an electrician, who worked at the tram depot on Maria Louisa to finish the bombs, laughing as they imagined watching the blast and the fire from behind the police cordons, and if it so happened that a few geese walked on by . . .

That's how it had been. But only a year after, in the summer of twenty-four, he and Ikonomov had a falling out, and the latter left Kilifarevo without so much as saying goodbye.

[Sunday, July 14, 2013]

If the topic ever came up, Sheytanov and Georgi Popov couldn't see eye-to-eye regarding that same camaraderie with the communists, but when, at the beginning of August, Sheytanov learned the identity of the two cops who'd desecrated Popov's corpse—wrath engulfed him. He took Zhelyo and three other men from their pack of anarchists, went down to Kilifarevo, and burst into the police station where he personally executed one of them, and Zhelyo took care of the other. Then they left. The guard outside the United Industries bank started screaming from the other end of the square: "Help! Thieves! Help! Bandits!" Sheytanov called Zhelyo over and told him to go tell that moron to shut up. But the guard was already picking up his Mannlicher and Zhelyo had no choice but to shoot first. So he did.

That's how it happened.

[Monday, July 15, 2013]

Others couldn't let go of the fact he'd given fifty thousand leva to the poet to start *Plamuk*. They told him they could have started their own magazine with that money. What don't you like about the poet's magazine, he'd ask them. It's good, they'd answer, but it wasn't *theirs*! He didn't quarrel with them, but he also didn't like the darkness of the "us" versus "them": he'd seen it in Russia and knew how those things ended. "Us and them," he thought, "so they can kill us separately."

He roamed around a lot that summer—on this side of the Balkan Mountains and that, with Zhelyo, without him, greeted with a scowl, or with a firm pat on the shoulder. He saw a lot, he heard a lot. But the more he traveled, the more sobering his thoughts became. He became convinced that after the handful of chaotic post-war revolts, what lay ahead was nothing more than the harrowing dormancy of an entire people.

[Tuesday, July 16, 2013]
One August afternoon he made his way to the editorial offices—he walked along Tsar Osvoboditel Boulevard, toward Rakovski, and just as he got to Benkovski, he heard a slow and heavy stomp. He turned around and saw a black river of invalids spilling onto the street from the public gardens outside the palace. People on crooked wheelchairs or with crutches, with prostheses for arms and wooden pegs for legs, blind people with canes, most with dirty, worn out clothes, some with old and tattered military uniforms, with hole-ridden caps and with medals of honor on their faded tunics. There were so many of them that the first ones were already as far as the Russian Church, while the last were still stumbling over the curved tram tracks outside the palace gates. A dense police squadron waited ahead of them between the writers' gathering spot at Bai Yugrev's confectionary and the still-unplastered house of the businessman Nikola Shavkulouv, but the men dragged unyielding toward the cordon; the stomp of the dozens of lame legs was sinister. The cops dug their heels into their horses' sides and steered them toward the crowd, which was drawing out through the Rakovski intersection, passing by the Military Club—where the dark gazes of several young officers on the veranda followed the scene—and straight toward the National Assembly.

That's when he saw the poet: amid the swarm of broken down, spent, and gutted men. He strode, head lowered, with the prideful humility one adopts when he walks among his own kind.

He saw him, but he didn't call out to him. He never mentioned it. The poet never did, either.

[Wednesday, July 17, 2013]
That same night, it was just the two of them at 145 Rakovski, and somehow the subject of the dissolution of the co-op, Liberation, came

up. The poet immediately began to swear against the government. When the government starts confiscating and liquidating, it's no longer a government, it's a rabble of marauders, he yelled. Sheytanov let the poet get it out of his system and then calmly added that Liberation wasn't exactly what it should have been, either.

"Don't take it all at face value, Milev," he said, "don't believe everything they say. Half of them are dogmatists, the other half—total hustlers."

The poet was ready to explode all over again, but Sheytanov didn't let him get a word in.

"Milev," he said, "Liberation hasn't been a co-op in the true sense of the word for a long time. There's no way it can be a true co-op—its leadership is nothing more than a breeding ground for communist money-pigs. The people in charge of Liberation," he said, "they have fatty hearts."

The poet began to disagree, and challenged him, but Sheytanov interrupted him again.

"Let me remind you of something!" he said. "Lani Toudjarov practically broke his back going over there to ask them for something, anything for Smirnenski. Well?" he added, "Did they give him anything? They gave him the middle finger is what they gave him. They knew he was on his way out and that the only thing that could save him was a sanatorium, but not only did they not give him one *stotinka* for a sanatorium . . . what am I even talking about—they wouldn't even give him money for medication, let alone a sanatorium. Shady assholes. How many kindhearted shady assholes do you know? Think of how much they made just off his book alone. In one year they gave it two print runs, these Bolshevik swine. You're a publisher—you do the math. They could've sent him not to a little Bulgarian village, but to Davos, and just with the money they got from importing that soviet cement. You tell me, what kind of a co-op doesn't take care of one of its own?"

"Well, I don't know if Smirnenski was ever actually a member," the poet snorted reluctantly.

Sheytanov went black.

"He was a member of their party!" he argued spitefully. "Of their party. Isn't that enough? Let me ask you something. Last year you spoke at Smirnenski's wake, you spoke well, I was there, I heard you, but where, exactly, were his comrades? Or had their permission not yet arrived from Moscow—or maybe they weren't required to be present by the Central Committee of the Bulgarian Communist Party. I wouldn't be surprised if it turns out that what people are saying is true—that Minister Roussev gave his people from Public Safety a warning after June ninth. Do you know what he supposedly said to them? *We won't touch the communists*, that's what he said to them. What do you think of that, Milev?"

He gave a hopeless wave of his hand.

"Do you know what they say where I'm from," he added, "the goat and the Bolshevik are never sated!"

They sat around a few minutes more, then went their separate ways with furrowed brows.

[Thursday, July 18, 2013]

Summer was wearing off when he brought Mariola to the poet's house. Both the poet and his wife welcomed her warmly, Mila quickly put together something to eat, the two men sipped from the Yambol grape rakiya Sheytanov had brought, and they got to talking about the confiscation of the sixth issue.

"Listen to me," Sheytanov said brightly, "when you think about it, a confiscated magazine is a big deal. People will be dying to exaggerate its contents with God knows what. And curiosity does help a lot. Hey!" he added, "it's not you who's behind the whole thing, is it? Tell me if you are, you'll feel better about it too."

"You're laughing!" the poet took offense immediately. "You think the whole thing is funny? People *are* exaggerating, I even hear that it's being passed from hand to hand, but it's not available in any shops. I can tell you what to do with fame when there's not a single sale behind it. The bookshop owners shrug their shoulders, sorry Mr. Milev, they tell me, the police came and took every last one, I couldn't sell a single copy.

You go and try to prove they did or didn't, if you've got nothing better to do. Thankfully we got the issue to all of the subscribers before it was confiscated, maybe we'll get a couple of leva from that."

He added that he'd already written his thoughts on the confiscation—he'd show them!

"The way I've written it," he said, "the way I've written it, I'm telling you, it's going to start a fire under their asses, theirs and their talentless mothers', pardon me, ladies. This is nothing but a police-driven critique!"

[Friday, July 19, 2013]
Later that night, when the rumpus from the convivial public drifted from the boulevard up through the open window, the poet suddenly declared:

"Listen to me now, Sheytanov, I came up with something, I want your opinion."

He got up, lowered his head and began: *"From the dead womb of night, the age-old venom of the slave is spawned."* Sheytanov was surprised and started to ask something, but decided against it and did not interrupt the poet. The poet was not reading from a piece of paper; he spoke confidently and Sheytanov quickly figured out that he and Mariola were far from being the first to hear the thunderous words. He saw, too, that Mila's whole demeanor darkened, and knew at once he'd been right: many must've already heard these verses. It occurred to him that Mila likely already saw herself a widow with fatherless children. The thought was heart-wrenching. The poet recited with his hands in his pockets, but his entire body moved to the rhythm of the words: the verdant dusk inside the room thickened, and the poet's shadow on the wall alternated between swinging as if in a heavy march, and crouching like a beast before pouncing . . . all the way to the end of the poem, with its unexpected *"No god! No master!"*

"Earth shall be heaven!" the poet threw out deafeningly. *"It shall!"*

Quiet overtook the room. The poet laughed and asked:

"What do you think, Sheytanov?"

Sheytanov shrugged.

"Wasn't it supposed to be about Prince Marko instead," he said, "Prince Marko, Musa Kesedžija . . . ?"

"Those two can wait," the poet responded. "Their time will come too, just not right now, because right now . . . wait, I missed something. Did I tell you what the title is going to be?"

"No," Sheytanov furrowed his brows. "What will it be?"

"September!" the poet yelled victoriously. "September, my brother, September. Now tell me, do you like what I've written?"

"Well," he attempted to answer, but quickly bit his lip, because he heard how Mila sighed painfully.

But the poet heard her too!

Since losing his right eye—and with a left one rapidly fading, he'd soon have been completely blind—the poet had the hearing of a bat. He heard her sigh.

"None of that, Mila!" he thundered. "This is a work of art, what are you sighing about? You could say 'Well done, Geo, you're incredible,' it would do the job better. Don't make me second-guess myself!"

He said this, but then he darted around the table and embraced her.

"It's a good poem, don't be afraid," he said and pushed her glasses down her nose with guilt. "You shouldn't do that, it's no

[Sunday, July 21, 2013]
[NB!

"Only in Russia poetry is respected—it gets people killed. Is there anywhere else where poetry is so common a motive for murder?" Mandelstam.

Look at that, how peculiar. Did Mandelstam really think that? In the thirties, no less, when . . . And if he did think it, did he believe it?

Peculiar indeed.]

[Sunday, July 21, 2013]
good to think like that," he said, "please, smile!"

[Four]

Ваше Величество,
На двете ми молби, отправени до Ваше
Величество, нямам отговор.

"*Your Highness,*
I have yet to receive a response to either of my
previous appeals sent to Your Highness."

—From Milyo Kassabov's
third letter to Boris III,
December 5, 1925

15.

During that entire month of April in nineteen twenty-five, the sky was leaden and sepia rains poured out of it: they poured relentlessly, scalding the still delicate virescence of the trees. It was then that three Englishmen, Labour MPs, appeared in Sofia. Their names were William Mackinder, Cecil Malone and Josiah Clement Wedgwood. Lieutenant Wedgwood was a distant relative of Charles Darwin—yes, that same Darwin! He was also a bearer of the Order of Merit for services to the army, a member of the king's secret council, dry and pleasant, as any real Englishman who came from good stock ought to be. He was in superior ranking to the other two men accompanying him.

In any case.

The three were escorted by pastor Reuben Markham—so he could direct them where to go and translate for them—and the men went all over asking and interrogating so they could get to the bottom of what in God's name was happening in this blighted little country.

They queried the Bulgarian MP, Grigor Vasilev, too, who'd received his law degree from Geneva before coming back to Sofia to work in Parliament. He stared sullenly at the three men and answered most of their queries with a grunt, but when they said they'd heard that at least six thousand had been arrested following the attack on St. Nedelya Church, he couldn't restrain himself.

He slammed his fist on the table and yelled that was completely preposterous!

"This is a repugnant fantasy, gentlemen!" he exclaimed. "It's not that crazy to think that after an attack of this magnitude—which resulted in the deaths of over one hundred seventy-five people, and wounded more than eight hundred—there would be arrests, but six thousand . . ."

"Well, how many, then?" Lieutenant Josiah Clement Wedgwood asked courteously. "Approximately."

"Well, I don't know exactly how many," Grigor Vasilev became more infuriated. "In any case, the maximum number of people arrested was never higher than a thousand. After all," he said, "one must strive to eradicate society's tumors!"

"Could you please repeat that?" Wedgwood interrupted him in that same courteous manner. "Did you say a thousand?"

"Give or take a few!" the Bulgarian MP responded triumphantly.

Lieutenant Wedgwood wrote this down and asked:

"To what extent is it true that there were people detained throughout the entire country? For instance in Ruse, Varna, and Bourgas?"

Vasilev shrugged.

"*Mais bien sûr!*" he said. "It's true. These rats are everywhere, gentlemen!"

It was then that Josiah Clement Wedgwood raised his eyebrows.

"Let me see if I've understood everything correctly," he said. "You, sir, are telling us, that the entire horrific plot to murder innocent people via an explosion inside the cathedral was planned by *one thousand people*, give or take a few, all scattered three- to four-hundred kilometers apart from each other?"

He took a breath and then sighed.

"To be honest, this must be the most puzzling plot in the entire world history of conspiracy theories."

Grigor Vasilev's face went scarlet and he opened his mouth to speak, but Josiah Clement Wedgwood, grandson of Darwin himself, the man whom George V once personally sent to Siberia to keep an eye on the Bolshevik's handle of the situation, so that he would remain free of suspicion from communist affiliation, at once shut his leather notebook.

"Interesting," he said dryly. "And where might you suppose these one thousand people, give or take a few, gathered to plot the attack?"

[Monday, July 22, 2013]
But anyway.

The Englishmen continued to putter about Sofia, but the city was desolate. Even the otherwise lively cafés and confectionaries were empty that April. Markham remained hopeful and took to visiting people's homes; people with whom he was acquainted and whom he was certain would talk.

But they didn't talk! They didn't, in fact, even open their doors.

Everyone had bolted up the locks and peered pitifully out their peepholes.

Only the poet did no such thing.

He invited the men into his office with the embrasure-like window, and using the most perfect English they had heard since setting foot in Sofia, explained everything. True, he spoke with the strong accent of a someone from the South of Europe, but he was as precise in his wording as he was in his manners.

As soon as they all sat down at the round table with the lace cloth, he warned them that he wasn't sure exactly what sort of new information they were hoping to learn, but they'd do well to keep in mind that those in office in Bulgaria were in a perennial war with their citizens. A bona fide war. And as with any war, everyone yelled "God help us! God help us!" but it would appear as though this time God was on the side of the machine guns. Those in power now, according to him, did little to hide their real intentions. He read them something he'd written in his own magazine a year before. The black sun on the ninth of June, he went, rose in the name of such glorious things as freedom, the constitution, trampled human rights, social justice, culture, and national prosperity, and it burned all too brightly into the eyes of the people.

"This is how it is over here," he said. "They arrest you, beat you, kill you—in the name of the Law for the Protection of the Nation. And when you try to fight back using the same tactics—that's called terrorism. Full stop."

He spoke tiredly and with dispassion, because as a man obsessed with new theater, he knew an icy tone and even voice were far more sinister than the screams and laments of the old school. But he smoked an entire pack of Sultans in three hours, and could do little to calm his nervous fingers, which continuously drummed the table. He was not embarrassed at having to wipe yet another rivulet trickling out from behind his glass eye, while the descendants of George V listened to him and urgently scribbled into their expensive notebooks all afternoon, and at least five men in long black coats stood on the sidewalk below, staring up anxiously and with malice at the fourth floor.

The Englishmen were very interested in what he had to offer as a way of a response to someone named Ernest Hemingway, who'd apparently been quoted as saying that Bulgarian intelligentsia is made up of people who, due to the excesses of their knowledge, had lost all honor and nobility.

The poet's face dropped and he in turn asked them where they'd read such a thing.

"A Toronto paper," they explained. "The *Toronto Star* or something of the sort. It's a rather big paper . . ."

"Well, I don't have the honor of being acquainted with the gentleman," the poet cut them off.

"Not many do," shrugged Wedgwood. "But it's an important paper. It has a good readership outside of Canada as well."

"I've heard of the gazette, but I have not heard of the gentleman," the poet interrupted again. "But he is correct. Unfortunately. I can't say whether this is really due to an excess of knowledge, since I doubt that immensely. As it happens, I've written something similar. The Bulgarian writer today has fallen out of favor; he cries in his coffee with a broken spirit, so foolishly servile was he during the previous regime's reign. And even if he desired to be valiant now, he couldn't muster it up. He's in no rush to do so, either."

He slapped the table and clarified that this too was warranted. Censorship.

"I call it *Police Critique*," he declared abruptly.

The other three nodded, as though they understood what he meant, but he countered that there was no conceivable way they could understand what Police Critique might possibly be.

"Police Critique, gentlemen," he stressed, "is when the authorities send the mutton-shunters to confiscate your magazine. When the mutton-shunters become literary critics, that's what I call Police Critique, gentlemen! That's a step below churlish critique. In lieu of debate, a baton. In lieu of reason, confiscation. This is what I mean by Police Critique, sanctified by the state!"

All of this had not, of course, begun yesterday. He told them that in nineteen twenty-two for instance, there was a typhoon of print lawsuits, ergo, lawsuits against journalists. A thousand in a single year! Just in the Sofia public prosecutor's office alone, there were over six hundred claims filed to prosecute journalists on account of the special journalism article, Article 235 of the penal code.

"A thousand lawsuits in a single year against the people who rely on print for their bread and butter. Can you gentlemen even conceive of such a thing? And it is the state that is suing them. The authorities are suing them, not some offended dimwit. Some unfortunate journalist exposes yet another abuse by yet another minister-sponger, and the whole ministry jumps up and sues. Not the greedy slyboots, mind you, but the journalist! A thousand lawsuits against journalists. This is one number that, as far cultural statistics are concerned, you, gentlemen, will be hard-pressed to match. Those unenlightened to the Bulgarian disposition will likely feel bewilderment or fall into a nervous breakdown for now, the written word is by law a political crime!"

He then threw down in front of them a state newspaper, with Bulgaria's Law for the Protection of the Nation, newly added in the cold month of March, where it was clearly stated: any literary works deemed antiestablishmentarian by the authorities are to be seized through a prosecutor's warrant; but the police had the right to stop distribution even without a warrant. The law made it so that even the owners of the printing shops could be charged as accomplices.

"Read!" he said. "Read my lords, read it. Article 6. They just added it in March. 'Anyone caught creating propaganda or setting in motion agitation, either by word of mouth, or in writing, or through the distribution of printed works, with the goal of subverting the political or economic order of the country through crime, violence, or terrorist activity, will be punished with solitary confinement in a maxim security prison for no fewer than five years and will be fined anywhere between fifty thousand and five hundred thousand leva.' Article 7. New as well. 'Anyone caught creating propaganda or setting in motion agitation, either by word of mouth, or in writing . . .' blah blah blah. Same thing: this many years in prison, this much in fines. Prison, fines, prison, fines. Brilliant, isn't it?"

He explained that his own magazine had been confiscated as well—twice. The second time they came straight to the printer's. He'd gone to four different printers just to print the same issue. Right when they'd start, they'd have to stop. Four times.

"Pure misery," he said. "And the printers? They act despicably too, out of fear."

The poet sighed and admitted he too had already been arrested once, to the exaltation of those same newspaper heels, and was awaiting trial on the fourteenth of May. He was being sued for writing a poem, which contained all of his own horror regarding an event he himself had chosen to write about.

"Just an *idea*, dear gentlemen," he stressed. "But the prosecutor filed a lawsuit. And why do you think he did that?"

He quieted for a second, surveyed each of the Englishmen and muttered:

"Because the poem is called 'September'! And if that title summons up the ghosts of someone else's conscience, it is not I who is to blame. Do you see what I'm getting at? Had the title been different, I'm willing to wager a bet that they would have, one hundred percent, overlooked the whole thing and wouldn't have made me out to be a criminal. But no, 'September' is what frightens them. There you have it: the Law for the Protection of the Nation, Article 6, Article 7, added just for me, surely. 'Anyone who by word of mouth, or through writing, or by the distribution of printed or other works, incites hostility, hatred or crimes against certain classes or echelons of the population or the presiding authority, and with these actions jeopardizes the social and judicial order of the country . . .' Hah, and this results in solitary confinement inside a maximum security prison for three to eight years and a fine of three hundred thousand leva. As though 'September' is a call to arms or a political proclamation. I'm at a loss as to how a poem can be classified as terrorism."

He laughed darkly.

"For God's sake! Hostility, hatred, crime, jeopardizing the social and judicial order? Crime against the state?! If we're talking about crimes against the state, this entire government of ours should be in prison, don't you agree? Just look at the penal code. Article 99, which states that every action that has as its core the aim of applying forcible change to the governmental order or the country's unity, constitutes treason. Well, didn't they do precisely this on the ninth of June, last year? They did, indeed! Not to mention the even more shining Article 247, whomever premeditates to murder another will be punished with death. Again, the government is guilty of this."

Out from underneath the blackened lens of his glasses, a single amber trickle made its way down his cheek again, and Mila quickly wiped it away with her handkerchief, while he groaned and reached for his cigarette tin.

"Allow me to get to the point," he said and raised his finger. "In conclusion, literary works are the same as inciting the people to rise up! That's censorship and nothing more. But when else has censorship ever been immortalized by a special law? They've done it in this country. And it's not parliament who did it, parliament's been useless since June ninth, nineteen twenty-three. Do you know who did it? The *nikolamilevtsi* and *borisvazovtsi*, the government and a certain person who signed it, *tout de suite*. And herein lies the most horrifying thing of all—once it's been done once, each successive government will feel free to do the same until every single newspaper in the world simply reprints the words of the prime minister, so there is no truth but the truth coming out of his mouth! Ah, to be led by *ibrikchii*."

The English gentlemen appeared quite confused, so the poet was quick to clarify:

"*Ibrikchii!*" he spat out again. "Grovelers, sycophants, toadies, political concubines, obligers, bootlickers, ordinary caitiffs. Long live the whores on Tsar Osvoboditel Boulevard, serpentine careerism, and the white lace valentines of the Stratievs and the Stoubelovs. On we go until each and every person stops thinking with his own head, declaring the truth to be that which is written in *Slovo, Mir,* and *Zlatorog.* The herd mentality, that's what the obscurantists want. Deprive one of the truth, it'll be easier for him to lie. Without censorship, the despot is impotent, because censorship is the mother of tyranny."

He began to dig about a pile of newspapers on his shelf, found what he was looking for, and yelled out victoriously:

"Here we have the dream result, my dear gentlemen. Is this," he said, "*Le Temps*? It is, indeed. The heavy artillery. Almost on par with your *Times,* perhaps even a bit better. Let's see what it says in the heavy artillery. Here it is . . . 'Before my visit to Bulgaria, the liberals warned me that Tsankov's government was very unpopular among the people. Now, after my two-week visit to this peaceful country, I'd really like to pose a question to myself and to the liberals: what does a popular or an unpopular government look like? Actually, let me rephrase the question: which is better for a country—an unusually popular prime minister, for whom the ladies clap, but whose ideas are inconvertible and inexecutable, or a prime minister who might make the hairs on your neck stand up just at the mention of his name, but whose word is the law?' Well, look at that! His word is the law and the law is his word!"

He threw the paper over his shoulder with disgust.

He sighed and went on, but his ire seethed underneath his ostensibly dry tone.

"As he understood things, the most horrifying thing about censorship is that it destroyed Voltaire's words forever: *'Je ne suis pas d'accord avec ce que vous dites, mais je me battrai jusqu'au bout pour que vous puissiez le dire.'* But now we have Jesus's nationalized *'qui non est mecum adversum me est et qui non colligit mecum dispergit.'* Or the even easier: 'Начальство лучше знает'—the administration knows better. Full stop. And if anyone questions it, the uniformed art critics show up at your door. It's true, my dear gentlemen, up until now, the only thing threatening the writer was starvation, now the threat is physical. I would not be surprised if they started murdering over poems and short stories."

The Englishmen continued to fill their notebooks and likely didn't even notice how Mila's eyes grew darker and darker with worry and awful presentiments.

16.

Mila felt strange about Death. She'd nearly seen Death herself with her own eyes on the twenty-first of August, nineteen eighteen, when, after his extensive surgery inside Dr. Vayer's basilica-dark field hospital, they brought her husband, patched up by Johanes Esser's magic hands, back by ambulance to the exquisite Vereinslazaret Cecilienhaus hospital, located on Berlinerstrasse, originally designed by Walter Schpikendorf and Rudolf Walter as a women's hospital and maternity ward, used now as a military infirmary. The building at 137 Berlinerstrasse: the first of their many, many future addresses.

She had trailed on foot after the enclosed vehicle with the large red cross and the two horses in front of it, mournful like angels, and until the end of her life she would not forget the feeling she had as she walked. She felt as if she were walking behind a hearse. That she, together with this carriage of death, had already entered the world of the dead. It had been all too terrifying and all too real a sight: long trains of brutally maimed soldiers—victims of the still raging war—as close to death as you could get and suffering from the final indignity of not yet knowing it. Even the green veil she wore

[Wednesday, July 24, 2013]
resembled a mourning veil. She loathed Death for this reason. Regardless of whose death it was.

But she mostly despised Death because of her husband, because she saw Death every day—when she cleaned his porcelain eye, when she saw the pulsating blue veins below the deceptively whole skin on his

186

forehead, or when she simply watched him trip over a threshold. He'd forbidden them—her and her sisters-in-law—to make any mention of his lost vision and of the small abyss behind the blackened right lens of his glasses, and they never spoke a word of it. But this didn't chase Death away.

Mila didn't know what the Englishmen may have thought, but she nearly fainted. For a second she saw herself a widow, and her children—orphans.

"He'll be all right, knock on wood!" she attempted to joke with the three men, but her voice was raspy and the joke fell flat: Death was already peering mockingly over her husband's shoulder.

[Wednesday evening, July 24, 2013]

[From: Hristo Karastoyanov hr_karast@hotmail.com
To: Georgi Yanev g_yanev_sz@abv.bg
Sent: Wednesday, July 24, 2013, 19:53:14 EEST
Subject: Mila Geo Mileva

My Dear Mr. Director Yanev,

I have turned the entire world wide web upside down, but I have as yet been unable to find so much as a grain of information about Mila Geo Mileva's death. Isn't that strange? I find it rather strange. Do you happen to know anything on the subject?

I also wonder how she raised her two little girls—where they lived and how they lived after their father's death. Things of that nature.

Eternally Yours,
Karastoyanov

•

From: Georgi Yanev g_yanev_sz@abv.bg
To: Hristo Karastoyanov hr_karast@hotmail.com
Sent: Wednesday, July 24, 2013 23:10:13 EEST
Subject: Re: Mila Geo Mileva

My dear friend Karastoyanov,

Mila Geo Mileva-Keranova died on March 10, 1969. This is what it says in the obituary we have at the museum. I have no idea why the people inside that Internet don't know this.

As far as where she resided following Geo's death . . . in different apartments throughout Sofia. They moved frequently. She provided for her children alone, tutoring rich people's kids in four different western languages; she also worked on translations constantly.

After Geo Milev's disappearance, she began to work at the traveling theater of Nikola Ikonomov, who had been the best man at their wedding. It is how she was able to support her family. She hired a woman to take care of the children. In 1927, she went to work for her brother, Dimitar Keranov's troupe, where she joined a theater tour of Northern Bulgaria as the lead actress. However, the children were about to start school, and I am sure you can understand how Grandpa Milyo must have looked upon his daughter-in-law being written about in the papers for the types of roles she was taking . . . So Mila made the categorical decision to end her artistic career and to support her family from then on doing what I described above.

As to her personality, I have heard about it through her daughter, Leda. According to her, her mother was an incredible optimist. Unflinching. She'd laugh, recounting a story about the three of them renting an apartment from an affluent Jewish landlord. One day, he knocked on their door. Leda and her sister Bistra were by themselves, as their mother was away giving a lesson. The landlord politely informed them that their mother had not paid rent in two months and announced he'd give them until that evening to pay up—but no more than that.

"When Mom got home, we told her what had happened with sinking hearts," said Leda. "She only laughed and said 'There's a lot of time until tonight! We'll come up with something.' And she did! At dusk, she grabbed me by the hand and took me to the landlord's apartment. He let us in, and offered us coffee and chocolates right away. He was apprehensive as he began to speak, but Mom interrupted him. She said she was here to ask for a big favor. The landlord leapt to his feet, 'Of course, anything!' Mom explained that she had temporary financial difficulties, but was awaiting payment on her lessons. She asked him for a short-term loan, if possible. She even mentioned the exact sum she needed—one hundred leva. But, Madam, of course, he jumped from his chair again and pulled a drawer then counted several large bills and gave them to Mom. She took the money, counted a few back to him and told him that this was the rent money. The rest she would return very soon. We sure did treat ourselves splendidly that night!"

At one point Mila agreed to look after her sister's daughter as well (her sister died young). Her brother-in-law, Ivan Radoslalov, was a weird type; he lived in Plovdiv, where he worked as the library director, leaving his daughter alone in Sofia. Mila took her in and the girl lived with them for many years.

You should also be aware that before the Socialist Revolution of 1944, she harbored people on the run from the authorities without blinking an eye—anarchists, communists, agrarians. Who knows, maybe Mila had something of her mother's personality—her mother had been a highly energetic and lively woman, who loved to sing Russian romance songs, wonderfully, I might add, and had, at one point, been an actress; aside from that she was a socialist—not a communist, but a real socialist—which likely means she was a right-wing socialist.

Leda recounted that once, "Our mother asked us if we'd agree to take in a little girl to look after. She said they were giving a hundred and eighty leva for her. Mom reasoned that that way we'd help the girl and we wouldn't have to worry about food." So they became a kind of foster family to the little girl, and she grew up alongside Leda and Bistra, and Radoslavov's daughter like a sister. They paid for the girl's education and even threw her a wedding.

Now, comrade Karastoyanov, can you see why Geo Milev loved this wonderful and resolute woman, why Sheytanov trusted her, and why she in turn loved the former and remained in awe of the latter until her dying day? And if you only knew how stunningly beautiful she was, too . . .

An incredible lady she was, Mila Geo Mileva.

I leave you, and wish you good health!
Yanev

•

From: Hristo Karastoyanov hr_karast@hotmail.com
To: Georgi Yanev g_yanev_sz@abv.bg
Sent: Wednesday, July 24, 2013, 23:53:14 EEST
RE: Mila Geo Mileva

And so it is, Yanev, and so it is. We leave pale shadows of our former selves and we are forgotten by the ninth day. Shakespeare said it best:

> The evil that men do lives after them,
> The good is oft interrèd with their bones.

Thank you and I hope to see you soon!
Karastoyanov]

17.

[Thursday, July 25, 2013]

The Englishmen promised to relay his words verbatim, swearing not to use his name under any circumstances, but he only shrugged. He gifted each a booklet with his *poem* and saw them to the precipitous stairwell with its seventy-seven steps.

Markham stayed back and waited until the other three were already at the lower landing before admonishing the poet with a whisper. He was perhaps wrong to have spoken that way in front of the foreign gentlemen, and didn't he remember how Lyuben Karavelov had told the foreign journalists, "Bulgaria does not kill its people!" But the poet hissed back indignantly:

"Yes, of course, let them ignore us. Why don't we erect another silencing wall along the border to drown out our screams completely! Please don't give me advice I don't understand and even more, don't need."

Three days later, Wedgwood and his partners left Bulgaria, and as soon as they arrived in Vienna, the first thing they did was call a meeting with the journalists at the Hotel Sacher, that famous gathering spot for dynastic spawn of decaying empires, politicians, and international swindlers.

The hotel confectionary became a veritable babel—three weeks had barely passed since news flew around that a monstrous explosion had shaken Sofia's St. Nedelya Church, and news from the bloodied capital was still on all of the front pages of the newspapers in Europe.

Amid the din of the magnesium lamps and the buzz of the cameras, the MPs described their impressions of Bulgaria.

"There is no peace in Bulgaria," they said, "It is bloodshed. The victims are in the thousands," they said, "People in Bulgaria disappear without a trace. In Bulgaria," they said, "it is war."

The journalists leapt up, demanding to know if were they certain about what they were saying.

"What you are telling us is completely at odds with what your Prime Minister Baldwin said," they pressed on. "How can we be sure this isn't just the party line, that the subject of Bulgaria isn't just another reason for your leader Macdonald to squabble with Baldwin?"

The three replied that Baldwin would be judged by God, and that everything they were laying forth here they'd heard from a man they had no reason to distrust.

"And who is he?" the journalists demanded to know. "What does he do? Is he a communist?" they yelled. "Why won't you tell us who your source is? It's same as saying nothing at all! We've had enough of unidentified sources." They were screaming from all sides. "Give us a name!"

They yelled over each other until the MPs gave up.

"Our source," they said, "is neither a politician nor a communist. We heard all of the information from a Bulgarian poet . . ."

"The name, gentlemen, the name! No more melodramatics. We want the name."

It was then that Lieutenant Josiah Clement Wedgwood, bearer of the Order of Merit for his services to the army, distant grandson of Darwin according to the family's meandering genealogy, member of the king's secret council, opened his mouth and said:

"His name is Geo Milev!"

[Friday, July 26, 2013]

The newsmen jumped from their seats, dashed to the telephone and telegraph booths and frantically dictated what they'd just heard to the people in their editorial offices. That same afternoon, the name of the poet was already in all the evening papers as well as all the next day's early editions—from Vienna to Berlin and from Geneva to Paris.

[Saturday, July 27, 2013]

The news from Vienna reached Sofia like rolling thunder and infuriated Prime Minister Tsankov, as well as Minister Roussev, and Valkov, the other minister. In the ugly three-story edifice on the corner of Rakovski and Valkovich Streets, Tsankov hurled newspapers at their heads and screamed his head off—they'd only just managed to convince Europe and now this! How had they allowed such a thing to happen! In his office inside the National Assembly, Grigor Vasilev, the MP, was already writing an indignant letter to England, demanding to know whether the three men had been an official delegation or whether they'd visited Bulgaria as civilians, and was Lieutenant Wedgwood perhaps secretly a Bolshevik sympathizer, after all. One block over from the Council of Ministers, on 6th September Street, inside the Ministry of Interior, Chief Secretary Josef Razsoukanov was not about to stand on ceremony. He didn't mince words and pounced on the head of the police department, Skordev, and on that of Public Safety, Chemshirov, and they, in turn, got all of their subordinates up in arms—police guards, secret agents, everyone without exception—to seize any and all foreign newspapers they laid their eyes on, regardless of what newspaper it was or if it even contained anything about what the poet had said inside. Were they to spot a foreign alphabet—directly into the truck, and from there—directly into the furnaces beneath the Police Directorate!

Only thing was, they were too late: the people had already purchased their newspapers en masse.

And they all saw the poet's photograph, with his forelock of hair above his smashed-out eye, and they all read what he had told the Englishmen.

And the people whom it all concerned—*were never going to forget it* . . .

And so it was.

18.

[Tuesday, July 30, 2013]

Winter returned in March of twenty-five, after the short-lived, craven February spring. Snow fell again and the mothers put their babies in their strollers and headed out into the freezing cold to the Borisova Garden, because some new method to toughen up babies propagated by the government said they should do so: it was how the children would grow up to be strong Bulgarians.

Then came the endless rains.

[Saturday, August 3, 2013]

The last time they saw each other, at the end of April, the rain had seemingly stopped, the frigid, silver sun had seemingly begun to shine through from behind the clouds, even the tulips across the street in front of the bathhouse had blossomed, crimson and impatient, but at dusk, somewhere around the edges of Sofia, distant thunder grumbled yet again. It had all been too strange—as if some sort of bad presentiment weighed over the entire ostracized country that spring.

At that time, the poet's main worries centered on a labor of love—the anthology he was editing. He'd proposed the project to Philip Chipev right after the New Year, and Philip Chipev had been a man of his word. They arranged all the details in a flash—the size, the paper, the font, the honorariums—all of it. Metzger, efficient as ever, sketched the authors' portraits, as well as one of the editor himself—nineteen portraits all in all. They constructed the engraving plates and only two weeks later, and the presses started sometime at the end of January. They were mounting the last quire on the big machine when Chipev noticed that the poet had not included himself in the anthology. And as publisher, he'd given specific instructions that the poet include some of his own work—which is why he'd asked Metzger for a portrait. "What's happening?" he asked every other day. "Where is your work, Milev? The only reason I agreed to publish this anthology was to include your work!" The poet waved his hand—no problem. "My work is still in the queue, Chipev, don't worry about it." So it was. And when they did mount the last quire onto the press, and the poet's work was still nowhere to be seen, and Chipev again began to yell, "What are we doing? What are we doing?" the poet roared with laughter and replied that this was how it should have been done. It would be embarrassing for the editor of the anthology to parade his own work on the pages of the very anthology he was curating! Chipev yelled and screamed in protest, but to no avail—the big machine already rumbled and thundered . . .

[Wednesday, August 7, 2013]
[Would you look at that . . .

Daily horoscope: When you make plans for the future, keep in mind your past plays a very important role. Connect the two, and only then decide on the best way to go forward.

Jesus, the past plays a big role in your life, apparently.

Fuck your dumb horoscope!]

[Saturday, August 10, 2013]
The *Anthology of Bulgarian Poetry* was praised by many, but the big blow came from the least expected source—his own brother-in-law, Radoslavov, who took up an entire five-page spread in his magazine, *Hyperion*, to tear apart the work. He wrote that the collection was happenstance, unsystemic, politicized unnecessarily through the publicism apparent inside the authors' introductions. He wrote that the editor, Milev, likely hadn't even the slightest idea what a literary trend might even mean, since he'd introduced Peyo Yavorov as the founder of some European literature or other. To top it all off, his brother-in-law declared

the anthology a capriciously contrived collection. Collection! Not an anthology, but a collection. That part hurt him the most.

And the poet decided this person was dead to him. The man had rubbed salt into his wounds and he would cross him out of his life.

He thought of Hristo Botev's words:

"As if being all scabbed up wasn't enough for the donkey, now the flies wanted a piece of him, too."

But so be it.

[Sunday, August 11, 2013]

Sheytanov appeared in the late afternoon. He did not come in, he suggested the two of them go out and walk around a little bit, despite Mila's courteous protests that he so rarely graced them as a guest, that she had not seen him in so long, would he stay for a chat and so on—and the two exited the gloomy red and brown building on Maria Louisa Boulevard.

[Friday, August 30, 2013]

They crossed Banski Square, continued on Turgovska, turned on Dondoukov, and ended up going into Rosa—situated right across from Chipev's old bookstore. The streets were nearly desolate, but that didn't keep them from running into three separate patrols, whose cops had looked them up and down probingly. As they walked, the poet recounted that on the previous day he'd given a lecture inside the university's largest auditorium, the one at 145 Tetevenska Street: some young people from the neophilological association had invited him to speak, and even arranged for an honorarium. They charged students and school-children three leva, city residents five leva, and although they never paid honorariums, made an exception for him.

"They must know of my dire straights, the silly fools," he snorted contently. "But never mind that, I didn't refuse, obviously."

The students wanted a lecture on *The Art of Poetry* by Boileau, so he gave them one. He could speak on any subject, why not? They'd all loved it, and how could they not, all of their professors gave their lectures in

French, while he spoke in Bulgarian. At the end, the treasury secretary counted out two hundred fifty leva for him.

"That's why today, it's on me!"

He added that the day after tomorrow he was going to Kazanluk to speak in "Iskra" on Russian poetry; they'd promised to pay him a fee there as well, so Sheytanov shouldn't worry about him. Then he triumphantly pushed open the door to the confectionary.

[Saturday, August 31, 2013]

It was far too quiet for this hour inside the confectionary, a place one could barely find a seat otherwise. They climbed the steps into the gallery—the poet led the way and affected a confident swagger, but Sheytanov saw his foot searching for the step. The poet's good eye was dimming ever so quickly and Sheytanov knew it.

They sat at a small marble table, ordered, and tried making small talk, but the conversation felt awkward. The poet was tense and absentminded and Sheytanov understood why: *Plamuk* had been halted immediately after its January issue, and although the last booklet of the previous year contained an advert and call for submissions for a new magazine—*Zhar*—the eponymous *ember* never did catch fire . . .

[NB! In reality, the whole thing had been far messier. October's double issue contained an editor's note from the poet stating that all queries from subscribers as to the future of the magazine were baseless—the magazine had not halted publication, nor was it, thank God, terminated by the authorities. "The publication," it was written, "is absolutely guaranteed to come out!" "*Plamuk*," it said, "will continue to come out next year; and we can guarantee the following: it will do so with absolute punctuality and regularity, with no dependence whatsoever on the whims of printing shops or other "rogue agents."

It was this issue in particular that was even more fiercely confiscated down to the last one.

Because it contained the *poem*.

The issue that followed, now in December, had the following note, clear and imperturbable, on the back cover: "*Plamuk* will cease publication."

What would there be to be happy about?]

The poet lost it. He didn't yell, he didn't slap the marble on the table, but Sheytanov knew him so well that as soon as he saw the poet's upper lip start to quiver—that otherwise imperceptible tic—it was a surefire sign his mercurial ire was about to rise. Indeed, the poet suddenly grunted. Why was everyone all up in arms over "The people this, and the people that!"—who, exactly, were "the people"? A pitiful handful of do-gooders, an absolutely indiscernible minority drowning in milquetoasts and bastards.

Sheytanov refrained from interrupting; he let the poet go on. Here we were, almost half a century after Bulgaria was seemingly liberated from the Turks, out of the Yoke—five hundred years of slavery—yet the slave remained a slave. And if you robed the slave in power, the only thing he was capable of doing was committing outrages over others.

"Did we not see all too clearly what the slave is capable of in these last four years, did we not see what the slave could do when you hand him a bat? Goddamn it," he said, "in the end, it will be the slave inside our souls who proves ineradicable."

The poet recalled the long, painful conversations with his father from before the wars, when he feverishly contended that a people is something pure and bright, something pristine and angelic, but his father mournfully challenged him, was Gocho Kuymuyra pure, pristine, and angelic? At first the poet had no idea who the old man was talking about, but one evening before he set off for the military academy in Kniajevo, his father finally told him the story . . .

"And now allow me to retell this very same story, Sheytanov," said the poet while they sat in Rosa. "The Russians got to Stara Zagora sometime around July tenth, eighteen eighty-seven. But Suleiman wasn't to return until the nineteenth! Hence, between the eleventh and the eighteenth of July, the Bulgarians ruled, just as people like Hristo Botev had long dreamed of. But here's what happens. Someone named Gocho Kuymuyra is made a guard. And this Gocho, this *Kuymuyr*, is then given a gun. He takes his gun, and he goes to the house of some higher-ranking Turkish guy. And he tells him something to the effect of, 'They're asking for you at the tent!' The Russians' marquee, in other words. Our Gocho takes the poor man, makes him turn down some crooked street, and kills him. Then he goes back for another. Liberty, right? Down with Turkey, right? There you have it. Take that, Turkey!"

He emptied the last of the vermouth down his throat and pointed his empty glass toward the waiter.

"My father always wondered," he went on, irately. "Wasn't the old Slaveykov—Pencho's dad—in the city administration, did he really not have any idea what these Kuymuyri were doing?"

He went quiet for a beat.

"Come to think of it, I'm not sure he was wondering. Not at all."

[Monday, September 2, 2013]

His father had then told him about Nanuy Dimitrov, too. This Nanuy was a teacher at the time, a well-read man, knew a bit of Russian, so they made him a translator at the Russian état-major in Gabrovo. The Russians had just destroyed Veissel Pasha in the battle at Sheinovo, and took his entire central army as prisoners—three pashas, countless European-educated officers, and twenty-two thousand soldiers. It was then the Russian generals Fyodor Radetzky, Sviatopolk-Mirsky, and Mikhail Skobelev himself sat down and decided that this unprecedented number of war prisoners must be sent to Russia. They call Veissel and his entire staff and tell him all this, and Veissel just mournfully nods. Then he asks if the hostages could be officially convoyed by Russian soldiers on their long trip to Russia, because he knew what would await them, had they given them over to

[Tuesday, September 3, 2013]
the Bulgarian army volunteers.

And Nanuy the translator kept on translating and translating.

What did he end up translating, you might ask? He *translated*—very convincingly—that the Turks *wanted to be convoyed by the Bulgarians*, because the Bulgarians knew Turkish and this way, the captured soldiers would be alleviated on their long journey into exile. The Russians just shrugged and said, whatever Veissel Pasha wants, Veissel Pasha gets. And they turned all those thousands and thousands of poor souls over to the Bulgarians.

On that January day the endless column of men lined up to embark from the snow-covered Gabrovo, Nanuy came out to watch the Turks take off for Siberia. The poor wretches now saw all too clearly what would ensue; many officers were already crying, and Nanuy watched in horror as one of them pointed directly at him.

Years and years later, this same Nanuy told the poet's father that he could never forgive himself this heinous deed and he wasn't even sure how he was going to answer to God, and Milyo Kassabov then in turn hollowly explained to the poet that Nanyo was right to agonize over his soul: before they'd even reached Turnovo, just forty-five kilometers from Gabrovo, the road was already paved with the corpses of the Turkish soldiers; by the time they reached Russia, only half remained, even as little as a third . . . "This is what you can expect," his father had said, "from that slave, the Bulgarian."

[Wednesday, September 4, 2013]
"That's what you can expect," the poet repeated, "from that slave, the Bulgarian."

"You know," Sheytanov spoke emptily, "what I find to be the most repulsive part of that law to be? It's obscurantist, it's fascist, it's all of that. But for me, the most horrifying part of that law is that it is a dishonorable law. It's antihuman, my brother."

"Joseph Herbst calls it *dissolute*," the poet added.

"It's all the same," Sheytanov sighed. "You know better than anyone, and you just said it yourself: Bulgaria's Law for the Protection of the Nation is contingent upon the slave mentality of the Bulgarian. It isn't even that dependent on guns as much as it relies on our servile little souls. The first ever law to egg on earwigging. Anyone who might be aware of a premeditated, imminent criminal action breaking this law, and does not inform the authorities . . ."

". . . will be punished with solitary confinement," the poet finished the sentence. "From the new article, Article 18. Lest I forget."

"I know you know it," Sheytanov nodded. "Never mind the fact anyone can just point you out to any random cop on the street."

"That too!" the poet grumbled again. "Any member of a pack who turns himself in before any planned criminal activity, and also turns in his accomplices and points to their whereabouts, can walk! To hell with this piece of shit law."

"Curse all you want, it is what it is," Sheytanov added, even more emptily than before. "A law to make brothers eye each other with suspicion, a father to rat out his son. . ."

". . . is a law that might as well announce the Bulgarian is ready to be a slave once more!" the poet concluded. "I know this too."

He started to light up yet again, but the lit matchstick in his hand kept missing the cigarette.

"I know you know," Sheytanov agreed again. "But the worst part is, this law is now a precedent. From here on out, whatever happens in this country, each successive repressive law will persecute non-informants. Mark my words! Anyone who comes into power will by any means necessary punish non-informing as a crime against the nation."

They looked out toward the deserted boulevard, where only the trams swung back and forth either west toward St. Nedelya Church, or back east toward Ferdinand, and the poet suddenly remembered how two months earlier, right in the middle of the day, just a few streets over—right outside 17 Dondoukov street, which was right across from the First Men's Academy—they had assassinated Nikola Milev. The poet had gone to see the ordeal with his own eyes, but by the time he arrived at the scene, the stretcher-bearers had taken the body away. Only the blood still remained on the pavement, making the boulevard seem even grimier than other days. And even the iced-over puddles had been turbid and pink that Wednesday.

He couldn't resist asking Sheytanov whether he'd heard of the story, and who may have taken it upon himself to kill the professor.

"Some are saying one thing, others another . . . what have you heard?"

Sheytanov stood quiet for a second then answered nonchalantly:

"I haven't heard anything," he shrugged. "Zhelyo shot him. Zhelyo Grozev. You ought to remember him. I introduced you once."

"And you're telling me this like it's no big deal?" the poet was amazed.

"Why?" Sheytanov asked dryly. "You don't feel sorry for that piece of shit, do you?"

The poet did not mourn Nikola Milev in the least—he'd had far too many headaches courtesy of the man's newspaper to pity him in the end—but he'd been stunned by the nonchalance with which Sheytanov had dropped the information on him, as though the murder were nothing but a fact of life.

Sheytanov gestured dismissively with his hand and recounted having gone to the university with Zhelyo to hear one of Nikola Milev's lectures. The two were quite eager to hear what he had say to the students, this same man who—regardless of his position as chair of the Union of Bulgarian Journalists—stood as the real inspirator of a law whose sections, letters, and subparagraphs dripped with blood. They heard exactly what they thought they would hear. "Dear students," the professor had said from the podium, "colleagues! The anarchists in this country, as you know, are scoundrels and criminals. And such people ought to be exterminated like rabid dogs!" He put it in those words, more or less. The students sat in guilty silence, but Sheytanov and Zhelyo just looked at each other and later intercepted the professor right outside the high school. Milev, of course, was flanked by security on orders directly from Minister Roussev, and the two bodyguards strode respectfully two steps behind him. Zhelyo and Sheytanov stopped Milev, and Sheytanov greeted the professor and informed him the two had just been at his brilliant lecture . . . "Yes, and?" the other said, while his two bodyguards seemed at a loss for what to do: Zhelyo and Sheytanov were elegantly dressed, well put together, speaking politely to the professor . . . they could neither intervene, nor stay away.

"And so," Sheytanov shrugged, "I said to him, 'We just listened to what you said to the students—that anarchists should be exterminated like dogs.' The man felt we were up to something and looked over at his security detail, who were startled and reached for their holsters, but I went on, ever so politely, 'Well, isn't it strange, dear professor, that you call anarchists rabid dogs, just as the late Stamboliyski did. Correct me if I'm wrong, but wasn't Stamboliyski your mortal enemy? Would you be so kind as to clarify for us, professor, which of you, exactly, borrowed the political term of endearment from whom?' But before I even finished the sentence, Zhelyo had already shot him in the head and I took care of the two guards. And that was that."

On the boulevard outside, a red tram passed with a consumptive rattle, strewing sparks into the descending Sofia dusk, and Café Rosa's vitrines and the chandelier above both men's heads clinked quietly.

"All this, right on Friday the thirteenth," the poet spoke up, "and they tell me not to believe old wives' tales . . ."

He suddenly came alive and waved his hand in the direction of the bored-looking waiter.

"I'll take some *boza* and something sweet for the kids!" he said.

He then grinned heroically and added:

"And ten crème caramels for me."

[Thursday, September 5, 2013]

They went in opposite directions. The poet took Turgovska Street back, with a paper bag in one hand and the bottle of *boza* in the other. He strode with impatience, thinking the kids were likely in bed by now and he and Mila could devote themselves to doing that which would bring his wife to that blessed, regally glowing state borne out of the new life growing inside of her. And he did not doubt, not for a second, that this new life *would be a boy.*

When he'd first met her, he hadn't dared make an advance for a long while—even during all those months in that field hospital in Cecilienhaus in Germany, crammed with those excoriated unfortunates. He'd been such a savage in his passion that even on their wedding night on June thirteenth, nineteen nineteen, he'd jumped on her like a young soldier inside their tiny apartment at 14 Tsar Samuil Street, so that nine months later, Leda would be born—just as God and nature had intended.

Mila had gradually taught him to appreciate the prolonged sweetness of these things.

[Friday, September 6, 2013]
Sheytanov, in turn, took off along the quieted Dondukov Street, turned on Stara Planina, and went straight to see Anton Strashimirov.

[Sunday, September 8, 2013]
He found him just as he'd always been—with his gray coat thrown over his always-cold shoulders, slouched over his table with its green lamp and the books, with the scattered notebooks, white sheets, chewed up pencils, and that same obituary, which read, *"They've killed my brother, Todor! May God save us all!"* The only difference was that now, his pugnacious Don Quixote beard hung bedraggled and crestfallen. He was a little over fifty, but he already looked befallen by a premature old age, his blue soldier's eyes paling.

He was happy to see Sheytanov for a second, but his face quickly turned anxious, and he warned him something awful was coming, that he ought to get out.

"Look, Georgi," Strashimirov said, "You're a man held in high regard. Run and save yourself!"

"Run from where, Bai Anton?" he laughed. "Do I look like someone who runs?"

"Don't laugh, boy!" Strashimirov scolded him. "Now is not the time for laughter and heroic ballads. Get out of Bulgaria! You've crossed the border illegally so many times anyway. Here's ten thousand leva, run and save yourself, my boy!"

"Bai Anton," Sheytanov suddenly became serious. "I appreciate the gesture, but I don't want anything. I'm not leaving. It's a little late for me to become a deserter, don't you think?"

Strashimirov let out a slow, heavy sigh and shook his head for a long time.

[Sunday evening, September 8, 2013]
[Who can say if that's how it happened? But I imagine it did indeed happen so.]

[Monday, September 9, 2013]
[NB! Before I forget. This is important: When Geshev officially begins working for the police in May, Bulgaria's Law for the Protection of the Nation has already been amended twice—once on March sixteenth and again on April twenty-ninth; a little bit later, on July fourth, the Law for Administration and Police is passed. The Police Directorate is erected during that time, built on the Austrian model and under the expert guidance of General Edmund Heidenfeldt of the Viennese gendarmerie. Dogs are brought in—again from Austria, directly from the Vienna police factory—and their trainers educated in their craft. Somebody named Yordan Petrov Schwartz (I couldn't find him anywhere), was, in turn, in charge of the trainers.

Now everything's new, modern, and European.

So be it . . .

It is also somewhere around this time that Geo Milev is murdered.]

[Tuesday, September 10, 2013]

MAN ON A WIRE

A short interlude

. . . Meanwhile, a tightrope walker had arrived in Bulgaria from Sicily, Montagnani someone or other, Giorgio, or something of the sort—renowned in all of Europe, a man invited, as *Dnevnik* and *Utro* detailed, to the court of none other than George V himself, king of England, and so forth. The flashing chrome and bronze and the gleam of the Hispano-Suiza's black paint, with its stork figurine mid-flight atop its grill—trailed by two mottled trucks, carrying the gear for his dangerous art—traveled from city to city, and his dexterous workers erected the pylons with their circus-like red flags, together with the blue and yellow streamers, pulling the rope tightly across the market squares where he walked high above people's heads, once at ten in the morning—for the kids, students, and the soldiers, and twice more in the afternoon—for the remaining fawners.

He traveled with those same caravans, making the rounds at all the spring fairgrounds under the blue skies of that splendid May. Just like Signor Montagnani, they too unpacked their giant drays, unloaded their lorries, and raised their tents up at the empty places around the markets and hung their colorful signs, and the whole town echoed from the clangor and the children's enthusiastic commotion. There were fire-eaters, Indian wizards, shooting galleries called "William Tell" and "Good Aim," walnut trees festooned with garlands and targets enticing players with a promise of "A bonbon from Mimi," two tough guys riding their motorcycles around inside a giant wooden barrel, causing an even louder roar—once from the bikes, and again from the creaking of the wood. There were wax-work exhibitions and large jars where dead calves with two heads swam in formalin, there were mysterious species of fish and snakes and turtles and unborn fetuses, there were zoo corners with black

Malayan Sun bears, Siberian wolves with blue eyes, monkeys, and tiny lazy crocodiles, a lion, by turns molting or well-groomed, and finally, in some other tent—the obligatory woman born to a human mother and an orangutan father. The fire-eaters and Indian wizards were nothing more than ordinary Bulgarians, of course, with turbans on their heads; the woman begotten by a Siamese monkey sang a melancholy song of her mother's travels on a steamboat, and that same steamboat's unfortunate sinking by the banks of distant Asia and the horrible death and mass drowning that ensued, but it was her mother—the sole survivor—who somehow escaped, only to be captured in the jungle by the orangutan . . . and who knows why, but the song the woman mumbled in that sweaty tent was in Bulgarian.

But moving on.

The red placard announcing this same Montagnani featured a rope with the tightrope walker himself sitting on it—this had been his trademark party trick: to sit cross-legged on the rope, the long stick resting on his lap, pretending to smoke a chibouk while two Italian ladies below, head to toe in sequins and lace, yelled up "Ole!" The photo was headlined: "*Sir Montagnani, the king of the tightrope!*"

Geo Milev was really impressed by the placard. One afternoon, as he made his way back from one of the printers, he couldn't contain himself: he carefully ripped the poster off someone's fence somewhere along Dondoukov Street and brought it back home, where he carefully pinned it to the door with four thumb-tacks, taped a piece of paper over the name of the Italian circus performer, put a dash after "the king," and another little piece of paper over "tight," so that it now read: "*King on a rope!*"

He admired his work and called Mila and the children to see it too. Leda and Bistra loved it, but Mila didn't.

"Wait, wait a second," he said, "What better advertisement for the government! 'King on a rope!' It's funny!"

Mila didn't feel like laughing. She looked around at the other doors on the floor—they all had eyelets or small windows in the middle and may as well have been watchtowers—and she only shrugged.

"Oh, come on!" Geo Milev groaned, affecting disappointment. "You just don't get the joke!"

He guffawed, reached over and pushed her glasses down her nose like a schoolboy.

The kids snickered, Leda immediately launched into *"Babo dear, Babo sweet,"* Bistra fell over laughing, but Mila again failed to see the humor.

19.

[Wednesday, September 11, 2013]
[This, I didn't know.

The Trial of Viktor Jara's Killer

The former officer from General Pinochet's junta—Pedro Pablo Barrientos—will face criminal charges in Florida for the torture and murder of singer Victor Jara in 1973. Victor Jara, then forty, was a member of the communist party and one of the most popular protest-song performers in Latin America. He was arrested by the junta after the coup of the eleventh of September, 1973, together with thousands of students from the Santiago University of Technical, where he taught. They were then taken to the main stadium, held captive, tortured, and murdered by soldiers from the junta. Today this same stadium bears the name of Victor Jara.

The criminal trial against a former officer of Pinochet's army—Lieutenant Pedro Pablo Barrientos—began on the eve of the tragic forty-year anniversary of the bloody military coup in Chile. The claim was filed on September fourth at the Center for Justice and Accountability in San Francisco by Victor Jara's widow, Joan, and their children. They were adamant that the regional courts in Jacksonville convict the sixty-four-year-old Barrientos—an American citizen since 1989. The claim pointed to the fact that Victor Jara's killer, residing in Daytona, Florida, should be subject to criminal investigation in compliance with the articles set forth in the Torture Victim Protection Act of 1991. In December of last year (2012), the Chilean court charged Barrientos and another officer from the junta—Hugo Sanchez—with the murder of the Chilean singer. Six more soldiers and officers from the junta were named as defendants in the same suit.

After Pinochet's military regime ended, out of fear of retribution, Barrientos decided to hide from the authorities by running away to the United States. Last year, a team of investigative journalists from Chile managed to track down Victor Jara's killer in Daytona. But Barrientos adamantly denied being responsible for Jara's death, or that he was even present inside Santiago's stadium during the mass killings of Salvador Allende's supporters. However, testimony by Barriento's former soldiers unequivocally proved his guilt. One such subordinate—Jose Paredes— testified that Lieutenant Barrientos and other junta officers personally tortured Victor Jara, and more than once and alongside other captives, beat him unconscious. "I personally saw Lieutenant Barrientos take out his gun, spin the cylinder, release the safety, and step toward Victor Jara, who was sitting on the grass with his arms tied behind his back. He then shot Jara point blank, and the other officers followed suit. Victor Jara slid face down onto the grass, dead, entirely covered in blood."

Although the Chilean Supreme Court gave a judge the power of attorney to ask for Barrientos's extradition from the United States in January of this year, the Chilean government has yet to send an official letter to the relevant American agencies. According to the Chilean foreign ministry, the reason for the delay was purely technical: the translation of the documents accompanying the trial—543 pages in all—simply hadn't yet been completed.

After Victor Jara's murder, his wife Joan Jara—a British dancer—left the country together with their two daughters. She did not return to Chile until 2001, intent on finding justice and retribution for the death of her husband and the other victims of Pinochet's junta. Joan Jara filed suit, asking that Lieutenant Barrientos and his accomplices be held responsible for the 1973 murder. Over the next 35 years, the case was repeatedly delayed, dragged out, dismissed, and renewed.

In 2009, Victor Jara's remains were exhumed because of the pending medicolegal investigation and reburied, while the details surrounding his murder have been painstakingly pieced together over several decades from the testimonies of dozens of witnesses.

The prosecution's case against Pedro Barrientos now states he must claim responsibility for a number of crimes, including torture, execution without trial or conviction, cruel and unusual treatment of prisoners, holding people captive against their will, and crimes against humanity. Joan Jara is unequivocal in her petition that she is looking only for justice for her husband's killers, not financial gain. "No money can ever make up for the pain and suffering caused to Victor Jara. I have personally lived two lives, one before 1973 and one after."

Hmm, well, at least one other statistic is widely known: "Officially, the number of those disappeared without a trace is three thousand one hundred ninety-seven people. In the period between nineteen seventy-three and nineteen ninety, between one hundred fifty thousand and two hundred thousand people went through camps and prisons, and the number of those killed reached nearly ten thousand . . ."

"In the year two thousand, Pinochet was named in over two hundred criminal lawsuits involving mass killings, kidnappings, and cruelty to prisoners. Every one of them is deferred, citing senility."]

[And so it goes . . .
 Everyone gets away with it!
 That's how it works. Time flies and it turns wildly in the night.
 Think about it.]

[One can't help but wonder, why I remember *that* September eleventh—and I really do—I was in the library.

Two years later, I saw Joan Jara. She was surrounded by the Young Communists, who wouldn't let anyone get near her. They only showed her face in press conferences.

I remember April twenty-fifth, nineteen seventy-four, too, goddamn it!

At the same time I'd seen Joan Jara, I also saw singer José Afonso. The Young Communists guarded him like a president, too, but they must have lost track of him one day, because I ran into him inside the courtyard of the Rila Monastery and we quietly sang that song of his, "Grândola, Vila Morena," which had sparked everything in Portugal. José Afonso died in Setubal in nineteen eighty-seven. He was fifty-seven years old.

Coups, putsches, revolutions, carnations . . .

And so be it.]

[Thursday, September 26, 2013]
[Suddenly, fall has come. Yesterday, the first fog settled and now the first September rain is falling. That's how it'll be. The days are so long, yet the years fly by. And while you're wondering when goddamned Wednesday will become Friday, a new year has already begun.]

20.

[*Friday, September 27, 2013*]

On January fifteenth, nineteen twenty-five, the poet hosted a gathering for his friends: he was turning thirty. A lot of people came and somehow they all managed to fit inside his office—two to a chair and knee to knee on the couch. Behind the windows, the beautiful falling snow resembled a meshwork painting, the city had quieted and cozied, and the air inside was fragranced by winter wine and the smoke curling from the sizzling *sujuk* Mila was frying up on the stove in the kitchen. Leda and Bistra puttered about, their flowy, taffeta dresses rustling, which their mother had purchased after a long haggle with a reseller. A neat pile of freshly printed, still-warm issues of *Plamuk* sat on the shelf, a proud "Year II" on the cover and the start of the poem "Hell" . . .

[. . . Whose ending on page nine declared there would be eight more circles of suffering—seven deadly sins and eight infamous contemporary crimes. "Hell"—it said—is the first part of the trilogy DIVINE COMEDY: HELL—PURGATORY—HEAVEN."

And that's it.

What remains is silence.]

When everyone's glasses were full, the poet stood up and roared:

"Dear convivial folk! You shall now be quiet, because I have a very important message. I," he said, "am turning thirty years old! I can hardly believe it. From here on out," he declared celebratorily, "I will count each successive year as a gift from God Himself! If He gives me fifty more—I'll take it! If he gives me a hundred—I'll take that! I'll take whatever I can get. I won't be nitpicky with Him. In that vein, *nazdrave!*"

"*Nazdrave!*" everybody yelled. "You're going to live forever!"

[For his birthday, the poet got decked out in a suit made of that same terrible plaid fabric everybody called "commissary" because it was given to poor people for stamps by the provision commissaries.]

[Saturday, September 28, 2013]

Not ten days later, he was arrested.

The examining magistrate assigned him to house arrest and monetary bail of five thousand leva, and Mila had immediately thought, "My God, it's all beginning."

At dusk, Sheytanov brought her the money (ten pitiful, violet bills depicting the Varna port).

Mila looked at him, frightened. He told her there was nothing to worry about, but he didn't believe his own words.

[Five]

ще преувелича, ако Ви призная да Ви,
че мъката ми за Гео щеше да загуби
много от горчивината си, ако Г. Ш. Беше
останал жив.

*"It would not be an overstatement to admit my agony
over Geo would be far less bitter
had G. Sheytanov remained alive."*

—From the letter Mila Geo Mileva
penned to Dr. Konstantin Kantarev

[Friday, September 27, 2013]

. . . Nikola Geshev was clear where he stood on Death: he spited her. He thought her something wholly superfluous and bad for business. She was, of course, a necessary evil, but he couldn't understand why you should have to cut off the chicken's head right away when this same chicken could one day lay you golden eggs. Death was useless. That's why he felt the aversion he did for the anarchists. The communists he could handle, the social democrats weren't a problem, the fascists were still wet behind the years—not sure if they wanted to fuck or piss. They weren't in the way, either.

But the anarchists, they crawled on his damn nerves and he couldn't get a wink of sleep at night because of them. They got under his skin—he could never understand why they wouldn't simply give up like everyone else! Were they just too full of pride, or were they simply the worthless offspring this new tribe of anarchism-worshippers had spawned—that's what he couldn't understand. They got in your face, they fought with boundless impertinence, and at the end they split—if they even got that far—and if not, they shoved the barrel down their own damn throats.

He hadn't yet been hired by the criminal pursuit agency, when, right on Three Kings' Day, the nineteenth of January, in the Dolni Lozenets neighborhood, which half of the town still referred to as *Kurubaglar,* the police got hold of some anarchists. As soon as he heard the news, Geshev locked up his dusty chancery at the housing commission with lightning speed and jumped on the tram heading in that direction. He saw what went down and would remember it with real despair—it had been a

217

true battle. The police and gendarmerie shot up the building for several hours, but the guys inside wouldn't give up and that was that. Late in the afternoon, the police were left with no choice but to call for help from the army. The army! For help! And it was then Geshev witnessed how the military folk drove up with several small trench mortars and started to shoot up the house with cannons! They disemboweled the structure almost entirely—if you looked through the windows you'd see the sky. When even the cannonade wasn't enough, they brought in the fire trucks. And they lit the whole place on fire. The flames twisted around the walls, licked the eaves and then vehemently swallowed everything, all the while the guys inside shot back relentlessly. In the end, a second before the beams collapsed amid sparks and thunderous creaking, in that scarlet January night, the following tortured and sorrowful, yet proud curse echoed through the fire: "Fuck you, you fucking murderers!" they yelled from the inside, "Catch our dicks, if you can! Roast us, you fascist fuckers!" The house was then eviscerated, the roof collapsed and buried them under the heavy blustering flames, and their vile curse was the last and only thing the military, the police, and anyone else within earshot would ever hear from them. A few soldiers then entered the smoldering structure and dragged out the tattered and seared bodies, and it was then it became clear the entire epic battle was fought by just two men. Just two! Two men with toothy grins and staggeringly short and wrinkled corpses. The soldiers leaned the dead bodies up against a cannon and the journalists buzzed around taking pictures in the beam of the headlights. Geshev grabbed one such journalist (the one who snapped away most feverishly with his flash) by the collar of his overcoat and hissed: "Stop photographing, you moron! What are you photographing, the nation's shame? Get the hell out of here before I break the camera on your head, dickwad." The other's tail curled between his legs and he ran off, but despite that, it was all the papers wrote about in the following days, and it was precisely from the papers that Geshev found out who the men had been—the until-then uncatchable duo from the *Heroes of the Night*—Stefan Efito and Hristo Baeto, one twenty-six, and the other not yet twenty-two. And that was that. "I'm surprised they didn't call an airplane to drop a couple bombs on them," he said to himself.

The year had started off badly, very badly. Next to the comparably calmer nineteen twenty-four, it now appeared that

[NB: No, I must have something wrong here. Nineteen twenty-four was far from calm. It may have been calm for everyone else, but not for the anarchists.

I better keep the following in mind:

THE BLOODY FACE-OFF WITH
THE ANARCHISTS IN THE CAPITAL

This past Sunday night, acting on information it was to host a gathering of anarchists, the Sofia police ambushed the residence belonging to one Al. Kotev, a postal worker, situated on the corner of Dorostopol and St. Ivan Rilski Streets. The following morning, a Monday, police officers attempted to enter the building to perform a search of the property, but were met with gunfire, which wounded the superintendent of the third precinct, Zahari Georgiev, and two officers—Ts. Popetsov and G. Markov. The house was then surrounded by army troops, and gunfire was exchanged between the officers and the anarchists; the latter did not cease fire. Soon the house was engulfed in flames and the anarchists continued to shoot and to throw bombs at the police, all the while singing through the flames, 'Volga, Volga, our Birth Mother.' An agent from Public Safety, Dimiter Zhdrebev of Kyustendil, attempted to enter the premises and to capture the anarchists, but he was killed with a shot to the heart. Velko Andreev was another fallen officer. In the afternoon, the burnt corpses of three of the anarchists were pulled from the wreckage.

The dead anarchists were Georgi Todorov from Pazardjik
and Popeto, the first was killed by a bomb, and the second
had shot himself.

Illustrated Week, February 1924.

Take away the field artillery, and everything else repeats. It wouldn't be
faithful to the truth if Geshev hadn't felt the déjà vu!]

something was brewing. January had not yet ended when Geshev opened
Utro and read that a law student named Yankulov, an anarchist, of course,
young just like Baeto and Efito, had, quite impertinently, arrived in
Turnovo to defend those arrested in connection with the Kilifarevo
revolt. An agent from Public Safety followed him and arrested him. The
other seemingly went along with the agent, but on the way down to the
station, right in front of the Agrarian Bank, Yankulov took out his gun,
shot into the air, and attempted to ineptly run away.

The agent rolled under a horse carriage, another cop slipped inside
a shop and hid behind the piles of goods, a sergeant major ostensibly
pulled out his sword, but he too took to his heels . . . it wasn't until
Yankulov got to the county court that he was actually surrounded by
officers and soldiers. He opened fire. They responded. He shot. They
shot. Finally they got him. They took his identification and his gun and
the four wads of cash in his pocket along with his other gun. "Heroes!"
Geshev cursed out loud in his tiny, dusty little chancery, nearly chewing
the paper with his teeth. "Fuck your mother and your heroics! A single
person makes a mockery out of you, you fucking fags!"

February had barely begun when a pack of anarchists entered from
Serbia, assaulting Godech, and then pulled back, giving up not one of
their men. And so it was . . .

Later, when he was already at Public Safety, Geshev desperately wanted
to catch even one of them, just one anarchist. Had he caught one—the
rest would be easy. But he never had such luck. Anytime they found
them, the anarchists fought back like beasts, and if they didn't kill them

in the endless gunfire—they'd blow out their own brains. It was as though Death had been a preferable, more amicable place than being detained and going to prison.

That's what he couldn't understand!

That is why his hatred for them was vast: because with just one shot to their own head, they managed to escape.

The police, the army, the gendarmerie—they were good at what they did, no doubt. Just like the gangsters in America: shoot first, ask questions later. Geshev was beside himself any time he opened a paper and saw yet another photograph of a dead anarchist, sprawled on the cobbles of some square, with his shirt rolled up and his trousers pulled down, mouth gaping. "Bravo!" he hissed through clenched teeth. "Scrubbed him clean, didn't you. Now how'll you question him! He'll tell you everything, without a doubt! You dumb moron," he said to himself, "gas him up, put him to sleep, get his head spinning, and then capture him like a normal person." He wasn't sure which headline got him more roiled up: "The Escape of the Brave Anarchist" or "Anarchists Killed in Lozenets."

He resented the praise directed at the police for their killing of yet more anarchists, and he called it *cuntish*. Secretly he gloated when they shot down Nikola Milev: that vindictive poser got under his skin with his nonstop blabbing that the anarchists had to be exterminated like rabid curs. The guy was carried on everyone's shoulders and everyone walked on eggshells around him; he was even being groomed to become a plenipotentiary minister in Washington—just to hide him away somewhere far off, Geshev thought. They'd elected him member of the United Franco-Masonic Grand Lodge of Bulgaria, so his friends from the Lodge (the government was already crawling with them) got him twenty-four hour security detail, on which Minister Roussev—himself a mason as well, naturally!—had immediately signed off. There was not a single second day or night in which there weren't at least two armed policemen near him. And what of all of this? They had still gunned him down in the middle of the capital, in the middle of the day. On Friday, the thirteenth, no less.

What did Geshev think? That it served him right!

[The evening of Friday, September 27, 2013]
He fell into such deep desperation at times that he'd barge into any one of the many underground brothels and grab the first available whore: he would take her upstairs into the room where he practically tore her insides apart with the inconsolable rage of the ignored, while the other women on the floor couldn't figure out whether the wails drifting out of that room, and even into the downstairs, were screams of passion or of agony and terror. What he did had little to do with consummating relations—it was an act of hostility, a massacre. The woman cut his face and his back with her nails, screaming she would turn him into the police and he'd only hiss back, "*I am* the police, you fucking whore." And he mercilessly poured his seed inside of her. He stopped going to the brothels once he had to visit Dr. Bogomil Beron's clinic, referred to as the *syphilis* clinic. He knew it would come to it sooner or later. Venereal disease was such an inconvenience; it'd become a real scourge after the wars and a good many folk moaned and groaned when they pissed. While he was in the clinic being infected with malaria, the resulting fever from which would kill off the goddamn bacteria, and they cured him with arsphenamine and quinine—the doctor told him something that blew his mind, and in the soft voice of a Bessarabian Bulgarian. In some village whose name he immediately forgot, a government census discovered that out of all four hundred forty people residing there, two hundred fifty-six had syphilis!

"Just think, young man," Dr. Beron said to him, "Eighty-two percent of the families there were diagnosed with syphilis . . . Nearly half the villagers had secondary manifestations in their mouths! That's truly disturbing, God help them." He threw his arms out, "Statistics, sir, what can you do?"

Geshev clenched his jaw, "Fuck this whole country!" And his teeth kept chattering through his synthetic fever.

[Saturday, September 28, 2013]

He sensed there was talk behind his back, accusations of never giving proper acknowledgement to his brother Georgi, but that had been a false accusation: as far as greeting his brother went, he did greet him, albeit out of the corner of his mouth, for the simple reason that his brother was the better chess player. Geshev also played chess, but always alone and locked up in his room, while Georgi, the youngest in the family, was already winning tournaments—true, school and town club ones, but tournaments, nevertheless. Anyone being superior gave Geshev the needle. After yet another solitary match, he would sweep the chess pieces back inside the box and stare out the window into the quieted midnight boulevard.

[Saturday, September 28, 2013]

Back in April of twenty-five, before they'd appointed him to work for the police, and Pane Bichev had personally called him in to help with the investigation following the bombing of the cathedral, Geshev hadn't felt the least bit of trepidation because he'd long thought about and imagined exactly *what* he would do and *how* he would do it—if only they'd take him into Public Safety! He'd waited for this moment a long time. Bichev heard him out carefully, signed off where necessary, and only a day later, Geshev had a desk and a chair inside the *criminal pursuit party*'s room.

And while Peter Amzel and his people kept searching for the organizers of the attack, Geshev would go to one of the higher ranking communists, someone, say, on the board of the *Liberty* co-op, and he would need only an hour or two before he'd let him go, but not before learning a slew of new names, which he would follow up with after.

His work was followed by the watchful eye of his boss, Bichev. He was taken aback when Geshev simply released those they'd arrested, but he didn't interfere. Right when he became irritated at himself for having hired him, just three days after the bombing, on Easter Monday on the Octave of Easter, he became witness to something he had a hard time believing could really happen. A member of the central communist committee—someone whom Peter Amzel had personally arrested, but whom Bichev had specifically arranged to be questioned by Geshev—stood on one of the staircase landings. The arrestee was not bound by chains. No chains, nothing; he stood and thrashed his arms, screaming at the serpentine file of arrestees trudging beneath him: "Rat them out!" he screamed. "Rat them all out," he yelled, "so we can put an end to this cannibal party once and for all!" The arrestees turned their heads up—some with fear, some with repulsion—but he just kept screaming for them to give up everything and everyone they knew, so that it could all end.

When he saw all this, Bichev called Geshev into his office and poured him a glass of cognac.

"I think I know what you're up to, young man," he said. "Keep on doing what you're doing and you'll get far."

Geshev wasn't sure if he was being threatened, mocked, or praised, but he chose to take the comment as encouragement. He wasn't ashamed of being a bureaucrat—just as he'd been in that tiny office at the municipality, and he wanted nothing more than to do the same at the police: *le bureaucrat qui vive.*

And that was that.

He kept on with an even greedier inspiration. "Control!" he thought. "Whacking these dregs did nothing, control is the mother of order in the nation. Keep an eye on them and then watch them squirm." He'd started to dream of one day tapping all the telephones—in Sofia and elsewhere—but he knew that even if he could, it would bring him neither what he sought nor respite: *anarchists never used the telephone.*

[Sunday, September 29, 2013]
Bichev's words had been praise, indeed, and Nikola Geshev, the lonely paper-shuffler from the sixth housing commission, was quickly promoted a rank. He clenched his teeth and said to himself, "Good!"

[Sunday, September 29, 2013—Monday, September, 30, 2013]
That spring, even the bells in the kingdom had tired of the endless funeral knell and no longer rang, but croaked and whanged. There hadn't been this many simultaneous burials since the September riots in twenty-three. Death had people's psyches stretched taut like drum skins, and their eyes betrayed a looming terror.

[Monday, September 30, 2013]
[Look at that, September's gone now too. So be it!]

[Monday, October 7, 2013; cardiology unit]
You could catch a lot of anarchists in your net that April and that rainy May, but you also risked catching a lot of small fish, too. Geshev could identify the small fish and wannabe bandits who thought themselves justice fighters with one look. There were also those who'd been sent packing by their own friends and who couldn't wait to squeal. At times the police went about it in the most vulgar way possible—they arrested the woman, beat her and tortured her, and the man they were after would run over to give himself up. Geshev squeamishly pursed his lips and said: "Dimwits. This is the extent of their anarchism!" and proceeded to kick out the first group and then the second and then the third, passing off the whole mess over to his other *colleagues*. Then he'd lock himself up in his office to do the crossword inside the omnivorous Atanas Damyanov's *Illustrated Week* (the first clue across was a work by Byron, the first vertical—a heroine from a work by Prosper Mérimée, and he'd bitterly fill in *Corsair* and Carmen). He'd never get to Ikonomov or Sheytanov with these idiots. Especially Sheytanov. The most wanted of them all— the man with the biggest bounty on his head.

Geshev couldn't care less about the bounty, of course. He would give anything just to have Sheytanov in his office.

[Tuesday, October 8, 2013; cardiology unit]
But Sheytanov was nowhere to be found. And when Geshev completed

yet another crossword, he turned to *Illustrated Week*'s gossip page: "Every-thing—About Everyone," where he read about the failed love affairs of movie stars, about the destruction of entire cities and humanity's lunacy, what with its chemical warfare; he read about Czechoslovakia's new post-age stamps, which the country would print in honor of its candidature for the next Olympic Games, an exercise costing one million two hundred thousand of their currency . . . things of that nature. Newspaper nonsense.

Illustrated Week also wrote about the "child killer" cult in Zhytomyr, Russia, where a murder trial was underway against one Zymbalnik some-one or other. This Zymbalnik was a member of a local cult, which called itself Korneavtsi, and had murdered his four children. According to the teachings of this cult, it was a sin to bear a child and, according to the testimonies of dozens of witnesses, the cult deemed children red devils who needed to be murdered before they went through the communist education system and grew up into the most fervent of communists. The Korneavtsi were avowed enemies of communism and looked at the com-munist leaders as antichrists who had come down for one reason only: to destroy humanity. Zymbalnik testified that he had acted simply of his own deep conviction and that God had come to him in a dream and told him the villagers should kill their own children rather than allow them to live and become communists. And so he did. This was printed inside the "Woman's Week" page—right between the articles "Dresses with Pleats" and "En Vogue: Low-Heeled Shoes," right under a photograph showcas-ing the latest Parisian styles and above the advertisement "Replace your phaeton with a motorized Ford! Quiet, with no fumes or odor!" Geshev was incensed at the garbage he was reading; he felt like going down to that idiot Pilgrim's office and tearing off his head. "He calls this propa-ganda," he cursed to himself, "that witless fool."

Geshev felt an inhuman aversion toward newspaper publishers.

[Monday, November 11, 2013; middle of the night]
In the days following the attack, the convoys of arrestees resembled gloomy rivers of lava, lazily flowing from all directions toward the

imposing edifice of the Police Directorate, above which a small bell
tower absurdly festooned with a protruding five-point star and a hammer and sickle, and the affixed bayonets and soldiers' helmets glimmered
like flashes of lightning underneath the razor April rain.

The building was still full of people even though it was May—
from the basement to the attic—as many as twenty, even thirty people
crammed inside a single room. The crowds of people sat and lay on the
dirty hardwood floors. In the evening, they moved them from room to
room and Geshev knew why—to torment them and to keep them from
forming connections. And to help them disperse the dreadful sense of
death looming around every corner. At night, the horror of anxiety set in:
around eleven o'clock, when the city descended into another uncertain
sleep behind darkened windows, the black camionettes arrived. They
came empty. They came to take away yet another hapless batch of para-
lyzed men to an unknown location. Inside the rooms, they all covered
their heads—with whatever was nearby—a blanket, a coat, a shirt—and
they fell silent, all ears, as the killers stalked the floors. Geshev sometimes
accompanied them while they *worked*: these people never called anyone
out by name, they just hit a head with their stick, and when the casualty
removed the coat or shirt from his face, they uttered one quick "Get
up!" and took him out into the hallway. Sometimes they got the wrong
guy, in which case, they grunted sourly, "No, not you!" and caned the
next head over.

[Tuesday, November 12, 2013]
Then they'd drive away, but back inside the building no one breathed
relief—it was too early to relax, the men with the sticks could come
back at any moment. It wasn't until dawn, when the windows facing
the boulevard grayed in the new rainy morrow that the people dared to
think they had survived, dared get some sleep in the knowledge they'd
live at least until that night.

21.

[Wednesday, November 13, 2013]

One day toward the end of May, the Directorate's hallways and floors echoed with news that Sheytanov had finally been caught. The blood drained from Geshev's face and he shot toward the telephone exchange. He barged in and demanded, "Is he alive?" When they answered him that yes, he was alive, there hadn't even been a shootout, he declared that from that moment on, he was to know of Sheytanov's whereabouts every second of the day. The telegraphers shrugged and moaned, yessir, but he yelled:

"And where is he now?!"

The telegraphers were startled because he had an awful look in his eye. One of them jumped out of his chair and handed him the dispatch, where Geshev read that the deputy district constable of Nova Zagora—Vrangelov someone or other, Ermia Vrangelov—was sending fourteen detainees to Sofia. The names were listed below, and Geshev spotted Sheytanov's name. He was eighth: immediately after someone called Andrea Petrov and right before Mariola Sirakova. It also said the detainees would be convoyed by First Lieutenant Kutsarov. The last detail nettled him—he knew the man personally and his penchant for causing trouble. He shook his head, knocked on wood just in case, and asked the telegraphers whether anyone else had seen the dispatch and the list of detainees. They explained over each other that it had just arrived and they were just about to take it to the chief, but Geshev nonchalantly told them he'd take care of it—he would bring it himself.

And he put the piece of paper in his pock

[NB! I've got the whole correspondence here somewhere—Sliven judges and prosecutors from Plovdiv demand to know Sheytanov's whereabouts for weeks and months on end, to assure a trial, while at the same time Turnovo's district court writes to the chief of Public Safety, "*where is he now, in some prison, killed in an attempted escape, etc.*," because any information is "*necessitated by the public prosecutor's office in order to carry out the verdict of the Turnovo district court: 10 years of solitary confinement inside a maximum security prison*" . . . And so forth. All of these institutions received the same response: the Police Directorate had "absolutely no information," a dispatch containing any of the alleged information was never logged, and appeared to be "*floating*" . . . Whatever that may mean.]

He put the piece of paper in his pocket and told the ill-at-ease telegraphers to report on every single word they got on Sheytanov.

"You know where to find me," he said to them and left the room.

[Friday, November 15, 2013]
The following day, one of the telegraphers did descend to the basement of the building with the ludicrous bell tower. He found Geshev, leaned over and whispered in his ear that First Lieutenant Kutsarov had indeed arrived with his entire party, but without the arrestees.

Geshev lost his ability to speak.

"What do you mean without the arrestees?!" he asked.

"Yessir!" the telegrapher responded. "Without the arrestees. And they were all fall-down drunk."

"Without even a single arrestee?" Geshev repeated, but the telegrapher only shrugged with shame.

Geshev sent him on his way and, now alone in the darkened room, mumbled, "They let them get away!" He cursed and slammed his fist on the writing table with the most impotent rage he'd felt in his entire li

22.

They unhooked the train car at the Belovo train station and unloaded
all the prisoners onto the black, mud-covered square outside, where
three bearded Macedonians already cursed impatiently. First Lieutenant Kutsarov told his men to unhook Sheytanov from the chains. (His
men were still wearing their winter, hoopoe-like guard uniforms—it
had been a frigid spring that year. The rain hadn't let up all of May.)
The Macedonians tied Sheytanov up using some disgusting rope, and
Sheytanov could only throw Mariola a glance before they shoved him
into the darkened vehicle.

Mariola Sirakova would stay with the other unfortunates at the train
station. First they took them to a tavern where they beat up the men and
raped the women. Mariola probably thought she was reliving the nightmare she went through in those carnal, blood-soaked basement rooms
at the police station in Pleven. There was no way she could have known
that this time the hell would end the same night: by morning they would
all be dead. Hell was no longer a place; hell was time. Hell could go on
for months, or it could end in mercy after only a few hours.

She had survived Pleven, but did not survive Belovo. Mariola was
not yet even twenty-one. She was seventy-eight days short of her next
birthday.

They brought the devastated bodies to the Gaitanovets region and
quickly unloaded them into the hole they'd dug—another mass grave to
hold yet more victims of that year, the year nineteen twenty-five.

Sheytanov might have only imagined what happened with Mariola—
there was no way to know. They took him to the other side of the mountains, to Gorna Djumaya, uttering not a single word, until he opened

his mouth to ask, "What are we doing now?" and they only responded: "Shut it!" His arrival in Gorna Djumaya was met by the same pathological murderers whose names had been on everyone's lips that year, the year an undeclared, repulsive war pitted neighbor against neighbor: Sheytanov knew who they were. As soon as he laid eyes on them he thought, "This is it." But he steeled himself and asked them not to play with fire.

"Me," he said, "you don't sentence. Me," he said, "you either shoot or you let go."

The group who informed him they'd be the ones to decide his fate— all those Vanchos, Ionkovs and Perovs—mhmmed bitterly and shut themselves in the other room to talk it over

[NB! Years later, one of them would say the following:

"Well, there was no other way! The Army League demanded Sheytanov's head at any price!"

And that was that.]

and he remained alone with two of their goons. They weren't the same ones who'd taken him up here, but they all looked alike—as though they were all begot by the same mother. They reeked like hell and their eyes were black with the opium they couldn't do without. He knew their type—the type who killed without a second thought.

"They have no first thought to speak of," he thought, and immediately vowed to remember the joke and share it with the poet when he saw him in the coming days. Geo Milev could surely use it in a poem or in one of the angry diatribes he published in the magazine.

Suddenly, a poem came to him. *What kind of epoch is this, / Which drowns our souls in crimson and gold, / Which, when our hour strikes bare—conspires to send us to death, with fanfare . . .*

He would give it to the poet for his next magazine—there was bound to be another magazine sometime! But he had no way of writing the poem down: he was all tied up.

So he began repeating it—once, a second time, a third, many times over, so that he wouldn't forget it. *What kind of epoch is this, / Which drowns our souls in crimson and gold, / Which, when our hour strikes bare—conspires to send us to death, with fanfare . . . / What kind of epoch is this, / Which drowns our souls in crimson and gold, / Which, when our hour strikes bare—conspires to send us to death, with fanfare . . . / What kind of epoch is this, / Which drowns our souls in crimson and gold, / Which, when our hour strikes bare—conspires to send us to death, with fanfare.*

And that was that.

23.

[Monday, November 18, 2013]

. . . Inside the Police Directorate's jam-packed rooms, some of the detainees took to etching small notches on the smoke-blackened walls: seemingly to mark the days, but they quickly lost count, because each night they were moved from floor to floor and from room to room, where they were met with a whole new set of days and itchings to match. The poet did no such thing. He saw no reason to—so certain was he that those men from the police were obligated to release him any moment now, and bring him to the prison where he could start serving his sentence. Instead of marking notches on the walls, he protested loudly for being detained, threatened inquiries, and yelled he would write about this in every European newspaper. He made a lot of noise and hullaballoo, but no one paid any attention. "Write all you want," they said to him. "We won't read it." Then they moved on and he pounded his fist into the wall and spit out all the worst profanities he'd learned at the Kniajevo Military Academy.

He thought about Mila and the kids incessantly. He wondered what could possibly be keeping them from coming to see him. Right before they took him in, Bistra had been on the verge of chicken pox—feverish, sneezing and coughing, her little nose constantly wet—all those sure signs of measles the old people would call *brusnica*—and the poet's heart broke remembering how torturous it had been for Leda, who'd had it when she was two. He wondered why there was no sign of his brother, Boris, either. True, he was on friendly terms with the new government, but the poet refused to believe his brother would give up without looking for him. He knew his brother loved him the most out of everybody in the big Kassabov household. When they were children, Boris had trailed him devotedly, picking up all those flying pieces of paper and notebooks—batko's magazines! The poet tore them up, and Boris would race to pick it all up. The poet drew, tore, and threw away—and Boris picked it all up. The poet tears—Boris picks up. When he collected the pieces—he glued them all back together one by one inside his own small little notebook, which he then hid with yet another torn up magazine of the poet's in places he was certain were very, very secret and that only he knew about . . .

For this reason he knew, he was certain Boris was out there looking for him—somewhere outside the walls of this cursed building.

The days came and went, people disappeared and others came, but he was not afraid, he was simply beside himself.

[Tuesday, November 19, 2013]
What do you know—one Saturday night, when, according to his estimations, May was already on its way out, two police officers came in, pulled him out of the airless room, and led him down the muddy staircase. He looked at his watch and saw that is was a quarter to eleven—the same hour in which they usually came in silently and took out yet another person. But he still wasn't afraid. The silence in that enormous building was broken by all the noises of men crammed together and only the black shadows of Kocho Stoyanov's Macedonians scattered in the hallways.

They descended down the stairs, going all the way down to the first floor, but they didn't stop there, nor did they take him outside as he thought for a split second; instead they kept climbing down.

They went all the way down to the basement, and led him inside a room.

The room had a chair, a warped writing desk and a weak, bare light bulb.

And behind the writ

(Crossed out)

[Saturday, November 23, 2013]
[Goddamn it! My thoughts at this point are so convoluted and mired that I'm going to need a good amount of time to pull the right one out.]

(Crossed out)

. . . but this time the poet recognized him immediately. The same young clerk, the braggart who had once upon a time validated his address registration, whom he had seen carry Blagoev's coffin with his own two eyes, who had only just recently come inside his home for a midnight check up.

Geshev. Nikola Geshev—he truly recognized him now.

"Well, Mr. Milev," said Geshev, "we're alive and well to see each other again, what do you say?"

"Yes, hello, hello," the poet mumbled. "But enough with the hellos, would you be so kind as to explain what I'm doing here? I've been held for two weeks, I have no idea why they even brought me here, why aren't I in prison? I haven't spoken with my wife, or my children—what's happening here!"

"Milev, Milev . . ." Geshev sighed, his eyes becoming as black as two lifeless coals. "I asked you to introduce me to Sheytanov, didn't I? Had you done that, you'd still be alive."

"But I am alive!" the poet countered surprised.

What Geshev said next he said with bite, looking at the poet at once with worry and impatient anticipation.

"No, no you're not," he groaned. "You are no longer. You just don't know it yet."

He nodded to the two men, who stood like black clouds in the rusted dusk and whom the poet hadn't even noticed. One of them approached him, took the thick bludgeon from the desk, and swung with all the might of his muscular body and unloaded into the poet's head. He did so from the left—where the poet's only good eye was. The entire room echoed with the ugly sound of a cracking skull, and the good eye flew out of its wrecked orbit.

Geshev sighed and left the room.

(Crossed out)

[November 25-November 29, 2013; Germany]
(Crossed out)

[Sunday, December 29, 2013]
[This is something! It is true that the days are long, but the years fly by. And while I'm wondering when the Wednesday will become a Friday—the whole year has gone by.

A whole year, and there's still no end in sight for this diary . . .
God help me!]

[The hour of death]

"The following is given to Mila Geo Mileva, regarding her inquiry #823, so she may use it wherever is necessary."

—From the certification given to Mila Geo Mileva by the Police Directorate and the Sofia Police Commandantship on August 6, 1925

[Monday, December 30, 2013]

Mila searched for the poet day after day. She went to all the Sofia police precincts, stood for hours outside the prison, visited the civil prosecutor and the field court prosecutor. Nothing. Public Safety told her they had no copy of an arrest warrant issued in the poet's name, the prison said he'd never been brought there. It was the same thing everywhere she went. When she heard detainees were held at the First Infantry Regiment—she immediately went down to the First Infantry Regiment. She went straight to any place rumored to be housing arrestees. She'd been to the Fourth Artillery Regiment, and inside the Military Academy—everywhere! After which she returned to the throngs of people by Lavov Most.

Heavy clouds hung over Sofia, and Mila didn't think they were clouds at all, but the souls of all those who'd been gathered up and disappeared that spring, summoned to silently keep vigil somewhere high up—at the threshold of heaven and earth.

One Thursday she overheard that the Fotinov School was also full of arrestees. She went there too—rushing off along the river and turning down the boulevard. The school was occupied by an army, but an officer came out from his post to speak to her, and when he heard *whom* it was she was searching for, he immediately let her go inside to the gymnasium to see with her own eyes they had no such person. She was shocked by what she saw inside, but not by the sight of a hundred or so men meandering about between the wall bars, gym horses, and climbing ropes. The astonishment came from the men's complete lack of consternation. Quite the contrary, right as she walked inside the stale-aired gym hall that reeked of rot, sweat, horseradish, and goat shit, the detainees were falling over with laughter as three hapless men—arrestees like all the rest—had pushed three tables together, climbed on top, and were now performing a satirical *skit* and *singing* a dirty song.

So repulsed was she at the men's bubonic cackling, she never stepped foot inside that school again.

But she did keep visiting all of the police precincts and heard the same thing everywhere, "Geo Milev has never been here!" One day, amid the soundless crowd outside the Police Directorate, she spotted Viola Karavelova: she was dressed head to toe in white and had pinned to her skirt a photograph of her husband, Joseph Herbst. The women stood so close to one another that Mila could see into Viola's eyes—blue, piercing, and vacant. Mila at once thought *this is it*—our lives were sundered and this is what remains. Their men were never friends, their paths had not crossed, and they did not share the same acquaintances, but now *the two women would wander the city together, looking for them.* Together. The same places, the same reason; they'd wade through the same mud beneath the same May rain, united by a common nightmare from which there was no waking.

Her face darkened with each barren day, her exquisite femininity betook itself into the black hole of unease. It was as though all those old premonitions of woe now befell them and she chased them away, and just when she felt like she might keel over and give in to the desperation and her world reached the brink of collapse, she would get up and take off to yet another place someone tipped her off about, with even more determination.

[Tuesday, December 31 2013]

The very next day after they took the poet away, Mila's brother-in-law, the poet's little brother, Boris, immediately arrived in Sofia from Stara Zagora via the overnight train. He jumped into the first available taxi or phaeton—and went straight to Nachev. He wasted no time going to the Police Directorate, he went straight to the man's house, because the two of them went far back, they'd served in the same regiment together

. . . It wasn't easy to get to Nachev in those times, it was a known fact the communists had issued him a death sentence and hence the man was fiercely guarded. But they let Boris in. Only after that did Boris go to his sister-in-law's house on Maria Louisa, but he had a bewildered air. He told Mila everything would be fine, Nachev had given his word he would look into it and take care of it—they'd been friends, after all—but Mila felt as though he was afraid to look her in the eye. She had reason to be anxious: Nachev had promised to call first thing the following day, but he did not—perhaps because the following day had been a Sunday, Boris thought. But on Monday, concerned the man may have forgotten what they'd talked about in the diabolical chaos following the attacks, Boris again up and went into the Police Directorate. He did not return until the afternoon; even more disconcerted, he now looked afraid, plain and simple, and his eyes were red. Mila and Boris sat down and wrote the first official complaint letter, and Boris departed for Stara Zagora the next day.

It was already the nineteenth of May. On the twentieth, a Wednesday, Mila's father-in-law, Milyo, arrived in Sofia. He came into town but got a hotel; he didn't stay at their house on Maria Louisa. Mila knew the man did not care for her, but her getting angry at him about it now was futile. Her father-in-law went around and did what he did, and on the twenty-fourth of May he caught the train back to Stara Zagora, because someone had told him the poet was in the Sliven prison or maybe in the Haskovo one, perhaps he'd be well advised to go check on it in person. He stopped by Mila's long enough to embrace Leda and let Bistra play with his mustache, gave them both a couple of leva bills and a kiss, and left, and Mila continued to make the rounds at all the police precincts, lodging yet more complaints.

One Thursday, she remembered her sister-in-law had had the idea to get all the writers together to make a stand on the poet's behalf. Mila immediately up and went to the imposing building of the Central Bulgarian Cooperative Bank, situated on the corner of Bazov and Rakovski Streets—right behind the National Theater. She knew the writer Konstantinov worked there as a legal adviser, in addition to being the secretary of the Writers' Union, and he was a close, trusted associate of the new union chair, Vlaykov, and had, for that reason, combined one with the other, and in addition served as editor of Vlaykov's magazine *Democratic Review.* He also signed everything as *Dushechka.* Mila found him and informed him what had brought her to him, all of which he was very *surprised* to hear! He shuddered and yelled that this was a grotesque disgrace, that he would at once *inform* the chairman, who, as a writer, lover of mankind, and a political man, would by all means be able to do something. Mila got the chills when she heard that a writer, the secretary of the writers, no less, was hearing about her husband the poet's disappearance from *her,* but she let it go. Afterward, she could barely wait for Monday to come—right after the twenty-fourth of May, the day of the Saints Cyril and Methodius, the day celebrating the written word, which that year fell on a Sunday—so she could go back to the bank. Dushechka wasn't in on that particular day, and the policeman at the entrance with the caryatids and the heavy, wrought iron gate, sent her to the Writers' Union—not too far, at 129 Rakovski Street. She went there, too, and Konstantinov told her mister chairman had gone to the director of the police, but he was told the writer Geo Milev had neither been arrested, nor detained there, and that they had no idea as to his whereabouts.

"And as I am sure you understand," he added, "Todor Vlaykov is not the type of man people lie to!"

Mila had begun to despair at that point, and she humbly insisted that they check once more. Konstantinov promised to do so, but who knows why he still avoided her gaze, and Mila did not return, not to the bank behind the National Theater, and not to 129 Rakovski . . .

[Wednesday, January 1, 2014, 12:17am]
On the last day of May, nineteen twenty-five, a Saturday, when she again returned to the Police Directorate building in the late afternoon, she was taken to someone called Nikola Geshev in the brigand criminal pursuit office. The office of those in charge of the pursuit was at the bottom of

the dark stairwell—somewhere far down the basement labyrinths, where dark men roamed and where the stench of the detainees mixed with the heavy aroma of opium. This same Nikola Geshev told her he knew her husband personally and greatly admired him, but he had not seen him as of late . . .

"Geo Milev was never here, madame!" he said. "Honest! Do you think I wouldn't know had he come here? I would never lie to you!"

His demeanor appeared convincing, but she saw the man was hiding something.

[Tuesday, January 7, 2014]
She got up and left without saying goodbye. She headed down Maria Louisa Boulevard, where the red trams rattled down toward the Lions' Bridge and back up the hill toward the gutted remains of the St. Nedelya Church, where soldiers with helmets, armed as if for war, strode tensely; she went inside her apartment building, across from the mosque—with the drug store at one end, and the boza fabric Radomir on the other, the post office on the first floor, and the import-export bank on the second, and the Bulgarian offices of Longine on the third. She listlessly climbed the seventy-seven steps to their then home, walked in, and asked her sister-in-law if she could watch the kids for just a little while longer. Maria hiccupped through her sobs and nodded, and Mila went inside the space, curtained off by an ebullient drape, which the poet and his wife considered their matrimonial bedroom. She lay down on the bed and before she could even think about how exhausted she was, she fell asleep and began to dream how

[Friday, January 10, 2014]
a snow-covered wilderness crawled with an endless procession of people clad in black. The line of people was so long that when, one day, those in front overheard the people farthest in back, crazed with hunger, had eaten a person, they had no way of knowing for sure—if they were to send someone all the way back to find out, he'd never catch up with

them again . . . And they couldn't possibly stop, either, for anyone who stopped fell and died on the spot: the road was blackened by hundreds of corpses that the eternal cold gave no chance of decaying. Every three days those up front lit fires, warming the people in back as they passed . . .

A long time ago, a man had told them about a faraway land, so far it was all the way at the other end of the world. The Promised Land. There, everyone would find a house, there would be work for the men, rose bushes, colorful flower beds, and vegetable gardens for the women to tend to, milk and ice cream for the children, wooden toy guns and merry-go-rounds for the boys, and for the girls—dolls and mirrors with pictures of actors on the backs . . . The people repeated this like a prayer chant. That same man had also told them not to fear the long road ahead—there was nothing to fear. They would cross many lands, he told them, and they would meet good people. And the good people would hire them for small jobs—to dig a well, to mix mud and straw for mud-brick, to erect a stone wall, to dig up beets and potatoes—and they would get by until they got to the Promised Land, and when they got there . . .

But they came across no good people who wanted to give them jobs. The bitter cold was permeating and no one dug wells or mixed mud and straw; the houses were made of red and black stone, the stone walls had already been erected in another time, and there were no potatoes or beets to speak of. The locals peered darkly through the narrow embrasures of their northern windows, and none came out to offer bread or cured meat to the travelers.

True, this had taken the people by surprise, but they kept on walking . . .

In the fourth year, when the glimmer of the Promised Land appeared on the horizon, the people spotted a somber horseman riding toward them. They stopped him and asked him whether he was coming from the Promised Land. He answered that yes, that's where he came from.

"Is it far now to the Promised Land? And," they went on, anxiously, "is there work waiting for the men, flower gardens for the women, and milk and seesaws for the children?"

The man gave them a long look.

"Nonsense."

The people grew anxious and began to fret, what did he mean, nonsense, but the stranger repeated:

"Nonsense! Flower gardens, seesaws . . . complete nonsense."

Frightened, they laid into him, shouting at him that he had no idea what he was saying.

"How dare you call that nonsense," they yelled furiously, "when a man told us about the Promised Land many years ago! He said there would be a house for everyone and work for the men, and rose bushes and flower beds for the women, and vegetable gardens they would tend to while the men were at work, milk and ice cream for the children, wooden toy guns and merry-go-rounds for the boys, dolls and little mirrors with the pictures of actors on the backs for the girls . . . We trusted him, that's why we set off in search of the Promised Land. He told us to!"

"He told you to. So what?" the horseman grunted. "He told you a fairy tale and forgot to mention it was just a story!"

[Wednesday, January 29, 2014]

[The snow is mixed with rain—exactly like in Chamonix in January, nineteen twenty-four. Then as now, the rain mushed the snow, and when the savage cold set in, it turned into a hellish ice slick.]

"That it was . . . what?" the people gasped.

"A fairy tale! Don't you know what a fairy tale is? The man wrote a story, read it to you in a church, and you went and believed him. Now you're dragging around like *meanderers without kin, you yellow, emaciated tatterdemalions . . .*"

He then dug into his horse with the gleaming spurs of a fallen angel and galloped in the direction from which they all came, past the entire train of people wrapped in black tatters, ragged blankets, and bedraggled scarves, who'd yet to realize they'd been duped.

24.

[*Thursday, January 30, 2014*]

Night had fallen by the time Mila awoke. The black sky behind the window had no moon or stars—only the Splendid company's diamond halo radiated from behind Banya Bashi's minaret as a late, lone tram clattered down toward its depot on the other side of Lions' Bridge.

The Market Hall's clock began to strike. It did so eleven times—any other year this hour brought Sofia's night to life in the sheer spring dusk, but on that night, only the clack of horses' hooves, the snore of a dense automobile, and that same lone tram cracked the dead silence.

She raised herself up and sat on the edge of the bed when she felt something inside of her tear in a scarlet hurricane of agony.

It was with that Mila Geo Mileva realized the little boy she and the poet had whispered about on so many of the cool, rainy spring nights in nineteen twenty-five would never be.

25.

[Monday, February 3, 2014]
[The End.]

[Epilogue]
After that night

[Friday, November 14, 2014]

> 1283 Милевъ Гео отъ Ст.-Загора, род.
> 29 I. 1896 г., синъ на Милю Касабовъ и
> Анастасия Касабова, писателъ, р. 160, к.
> ч., о. кест., н. прав., у. об., ц. б., инва-
> лидъ, (на черепа белегъ и дѣсното око
> извадено). На Соф. Прок., изх. 11300—926 г.

> *"1283 Milev, Geo, from Stara Zagora, b. January 29, 1896,*
> *son of Milyo Kassabov and Anastasia Kassabova; writer,*
> *height: 160 cm, eyes brown, nose straight,*
> *disabled (scar on skull, right eye missing).*
> *Prosecutor's office, Sofia, outgoing: 11300-1926."*

> —From the central police bulletin for
> missing persons, Sofia, June 10, 1926

Milyo Kassabov grew old in an instant.

He held himself together for an entire year after the poet's disappearance—he went around, he inquired, he came back home and went out again looking for his son. He wrote three pleas to the king, one to the National Assembly, and five to the ministers, growing rather surprised when, after a continuous, uninterrupted silence, he received the following lone response . . .

[Before I forget. This response arrived on the eighteenth of December, nineteen twenty-five. With outgoing number six hundred seventy, the king's clerks were responding to a plea sent to them on June of twenty-five. Half a year later! The response said only that his plea was forwarded to the Ministry of Interior and of National Health in November. For further investigation. That is all. Some fucking country.]

[Not that this constituted a *response*—it's that no one else had given even this much.]

He had forbidden anyone in the family to so much as put on an article of mourning, even marrying his oldest daughter Evgenia to one Zheko Velikov and sending Pesha to America to study in Chicago at the national academy for kindergarten teachers.

"Have you seen Georgi's dead body?" he demanded. "Have you washed it? Have you thrown dirt in his grave? I haven't!"

That's what he said.

And he always scowled at his daughter-in-law. He was convinced she was not doing enough, that she wasn't looking for Georgi as she should. He knew it wasn't true, but he scowled all the same.

But the following spring, when the yard and the garden on the other side of the hedge burst in the scant green of reawakening, he who hadn't yet turned fifty-eight years old, broke down. At the end of May, he wrote an obituary announcing the wake that would take place over the unknown *grave* of his beloved *departed*, he gave the obituary to be typed up, accompanied the servant girl to buy twenty loaves of bread, negotiated the lamb for the *qurbani* himself, and the service took place on Sunday, the twenty-third, inside the Church of Sveta Bogoroditsa (under whose arches the old king had once proclaimed the war manifesto). He'd chosen the twenty-third, because on another twenty-third of May, precisely three hundred sixty-five days and three hundred sixty-five nights earlier, someone had spotted his son through a window inside the grim building next to Sofia's Lavov Most for the last time.

[. . . The poet had retreated to a corner of his cell, writing something in his notebook: he'd promised to say a few words about Slavic literature the following day, May twenty-fourth, the day of letters, to the rest of the detainees, and perhaps this is why he'd been near a window.]

It was the last time anyone would see him.

And so be it.

On the eve of the wake, Milyo Kassabov opened his notebook No. 52 and wrote down the following with the decisive handwriting of a well-read man:

70 printed obituaries—100 leva
20 loaves of bread and a lamb—520 leva
Misc.—180 leva
Total: 800 leva

He now knew for certain this was to be the last money he'd ever spend *on* the poet.

He put the pen point back into the inkpot and as he raised his head, he saw in the darkened window not the strong and ambitious face of a big-time businessman, but the willowed countenance of a man on the threshold of agedness.

The dark outside stifled the fragrance of the rose bush that for years spiraled up toward the window, and that of the petunias down by the house, and although nothing was meant to have changed from the good old times his large family enjoyed, it was as though the May eve was now haunted by horrors and grotesque evils.

[Sunday, November 16, 2014]
Sunday, the twenty-third of May, nineteen twenty-six, was the day of the
Holy Apostle Simon the Zealot—the one with the Marriage at Cana—
where Jesus had been invited with his mother, who'd already arrived.
And when they ran out of wine at the wedding, Jesus's mother said to
Him, "They have no wine!" Jesus looked at her despondently, for His
hour had not yet come, but he asked the servants to fill the now-empty
earthen wine vessels with water, and take them to the steward of the
Feast. The man ladled the water, but it had already turned to wine, so
the old man reproached the groom, "Everyone serves the good wine first,
and then the inferior wine after the guests have become drunk. But you
have kept the good wine until now." But what neither of the two men
knew was that this had been the water Jesus had turned into wine. And
that he had just performed the first of His miracles.

Milyo Kassabov was thinking about something else entirely.

He thought that precisely a year ago—on the day someone had for
certain seen his son for the last time at the Police Directorate—it had
again been the day of Simon the Zealot, and that these three hundred
sixty-five days and nights were enough. He gave up.

He told his wife to put on her mourning clothes, hung the black
crepe on the gate, and sat down to write the obituary containing the
irreversible words *grave* and *departed*.

He no longer waited for a miracle.

[Thursday, November 20, 2014]
That year had been long and yet it flew past like a dark moment.

[Saturday, November 22, 2014]
Before that, all sorts of people kept wandering by, speaking to him with-
out moving their lips—like real ventriloquists. Half a year this went on!
The train of people started in June of twenty-five and did not halt until
Christmas. These people would swear up and down that his son was

alive, crossing themselves, and describing exactly where they'd seen him. One such degenerate came into his bookstore in July, wandered around obnoxiously and began to tell him that he knew: they'd only cut Georgi's arm off—the right one, so he'd never be able to write again—but that otherwise he was fine, he was alive and well and they were going to release him very soon, the arm they probably cut off out of vengeance and to make an example out of him. Milyo Kassabov heard him out, stood quiet for a minute, and then shooed him out. He did the same to some architect who came to tell him just how much he cared for his son, who'd encouraged him so patiently to pursue the artistic vein, and then told Milyo he was only passing through Stara Zagora, really he was on his way to Sliven, where he'd been sent by some extraordinarily secret organization to retrieve Georgi from his fate at the local prison. A third—this one an actor—assured him that he, too, knew Georgi was still alive and that his friends would never let him perish. And Milyo Kassabov sank deeper into depression because he realized that even people like that somehow managed to attach themselves to Public Safety as lowlife spies, provocateurs, and general contemptibles.

His daughter Mariika once told him about the Orphan—how he'd given his word he would show up as a witness for the poet on the day of his trial, but did not come, and how she ran all the way to his house to remind him, only to be met by the Orphanness, who told her her husband was stretching his canvases, but not in their beautiful house in Sofia, no, he was doing it all the way in their villa in Dragalevtsi, an hour away from the capital. And Milyo Kassabov had told her:

"Mariika, Mariika, by God, you must be turning into a socialist—you're delirious with camaraderie and solidarity. It comes from Christ, doesn't it, this solidarity and compassion. Well, let me remind you of something, my daughter. When Pontius Pilate's people arrested Christ at Gethsemane, did they arrest only him and no one else? Peter even cut off the ear of some poor slave, and still he didn't get locked up. That he cut off the slave's ear is written in the Gospel, but it says nothing of him being arrested. Why? Because, when they saw what was happening, they all ran, that's why. And Peter would have been the first to run. Fear is a scary thing, my child, remember that."

Maria looked at him, pale as the wall—but he went quiet and stayed silent, then added that all these books were written and then rewritten by those same cowards, and if not personally by them, then by their followers. And when they wrote, and crossed out and rewrote, they did it so they'd come out the heroes.

"That's how it goes," he said, "and if these same cowards one day rule, it is they who will write the history."

And he waved his hand dismissively.

[Sunday, November 23, 2014]
During that same rainy summer of twenty-five, old man Pavel, Bishop of Dragovitiiski and Metropolitan of Starozagorski, a diplomatic man well-versed not only in church doings but in secular ones as well, took off for Sofia to personally ask after and inquire about Georgi. When he returned, His reverence sent for Milyo Kassabov and told him he'd personally been to see General Valkov, and upon inquiring about Georgi, the general had replied: "I personally gave the orders in regard to him!"

"What orders did he give, your Eminence?" Milyo Kassabov asked drily, "Good orders or bad? Did he say?"

Who knows why, but the bishop pressed his hand to the enameled icon pendant on his chest, sighed, and spread out his arms.

"This man," he said, "is like a mire, Mr. Kassabov. You know neither how deep it runs, nor what might be hiding in the mud."

[Monday, November 24, 2014]
Milyo Kassabov crossed himself and left, and when he lay down that evening, he dreamt he found a stray kitten in the garden by the train station. He picked it up because he wanted to bring it to the children—in his dream they were still kids. But the kitten was skittish: it pulled away, twisting in his arms like orange lightning, scratching wildly and biting,

and Milyo Kassabov saw his hands covered in scratches that seeped with blood. He felt the pain even in his dream, but he still didn't leave the kitten. He got home and Georgi immediately reached for the kitten, but he told his son the kitten was wild and that it scratched and bit. "Don't try and be a hero with this kitten, now is not the time." But Georgi still took the animal from his hands and it suddenly became tame. It did not scratch, or bite, but quieted into his embrace and gave a vehement purr when Georgi scratched its pink ear.

He awoke, confused by all sorts of presentiments which he could not discern.

The day was the same as the one before it. It rained, as it rained nearly every single day during that summer of twenty-five, and raindrops large as gems fell from the shed's awning.

Milyo Kassabov thought he ought to construct some gutters, to keep the wood under the red bricks from rotting, then opened up his umbrella and went to his bookstore.

[Monday, November 24, 2014]
And it just so happened that on that day, Vladimir Nachev arrived in Stara Zagora from Sofia. His automobile—a polished Packard, with gleaming black paint and monstrous electric headlights piercing that June rain—pulled right up to the bookstore, and he entered wearing his ostentatious officer's cloak. Two civilian huskies stood guard at the door, with their black blazers and hats pulled low over their eyes, like caricatures of American gangsters. Inside, Nachev courteously removed his cap and announced he would not beat around the bush.

"Mr. Kassabov," he said. "I have not come to give you false hopes. Better that you leave any expectations you might have for Geo behind. I have ascertained from people in the know, that Geo has been taken out by rogue agents. Do not wait for him and do not look for him."

With an aching heart, Milyo Kassabov recounted this conversation with the old Bishop who'd been to see General Valkov; the latter had told his eminence that he'd personally given orders regarding Geo, but hadn't clarified as to the nature of those orders. When he spoke, he looked straight into Nachev's eyes—with hope, yet on the verge of despair. But Nachev's face had remained like a rock: nothing had moved.

"Well, perhaps it is I who is wrong, Mr. Kassabov . . ." and he replaced his cap, gave a polite salute, turned on his heels, and left.

Now alone, Milyo Kassabov felt such an overwhelming powerlessness and such a terrifying spite, that for the first time in his entire life, he braced himself on the edge of the chair behind the glass counter displaying postcards from Berlin. He had always stood while working inside his bookstore. Now, he sat as those same two black-blazered huskies outside ran back to the Packard—one nervously opened the door, while the other kept looking around—and Vladimir Nachev gathered the skirts of his cloak and dropped down heavily into the seat. The Packard jumped, hurled forward, and flew down the road toward the train station garden, its hefty tires tearing up the puddles with a silver hiss.

[Tuesday, November 25, 2014]

That summer—the summer of nineteen twenty-five—saw a large restructuring of the Bulgarian police. Edmund Heidenfeldt, general from the gendarmerie, arrived in Sofia all the way from Vienna to personally oversee the whole thing. No expense was to be spared. And that is how—in place of the uncouth disturbance comprised of yesterday's raffish and idle louts, sorry-looking and forever soiled by wine and *manja*, gummy-eyed and unshaven hicks, impertinent illiterates who tucked their lame rifles under their armpits like sticks, who staggered around, scatter-brained, their hats always the wrong way, with cracked and dusty visors—after just a few rainy months, Heidenfeldt and Vladimir Nachev saw in front of them

[Wednesday, November 26, 2014]

a new formation of sterling assassins.

And that's how it really happened.

[Wednesday, November 26, 2014]

3576 Шейтановъ Георги Василевъ,
род. 1898 г. отъ Ямболъ. По присжда 735
отъ 20. VI. 928 г. на Търнов. о. с. (гл.
1665—927 г.). На Прок. Търново изх. 11773--
929 г.   (А. 24923. 29.

Bulletin 3576
Sheytanov, Georgi Vassilev, b. 1898, Yambol.
Convicted by judgment 735, from June 20, 1928, by the Turnovo
District Court. Outgoing number 11773-1929 (A. 24923. 29)

—From the Central Bulletin for wanted persons, Sofia,
1929, declaring Sheytanov was still a wanted criminal

Kina Sheytanova grew old in an instant.

She'd buried three children, had even sent her husband to the next
world, and had still held herself together, but as soon as she learned that
they'd taken out her dearest, her Odjo, as she'd called him during the
entirety of his restless rebel's life, when she got word in that rainy spring
of twenty-five, she at once turned into a sorrowful, frazzled old woman.

She hadn't yet turned sixty years old.

[Thursday, November 27, 2014]

In the very beginning of November, nineteen twenty-five, just about a
week after the police lifted the curfew on the twenty-fifth of October,
and everyone could once again move freely at all hours of the day and
night, writer Anton Strashimirov arrived in town. He was to give ten
lectures at the National University—in other words, speak inside the
Suglasie salon, which reeked of floor wax and tobacco. Sofia University
had been a point of pride and happiness for the city that year: even the
eternally at-odds Yambolian newspapers *Thracian* and *Tunja* (specifically
Tunja and not *Tundja*, according to multi-page-long rhapsodizing in

the newspaper in defense of the latter spelling), buried the hatchet and stood side by side, of the same opinion. Otherwise, great battles were had by the editors of the two—one group drank only at the Kazacheto tavern, the others, only in Nova Bulgaria, and nowhere else. The *Thracian*, owned by publisher and editor Marangozov, appealed for a strong nation and a solid government, while the publisher of *Tunja*, Pavlov, and his editor, Assen Kurdjiev, seemed not quite sure of what, exactly, they were fighting for, but appeared to be heavily focused on the dirt in the streets and the pollution in the river.

In any case . . .

[Friday, November 28, 2014]
It wasn't his first time in Yambol. He'd also been in nineteen twelve, when the community center's management had spent a good amount of time debating as to whether even to organize his lecture, not to mention the question of actually paying him part of the proceeds. During those same times, Strashimirov had met a teacher in Yambol named Ivan Karanovski, but had not liked the man: Karanovski's ideas on literature had been far too outdated. Strashimirov came in nineteen twenty-one as well, when that same community center invited him of its own accord, and in spring he gave six lectures inside the crowded salon. He saw Karanovski there again, and again had not liked him: the man had fallen even further back in time with his ideas and appeared mildewed. But the general interest toward his lectures was one-of-a-kind, and the community center Magi did not hesitate but for a moment: they invited him to speak again in the fall of that same year for a second round, and this time, all of the proceeds—three leva from the citizens, and two from the students—would be for him. That time he spoke about the distinctive qualities of Bulgarian family life, about the remnants of the Bogomil movements in the then-everyday life of the Bulgarian person, he spoke about the Bulgarian woman, as she compared to the women of France, Holland, Germany, Scandinavia, and the other Balkan nations, about the despair of being a young person in Bulgaria, and, finally, about

the times of great moral decline according to the revelations of Arthur Rimbaud, Oscar Wilde, and Stanislav Pshibishevski.

This is why he liked Yambol—because the people here liked him too, and the community center paid well.

[Saturday, November 29, 2014]
Now his lectures were grouped under the common theme "Holy of Holies," divided into six separate discussions, such as what is sin, for instance, under the shadow of Tolstoy, sadism according to Pshibishevski, contemporary marriage according to Ibsen—all things of that nature. Later, *Thracian* would write that his lectures had been lush and exemplary of a high moral pathos and national ideal, while *Tunja* underscored the fact the discussions with Strashimirov had been a spontaneous fellowship between the celebrated author and his audience, who had followed his reflections with a heightened interest and hung, delighted, onto his every word: how truly great it was to have been witness to such responsiveness from people on questions of ethics and so forth.

That's what the two newspapers in Yambol would write, but that would be later; on the second of November, a Monday, as soon as he stepped foot off the mid-day train from Sofia, the first thing Anton Strashimirov did was to tell the group of young people from the university welcoming him at the train station to take him to Sheytanov's mother at once.

"First," he demanded dryly when he saw their alarmed reactions, "I want to see the woman, and then we shall get to our business. Don't get soft on me."

[Sunday, November 30, 2014]
The boys first paled from fear, then awe, and then nodded feverishly, and they all boarded the horse-drawn tram. The conductor whipped the two municipal horses and off they went from the station, over the German bridge, through the large park, over the other bridge across from the Turkish baths, and up by the Council of Officers. They got off at the

stop at Coburg Square, which was flanked by the imposing covered market on one side and Vassil Krastev's bookstore on the other, right in front of the Popular Bank and the large Singer store. They crossed the freshly paved Coburg Square, where, on this early afternoon, a crowd of men had gathered outside the Carmen ready-to-wear shoe store, owned by Robert Mefano, to look at the three new Opel automobiles parked there, and where the Modern Theater janitor brushed on glue to attached the placard for Douglas Fairbanks' *Robin Hood* over one announcing *The Thief of Bagdad*. The boys proudly declared that the Modern Theater was a big deal. They announced that the Brothers Kachulev had already taken care of the distribution of Emil Jannings' crowning achievement, *The Last Laugh*, and that the premiere of the exotic film *The Doll and Maharaja* would take place on the sixteenth of that month.

"The Brothers Kachulev," they said, "are very serious people. They promised to put electric lights in front of the community center, because it's really dark out there now and someone could fall and break his head."

The most important thing was, they said, that the following spring—at the latest!—they would open a movie theater in Yambol—a co-op, because the construction of the coming Svetlina Theater was also making great headway, and so from nineteen twenty-six onward, Yambol would have two whole theaters!

"What a miracle," Strashimirov grunted absent-mindedly. "Cinematography is dead! There's not a speck of future in that profession." And the boys turned red up to their ears.

Then they passed by the Jewish baths and went down the hill through the Jewish neighborhood, where the thinning Sheytanov clan had relocated from the Cargonne. As they descended down the precipitous little streets and stone stairwells, the icy, silver November sun—not yet winter, but not fall, either—shone right across from them and pierced the paling eyes of Anton Strashimirov, and the smell of smoke surrounded them. They arrived at the house and he crossed the yard, hunched over, walking under the bare apple trees, then by the fig tree with its velvet branches and leaves like cupped hands with their fingers spread, then under the vine, and climbed the wooden ladder to the second story. He was met by Penka—the sole surviving sister from the numerous siblings, all now departed. She recognized him, sighed, and invited him in. Anton Strashimirov took off his hat and stepped into the room with its air of apples and camphor, and saw an old woman: she was sitting on the edge of the couch and attempted to stand up, but Anton Strashimirov leaned down as if he were bowing and embraced her, kissed her on her dry cheek, and told her:

"Mother," he said, "you gave birth to an incredible person. He carried himself like a real man."

He said so, pulled back just a little bit, lifted one heavy, veteran leg, and stomped his heel against the hardwood floor.

"That's the kind of man he was, Georgi." He said. "Pity we couldn't save him. The ignorant killed him."

"Can I get you anything?" Kina came alive. "Can Penka make you some coffee, or bring you some jam?"

"Thank you," Anton Strashimirov replied, "but I am in a hurry, I must check in at the hotel and then get to the community center. I don't enjoy making people wait. But I will be here for a few days, and I will come again."

He said this, then left.

Penka walked back with him to the crooked, steep street, where he was awaited by the lads from Sofia University, casting glances back and forth, and while the two of them strode on the cobblestone path, Anton Strashimirov recounted asking around Sofia about how things had gone down with Sheytanov. He told her her brother had likely been taken out by Macedonian factions, but it was very likely the order had come courtesy of General Valkov. He told her that this general looked like nothing more than an army staff rat, but in reality he was also a coward and a murderer.

"This man," he continued, "when he wakes up, he hates the agrarians and the anarchists, but from lunchtime on, he hates the entire world."

He also told her the other general, Roussev, was the opposite: all talk and swagger, but a louse at heart. And everybody else in that cabinet was nothing more than a horde of opportunists, apostates and Pharisees: not a cabinet but a camarilla. They all detested each other, yet clung to one another.

Penka's face was sullen as she heard him out, but she did not interrupt. When she opened the gate, however, she looked him straight in the eye and said:

"I might be clothed in mourning, Mr. Strashimirov, but that is for my mother's sake only. If it were up to me, I would never dress in black."

Anton Strashimirov started and looked at her, confused, but she added, just as staunch:

"Have we seen Georgi's dead body? Have we washed it? Have we thrown dirt in his grave? I haven't!"

She said this, and continued to look him straight into his paling eyes.

"I am certain my *bratche* is still alive!" she sighed. "I don't know when, but I know that one day he will return. He might be in Turkey, or in France, but he will be back, I can feel it. I would never go against my mother, which is why I'm dressed like this."

Anton Strashimirov saw that her eyes were completely dry.

He shrugged and went out to the boys. He saw one of them smoking nervously and mumbled dryly:

"You leave that hobby alone, boy!" He then took off up the narrow streets and the white steps.

[Sunday, November 30, 2014]

Penka shut the gate behind him and went back upstairs to where her mother sat. The old woman asked who the man had been, who had stomped his foot, and who knew their Odjo.

"That was the writer, Anton Strashimirov."

"Was that really him?" Kina exclaimed. "My God he got old! I couldn't even recognize him."

[Thursday, January 1, 2015]

At any rate, life went on and nobody cared to remember the year nineteen twenty-fiv

End Notes

p. 14

Ilianski Base: Located in Ilientsi, a site for many military bases. It was there that those murdered by the "rogue agents" were buried. It became a residential district in 1961, and today is an industrial and commercial region.

p. 15

Rogue Agents: Unidentified persons who were in charge of murdering political opponents, much like the death squads in Latin America. The authorities used the term to justify the multitude of unsolved murders in 1925. Political agents—army and police reserve executioners acting on behalf of the government—abducted people in the middle of the night, and tortured and killed them, using government buildings for the purpose, such as the Public Safety building, military establishments, and police stations, but sometimes killed people right in the street. The government never took responsibility for any of these goings-on, blaming instead so-called "rogue agents," as though the persons were acting of their own volition rather than following orders.

p. 16

Sakarovs, Bakalovs, and Kabakchievs: Bywords stemming from the names of Nikola Sakarov, Georgi Bakalov, and Hristo Kabakchiev. They were representatives of the communist party whom the government detained, but never allowed into the hands of the "rogue agents," probably because it considered them more collaborators than opponents.

p. 23

Denounce the agrarian union: In June of 1923, the coalition of bourgeoisie parties took down the government of the Agrarian Union Party. In September of that same year, the Communist Party led an uprising, which was brutally suppressed.

p. 29

Tsankov, Russev, and Vulkov: Professor Aleksandar Tsankov (1879–1959) was a Bulgarian economist and politician who served as prime minister of Bulgaria from 1923 until 1926. General Ivan Rusev (1872–1945) was the Minister of Interior in Tsankov's government during his years as prime minister. General Ivan Valkov (1875–1962), was a longtime chairman of the Military Union; he also served as Minister of War from 1923 until 1929. Sheytanov mentions the three as a clear paradigm of a concentration of military power that has nothing to do with the people—the prime minister and his two generals.

p. 29

Aleksandar Stamboliyski: (1879–1923) was a leader of the Bulgarian Agrarian National Union, and a notorious anti-monarchist who lead the opposition to Tsar Ferdinand of Bulgaria. He became prime minister from 1919 until June 9, 1923, when he was ousted in the military coup. He was brutally tortured and murdered after attempting to raise a rebellion against Tsankov's government.

p. 29

Georgi Dimitrov (1882–1949) and Vasil Kolarov (1877–1950): Dimitrov was the first communist leader of Bulgaria, from 1946 until his death in 1949; from 1904 to 1923 he was Secretary of the Trade Unions Federation. Kolarov was a member of the revolutionary committee that launched the September Uprising in 1923. In June 1923, when Stamboliyski was deposed through a coup d'état, Stamboliyski's Communist allies, who were initially reluctant to intervene, organized an uprising against Aleksandar Tsankov. Dimitrov took charge of the revolutionary activities, and resisted for an entire week. But he and the leadership then fled the country and received a death sentence in absentia.

p. 36

Du lieber Augustin: From the song "*Ach du lieber Augustin,*" whose lyrics "Everything is gone!" tell of the desperation of the Austrian people in the late seventeenth-century, as they feared they would be besieged by the Turks.

p. 49

Vor! Vor! Pomogite!: From the Russian, "Вор! Вор! Помогите" meaning "Thief! Thief! Help!"

p. 50

Molodets!: From the Russian, "Молодец!" meaning "Brave man!"

p. 51

Lalyo Marinov: Real name of the Bulgarian poet and writer who went by the pseudonym Lamar. He became close to Geo Milev, and published his own magazine *Novis*, but unlike Milev or Sheytanov did not succumb to the government and lived until 1974.

p. 52

La Ruche: An experimental school founded in Rambouillet in 1904 by teacher and anarchist Sébastien Faure. At certain times, the school would have up to forty children from low-income families, as well as orphans. La Ruche's mission had been to develop libertarian and independent principles within children, to eradicate the feeling of class division: all children were treated equally. This educational experiment ended in the winter of 1917, however, when the school was shut down due to its inability to sustain itself economically.

p. 53

Peter Kropotkin: Russian philosopher, writer, and prominent anarchist advocating against capitalism, feudalism, and what he argued were the inefficiencies of a central government.

p. 55

It snowed from New Year's until after Christmas: Until the 1950s, Bulgaria used the Russian Orthodox calendar, and Christmas fell on January 7th.

p. 62

Atanas Damyanov: Damyanov (1876–1953) held the biggest printing monopoly in Bulgaria—United Printers for Publishing and Graphic Arts. He was the sole and enduring shareholder of the controlling interest of the company and the newspapers under its umbrella: *Utro* (Morning), *Zarya* (Fireworks), *Dnevnik* (Journal), and *Ilustrovana Sedmitsa* (Illustrated Week), *Nedelno Utro* (Sunday Morning) and *Kukurigu* (Cock-a-doodle-do).

p. 67

The Third Rome: The story of the "Third Rome" ("the second Constantinople") started in fourteenth century Bulgaria, under the reign of Tsar Ivan Alexander. He aimed to raise the prestige of his land and capital, introducing the name Tsarevgrad Tarnov (in comparison to the Slavic name of Constantinople—Tsarigrad), which was later supported by the words of Patriarch Callistus I of Constantinople in that "Tărnovo is the capital of the Bulgarians and second both in words and deeds after Constantinople."

p. 68

Karl Radek: It is said that Radek was keen on telling political anecdotes and double entendres. One such went as follows: "They told Stalin that Radek was telling jokes about him. Stalin became furious and called for him in the Kremlin. Radek walks in and says, 'My, what nice living quarters you have, Comrade Stalin!' Stalin responds: 'Soon, every Soviet man and woman will be living in something just like this!' Radek responds, 'Let's get something straight, Comrade Stalin, I'm the one who tells the jokes!'"

p. 70

Jukums Vācietis: Vācietis (1873–1938) was a lieutenant in the Russian Imperial Army, who quickly rose up the ranks of the Russian armed forces following the October Revolution. During the war, he was heavily wounded near Warsaw, but in January 1918, he squashed the uprising led by the Polish Corps of General Józef Dowbor-Muśnicki. By April 1918, he was already commanding the Latvian Riflemen. This same regiment is responsible for chasing away the anarchists, and in July he drowned the Socialist Revolutionaries, the SRs, in blood and mutiny.

p. 74

Alexander Blok: Blok (1880–1921) wrote "A Girl Sang in the Church Choir" (1905) to commemorate the mass shootings of the Saint Petersburg workers during their peaceful march toward the Winter Palace to present a petition to Tsar Nicholas II. (This happened in January of 1905 and is known as the Bloody Sunday Massacre.) According to another interpretation, the poem is a sad commemoration of the Battle of Tsushima (May 1905), and the Russian squadron that fell to Japan in the war.

p. 95

Hristo Botev: Hristo Botev (1848-1876) was a brilliant Bulgarian poet and revolutionary, widely considered a national hero. He was killed having not yet reached 30 years of age, as a vaivode of 200 rebels fighting to liberate Bulgaria from Ottoman Rule. Two years after his death, Bulgaria was finally freed from 500 years of enslavement. His words, "He who falls in battle for freedom lives forever," are eternally engraved in the Bulgarian consciousness like a battle cry.

p. 124

Geo Milev, "September," 1924; Translated from the Bulgarian by Peter Tempest, 1961

p. 138

Dimcho Debelyanov: Debelyanov (1887-1916) was a beloved Bulgarian poet and author whose premature death in the First World War cut off a promising literary career.

SEPTEMBER

by Geo Milev

1
From the dead womb of night
The age-old spite of the slave is born:
His passionate hate
Is great.

Where veils of mist are drawn.

From valleys in darkness
Before the dawn,
From all hills round,
From barren scrub,
From hungry ground,
From homes of mud,
From village,
Town,
Secluded courtyard,
Cot and cottage,
Siding, store,
Barn,
Farm,
Flourmill,
Loom,
Lathe:

By road and lane,
Past high
Scree, ravine, and boulder,
By ridge
And shoulder,
Through humming coppice
And autumn yellow-leaf forest,
Through stones
And water,
Swollen stream,
Meadow,
Orchard,
Vineyard,
Field,
Sheepfold,
Brambles,
Stubble burnt black,
Thorns
And sodden marshland track:
Ragged,
Muddy,
Hungry,
Haggard,
Toughened by toil untold,
Roughened by heat and cold,
Blunted,
Stunted,
Covered in grime,
      Long-haired,
      Feet bared,
Scarred,
Untutored,

Untamed,
Angry,
To madness
inflamed
      —Bearing no roses,
      No songs,
      No music, no gongs,
      No clarinet, sidedrum and drone,
      No trumpet and horn, no trombone:

Shouldering bundles in tatters,
Gripping—not glittering sabres,
But common sticks,
Peasants with stakes,
Cudgels,
Goads,
Axes,
Choppers,
Pitchforks,
Hoes,
Scythes
And sunflowers
—Young and old—
Down from every direction behold
They came
—A blind herd
Of beasts let loose,
Numberless
Thundering bulls—
Calling,
Bawling
(Behind them a stoneblack sky)

Without order
Forward
They flew
    Irrepressible,
    Terrible,
    Great:
    THE PEOPLE!

2

Night dispersed as the hills
Glistened.
The sunflowers
Turned to the Sun!
Slumbering dawn
Awoke
To the clatter of guns:
From the distant
Slopes
In leaden line
Mad
Bullets
Flew
With deadly whine.
The elephant jaws
Of cannon
Roared . . .
Fear it you must.
The sunflowers tumbled in dust.

3

"The people's voice
              Is the voice of God."
The people,

Pricked
By a thousand knives,
Dulled,
Degraded,
Poorer than beggars,
Deprived
Of brain
And nerve,
Arose
From the darkness and fear
Of their lives
—And wrote with their blood
    FREEDOM!

Chapter One:
    September.

—The people's voice—
—The voice of God—
O God!
Grant strength to the sacred task
Of hands grown hard and dark from toil:
Infuse great courage in hearts, we ask,
In such turmoil:
For Thou wouldst wish no man a slave
And now — we vow by our own grave
That it is we shall resurrect
Man free on Earth
—So with a will
We face our death.
For beyond:
The Land of Canaan blooms,
The Land of Truth

Promised
To us—
Spring everlasting of living dreams . . .
We believe it! We know it! We wish it!
God be with us!

4
September! September!
O month of blood!
Of rising
And rout!
Muglizh was the first,
Then Stara ⎫
     and ⎬ Zagóra
     Nova ⎭
Chirpán,
Lorn,
Ferdinand,
Berkóvitsa,
Sarámbey,
Médkovets
       (With Andrei the Priest)
—Villages, towns
From West to East.

5
The people arose
—Hand
On hammer,
Covered in soot, sparks and ashes
—Hand on sickle,
Numbed by the cold and humid soil,
Sons and daughters of toil,

Silently bearing it—
       (Not geniuses.

       Bright boys,
       Zealots,
       Debaters,
       Demagogues,
       Businessmen,
       Aviators,
       Pedants,
       Authors,
       Generals,
       Proprietors
       Of cafes and bars,
       Bandsmen
       And men of the Black Guards)
    But
Peasants,
Workers,
Commonfolk,
Landless,
Illiterate,
Boors,
Hooligans,
Boars
—A rabble like cattle:
           Thousands,
              Masses,
                 The people:
Thousands of faiths
—One faith in the people's cause,
Thousands of wills
—One will to obtain better laws,
Thousands of turbulent hearts

—In each heart a raging fire,
Thousands of toil-blackened hands
—In the reddening range of expanse
Eagerly raising on high
Red
Banners
Which spread
   Far
   And wide
Over a land in the grip o! alarm and revolt,
Ferocious fruit of the storm:
   Thousands—
   Masses—
   The people.

6
Over the homely hills,
Their navels turned
To the sky
And eternal Sun,
   Lightning
   Flashed
   —Thunder
Smote
Straight to the heart
The giant
Hundred-year
Oak.
Hill upon hill
Reflected the echo
Afar
Over peak and crest
To steep valleys,

In stone crannies
Where adders asleep
In coils rest
On hot couches,
To serpents' caves
And dragon lairs
And witches' hollow-tree haunts
        —The echoes mixed
        With the distant echo:
        Echoes and rumble
        Of waterfalls,
        Torrents,
        Gushing rivers,
        Rushing,
        Tumbling,
Thundering madly
        To the abyss.

7
The tragedy begins!—

8
Those at the head
Fell in blood.

A barrage of lead
Met the rebel flood.
The flags fluttered
In shreds.
The mountain boomed . . .
There on high
The near and distant horizon
Darkened with lines

Of men
—In black rows
Growing:
The paid, trained soldiers
And snarling police—
Each one of them knowing:
"The Fatherland
Summons its sons!"
             Exquisite:
             But—what land is it?—
The ferocious bark
Of the guns . . .

Those at the head
Fell in blood.

Beyond the faraway
Hills
Artillery pealed.
Towns
And villages
Reeled.
Slopes,
Hollows,
Roads
Were strewn
With blood-soaked corpses.
Guards drew swords
And rode in pursuit
Of routed peasants
—Finished them, shot them
With shrapnel and mortar,
Fleeing in terror in every direction,

Hounded into their homes
And there, where the eaves hang low,
Felled to the ground at a blow
From blood-wet knives
To the shrieks
Of horrified mothers,
Children and wives . . .

. . . .

9
The army advanced.
Under the menacing clatter of shrapnel
Even the boldest
Flinched:
In despair
Bare hands were raised in the air.
Fear without glory
Froze on each face—
Eyes beyond suffering.
            "Every man
            Fend for himself."
Now by all routes
Regiment follows on regiment
            —Infantry,
Cavalry,
Cannon.
Drums
Beat the attack.
Panic
Soars higher
Over the torn
Red banners,
Wielding its whiplash of fire.

There
As dismay increased
Alone
Andrei
The Priest
To epic boldness
Inspired
Fired
Round after round
From the famous cannon—
At last:
With the shout of
"Death to Satan,"
In fury magnificent
Turned about
His cannon:
Dispatched
The final shot
Straight
      —at the House of God,
Where many a psalm he had rendered . . .

And then he surrendered,
"Hang the Red Priest on the spot!
"No cross! No grave! Let him rot!"

He was dragged to a telegraph pole.
Close by stood the hangman
And captain.
The rope
On the ground.
Under the bitter
Chill sky

The Balkans
Frowned.
The priest stood full height,
Massive figure of man,
All
Calm as granite—
No regret,
No remembrances—
Christ's cross on his chest
And eyes fixed on the crest
Of the distant hills,
On the future . . .
"Butchers!
"You lower your cowardly eyes
"In the hour a man dies!
"But—one death—
"What does it mean ?
"Amen!"
Tight-lipped
He spat.
Then rapidly slipped
Himself
The noose on his neck
And
Not glancing heavenward
—Hung—
With teeth gripping
Tongue:

Majestic.
Magnificent,
Matchless!

10
Autumn
Flew by
In wild havoc
Of wailing and gales and deep night.
The storm clouds seethed
On darkening hills
—Gloom and glitter
And crows' croaking flight—

The Earth's back
Sweated blood.
Every hovel and home
Shuddered in cowering fear.
D e a t h   r o d e   h e r e!
Loud as thunder
The din
Split the heavens asunder.

11
Then came
The worst horror.
Smitten in fury
The alarum bell struck at their hearts
—Struck, smote, rang . . .
Darkness dropped to the ground,
Cast a dense, dread blockade
All round.
Death
—The bloodthirsty witch
Lurking in eddies of mist—
Shrieked
As she reached

Out through the night:
With endlessly long withered arms
Seizing, squeezing
Terrified hearts
At the back of each wall.
O night of nameless deeds!
—Both secret, and seen:
Again village greens carry scarlet stains.
Death screams in a severed throat are caught.
Again cruel clashing of shackle and chains
And the prison cells crowded.
In echoing courts
Of barracks and jails
Volleys ring to command.
Doors are locked,
Strangers knock.
In the porch with a gun
Sprawls a dying son.
Father hung.
Sister raped.
Uprooted from villages
Peasants are followed by troops
In grim convoy,
To be shot:
The order: "Halt!"
"Prepare to fire!"
                The bolts clatter:
                        Ku
                            Klux
                                Klan—
"Fire !"
                —Bullets spatter.
Ten bodies

Heavily
Plunge from the bank
Into the turbid grey River Maritsa,
Whose crimson flow
Carries away
Her sons in sorrow.
In distant deserted streets
Drums thud
As a band repeats:
"Maritsa murmurs . . ."
River of blood.

In the trampled
Thistle-grown fields
Where the grasses run wild
Roll scarlet heads
Defaced by knives.
Gallows outspread black arms
(Ghosts in a mist of death).
Ceaseless the merciless march of the axe
Against bone.
Villages blaze
Beyond the horizon.
Blood runs in torrents.
The death pyres' hot flame
Sacrilegiously licks
The foot
Of God's
Throne.
Live flesh roasts.
In high horror
The heavenly hosts

Exclaim
—A savage hosanna to God—

The end.

The hurricane ceased,
The storm
Stopped at last:
Over the land
Came
Peace
And silence.
The gods completed
Their bloody repast.

12
O Muse, now sing the Wrath of Achilles . . .

Achilles the strong brute,
The demon of war.
For long years the general
Of H. M. King Agamemnon.
Achilles the hero
With row upon row
Of crosses and medals and ribbons . . .
A pillar
Of order and peace
In the land . . .

But today
We no longer believe in heroes
—Not theirs, nor our own.

Troy burned, the city was razed.
Priam and Hecuba perished . . .
Achilles triumphs . . .
"What's Hecuba to him?"
His brute savage heart
Does not hear
The wailing of mothers distraught
Over nameless graves sprinkled with blood,
So many
They cannot be numbered.
"What's Hecuba to him?"
Achilles the hero.
Achilles was great.
God-sent scourge of God.
But Achilles shall perish in wrath and cursing.
—He perished,
          his fall was a fall of shame:
The killer was truly repaid.
Agamemnon killed Iphigenia
          —And perished:
Clytaemnestra killed Agamemnon
          —And perished:
Orestes-Elektra killed Clytaemnestra
          —They perished . . .
Alone there remains
Cassandra the seer,
Who stands and shall stay
Through the ages:
Speaking of vengeance
—A n d   a l l   s h a l l   c o m e   t r u e.
Constant amusement, pastime, caprice
Of the gods.
Perpetual bloom of gods' fury,

To whom all death is a jest,
All mourning revelry.
Death, murder and blood—
For how long must it be?
All-powerful Zeus,
   Jupiter,
   Ahuramazda,
   Indra,
   Tot,
   Ra,
   Jehovah,
   Sabaoth:
—R e p l y!

From the smoke of the fires
Rise
Assailing the ears
The cries of the killed,
The roars
Of the numberless martyrs
On blazing wood pyres

—W h o
H a s   b e t r a y e d   o u r   f a i t h?

Reply!
You say nothing?
Don't know?
—We do!
Look:
With one bound
We leap into Heaven:
  D O W N   W I T H   G O D!

—Heave a bomb at your heart
And take Heaven by storm:
      D O W N W I T H G O D!
From your throne
Send your dead
Down to the starless
Ironclad depths
Of the world's great abyss—
      D O W N W I T H G O D!
From the boundlessly high
Bridge of the sky
With levers and ropes
We'll bring down Heaven,
The land of our hopes,
Down
To the sorrowing
Blood-soaked
Earth.
All that the poets and philosophers wrote
Shall come true!
—No god! No master!
The month of September shall turn into May:
The life that men lead
From that day shall proceed
Ever upward, upward:
Earth shall be Heaven—
It shall!

Translated from the Bulgarian
by Peter Tempest, 1921

Hristo Karastoyanov is a multi-award winning contemporary Bulgarian novelist, playwright, and political essayist whose work has been translated into English, Turkish, and German. All seven of his novels have been shortlisted for the prestigious Helikon Award.

Izidora Angel is a Bulgarian-born writer and translator. She has written essays and critique in English and Bulgarian for the *Chicago Reader*, *Publishing Perspectives*, *Banitza*, *Egoist*, and others. She received a grant from English PEN for her work on *The Same Night Awaits Us All*.

OPEN LETTER

Inga Ābele (Latvia)
High Tide
Naja Marie Aidt (Denmark)
Rock, Paper, Scissors
Esther Allen et al. (ed.) (World)
The Man Between: Michael Henry
Heim & a Life in Translation
Bae Suah (South Korea)
A Greater Music
Svetislav Basara (Serbia)
The Cyclist Conspiracy
Guðbergur Bergsson (Iceland)
Tómas Jónsson, Bestseller
Jean-Marie Blas de Roblès (World)
Island of Point Nemo
Can Xue (China)
Frontier
Vertical Motion
Lúcio Cardoso (Brazil)
Chronicle of the Murdered House
Sergio Chejfec (Argentina)
The Dark
My Two Worlds
The Planets
Eduardo Chirinos (Peru)
The Smoke of Distant Fires
Marguerite Duras (France)
Abahn Sabana David
L'Amour
The Sailor from Gibraltar
Mathias Énard (France)
Street of Thieves
Zone
Macedonio Fernández (Argentina)
The Museum of Eterna's Novel
Rubem Fonseca (Brazil)
The Taker & Other Stories
Rodrigo Fresán (Argentina)
The Invented Part

Juan Gelman (Argentina)
Dark Times Filled with Light
Georgi Gospodinov (Bulgaria)
The Physics of Sorrow
Arnon Grunberg (Netherlands)
Tirza
Hubert Haddad (France)
Rochester Knockings:
A Novel of the Fox Sisters
Gail Hareven (Israel)
Lies, First Person
Angel Igov (Bulgaria)
A Short Tale of Shame
Ilya Ilf & Evgeny Petrov (Russia)
The Golden Calf
Zachary Karabashliev (Bulgaria)
18% Gray
Jan Kjærstad (Norway)
The Conqueror
The Discoverer
Josefine Klougart (Denmark)
One of Us Is Sleeping
Carlos Labbé (Chile)
Loquela
Navidad & Matanza
Jakov Lind (Austria)
Ergo
Landscape in Concrete
Andreas Maier (Germany)
Klausen
Lucio Mariani (Italy)
Traces of Time
Amanda Michalopoulou (Greece)
Why I Killed My Best Friend
Valerie Miles (World)
A Thousand Forests in One Acorn:
An Anthology of Spanish-
Language Fiction
Iben Mondrup (Denmark)
Justine

WWW.OPENLETTERBOOKS.ORG

**OPEN
LETTER**

Quim Monzó (Catalonia)
  Gasoline
  Guadalajara
  A Thousand Morons
Elsa Morante (Italy)
  Aracoeli
Giulio Mozzi (Italy)
  This Is the Garden
Andrés Neuman (Spain)
  The Things We Don't Do
Henrik Nordbrandt (Denmark)
  When We Leave Each Other
Wojciech Nowicki (Poland)
  Salki
Bragi Ólafsson (Iceland)
  The Ambassador
  The Pets
Kristín Ómarsdóttir (Iceland)
  Children in Reindeer Woods
Diego Trelles Paz (ed.) (World)
  The Future Is Not Ours
Ilja Leonard Pfeijffer (Netherlands)
  Rupert: A Confession
Jerzy Pilch (Poland)
  The Mighty Angel
  My First Suicide
  A Thousand Peaceful Cities
Rein Raud (Estonia)
  The Brother
Mercè Rodoreda (Catalonia)
  Death in Spring
  The Selected Stories of Mercè Rodoreda
  War, So Much War
Milen Ruskov (Bulgaria)
  Thrown into Nature
Guillermo Saccomanno (Argentina)
  Gesell Dome
Juan José Saer (Argentina)
  The Clouds
  La Grande
  The One Before

Scars
  The Sixty-Five Years of Washington
Olga Sedakova (Russia)
  In Praise of Poetry
Mikhail Shishkin (Russia)
  Maidenhair
Sölvi Björn Sigurðsson (Iceland)
  The Last Days of My Mother
Andrzej Sosnowski (Poland)
  Lodgings
Albena Stambolova (Bulgaria)
  Everything Happens as It Does
Benjamin Stein (Germany)
  The Canvas
Georgi Tenev (Bulgaria)
  Party Headquarters
Dubravka Ugresic (Europe)
  Europe in Sepia
  Karaoke Culture
  Nobody's Home
Ludvík Vaculík (Czech Republic)
  The Guinea Pigs
Jorge Volpi (Mexico)
  Season of Ash
Antoine Volodine (France)
  Bardo or Not Bardo
  Post-Exoticism in Ten Lessons,
    Lesson Eleven
  Radiant Terminus
Eliot Weinberger (ed.) (World)
  Elsewhere
Ingrid Winterbach (South Africa)
  The Book of Happenstance
  The Elusive Moth
  To Hell with Cronjé
Ror Wolf (Germany)
  Two or Three Years Later
Words Without Borders (ed.) (World)
  The Wall in My Head
Alejandro Zambra (Chile)
  The Private Lives of Trees